D1149438

RHYANNON BYRD

DEADLY IS THE KISS

MILLS & BOON

First published in Great Britain 2012
by Mills & Boon, an imprint of Harlequin (UK) Limited,
Eton House, 18-24 Paradise Road, Richmond, Surrey TW9 1SR

© Tabitha Bird 2012

ISBN: 978 0 263 901931
ebook ISBN: 978 1 408 97512 1

048-0812

Harlequin (UK) policy is to use papers that are natural, renewable and recyclable products and made from wood grown in sustainable forests. The logging and manufacturing processes conform to the legal environmental regulations of the country of origin.

Printed and bound
by CPI Group (UK) Ltd, Croydon, CR0 4YY

Dear Reader,

For those of you who have followed my PRIMAL INSTINCT series, you've known the characters of Ashe Granger and Juliana Sabin for a long time now. Sparks have always crackled between these two headstrong vampires, and yet we've never known why. In the past, friends and family have always surrounded them, making it too easy for Ashe and Juliana to ignore not only each other, but also the powerful feelings that neither is prepared to deal with. For nearly a year they've waged a fierce battle of wills, determined to resist temptation. But when a mysterious threat against Juliana and her family forces her to take drastic action, it's Ashe she runs to for help. Now it's just the two of them against a world filled with dangerous enemies and questionable allies. In order to survive, they'll need to overcome the secrets and fears that have kept them apart…and find the courage to embrace the stunning emotions that burn between them—before it's too late.

I truly hope you'll enjoy their story as much as I have, and endless thanks for making my books a part of your world!

Rhy

To Will, Cass and Conrad.
I love you guys more than you'll ever know.

DEADLY
IS THE KISS

CHAPTER ONE

THE HUNGER BURNING BENEATH his hot skin told the vampire that he needed a woman. Needed her until the bed was wrecked and her husky cries were filling his head. But despite the half-clad dancers eyeing him with hopeful yearning, Ashe Granger knew he wouldn't be touching any of the females filling the noisy London nightclub.

There wasn't any point.

He'd already tried screwing his way to relief through at least a dozen women in the past month alone, his hunger only mounting with frustration at each useless attempt to control it. Sex no longer brought him those satisfying moments of peace. Instead, it left him restless and in a foul mood—so he'd given it up for the time being, going cold turkey. It sucked, but at least he didn't have to face that bleak feeling in his chest every time he came inside the wrong woman. A bitch of a situation for a man to find himself in, considering he would never be coming inside the *right* one. And the idea of living like a monk for the rest of his life didn't appeal. He'd rather die.

"It's just for now," a voice said inside his mind. *"Just until you figure out a way to break the Burning."*

Burning. Baking. Being in heat. They all meant the same, each referring to the primal change that a normally cold-skinned Deschanel male experienced once he found his intended mate; that one woman meant to bring balance to his life. A violent, visceral wave of heat that twists and turns through his veins, growing more intense the longer he waits to claim her. It didn't always happen, now that their numbers were no longer what they used to be. But when it did, it was hard to miss, hitting the vampire's system with the punch of a nuclear assault.

With a snarl, Ashe shook his head, wiping his irritating thoughts clean. At the moment, he had more pressing matters to worry about. Namely, the man he was there to meet.

Ashe wasn't in the habit of conferring with anonymous sources who claimed they had important information they were willing to divulge. Especially when there wasn't a price attached. People just didn't tend to do things out of the kindness of their hearts. Especially the kind of people who sent anonymous notes to his hotel room, like the one he'd received an hour ago, telling Ashe to wait for him in this seedy club. And he hated waiting. Hated the way it felt. The way it coiled through his muscles, through his mind, leaving him edgy and restless...on the verge of violence at the slightest provocation.

The only reason he'd come was because the message had mentioned information about the Sabins. They were an extensive family, consisting of several generations, probably about fifty of them in all. For the past nine years, the Sabins had been serving time at their compound within the Wasteland. It was a vampire's worst nightmare, but then that was the point. Prisons weren't meant to be enjoyed, and that's exactly what the Wasteland was, only without the steel bars and armed guards. Instead, the vampires who had been banished to the desolate realm hidden within a Norwegian forest were bound within its borders by powerful magic. While the noncondemned could move freely in and out of the mystical realm, the prisoners were forced to permanently reside within the cold, bleak, dangerous pit.

An explanation for exactly why the Sabin family had been sentenced to the Wasteland was something that Ashe had been working to get his hands on for the past year, ever since he'd become acquainted with the family during a little quest he'd shared with a group of shape-shifters who were out to save the world. But despite his determination, no rulings by the Deschanel Council could be found in the record books. And no one he'd asked had been able to provide him with any answer other than that the details were "classified."

Ashe needed that information. Needed it badly enough that when he'd received the note saying to come to this club, he hadn't been able to ignore it.

Now he was sitting in a chair that was too small, sipping a beer that was too warm, while house music barreled its way through his brain like a hammer and the foul stench of sweat filled his nostrils. He wouldn't have thought this many people would be out clubbing in the early hours of the evening, but the annoying crowd clearly proved him wrong.

Maybe I'm just getting too old for this shit, he thought with a grimace, though at nearly two centuries in age he was still considered to be in his prime by vampire reckoning. Though not immortal, his species could usually enjoy long life spans, until such time as they took a mate. Then the man and woman's internal clocks aligned, ensuring that one never lived for long without the other. Most couples had little more than a hundred years together…but for the majority, it was meant to be one hell of a century.

Or in my case, he thought, *a hundred years of hell.*

Finishing the last of his beer, Ashe took another visual sweep of the steadily growing crowd, determining which of the writhing bodies on the dance floor were human and which were from the ancient clans—those nonhuman races, like the Deschanel vampires, who had lived for centuries hidden among their fellow humans.

Just as he decided that he'd waited long enough, a tall, lanky guy slipped into the empty chair on the other side of the small table. The guy's scent immediately told Ashe he was a vampire. Just not a very smart one, judging by the sour stench of drugs leaking through the male's pores. Spiky black hair shot out in every direction from the vamp's pale head, no less than seven piercings marking his face in different locations. Nose, lips, eyebrows and cheeks. Big black discs elongated his earlobes, at least an inch and a half in diameter. *Fucking ouch.* Ashe liked a little pain with his pleasure as much as the next vamp, but he didn't get how some guys could embrace it for the sake of an image.

The stranger shot him a nervous smile, revealing his crooked front teeth. "Hey, man. I'm Jax."

Ashe narrowed his eyes, waiting for the guy to get on with it.

Jax shifted in his chair with a kind of nervous

energy that probably had more to do with needing his next fix than it did with fear. Fiddling with his earlobe, he said, "So you're, like, a Förmyndare, aren't you?"

Förmyndares were an elite, highly skilled group of soldiers whose job was the protection of the Deschanel vampires. They were often considered the most ruthless hunters out of all the ancient clans…and they were not to be screwed with.

Instead of answering the question, Ashe just leaned back in his chair and glared. He had no intention of discussing his profession with the jonesing vampire.

Jax's nervousness was increasing, his right eyelid starting to twitch. "So, yeah, I'm, uh, here to give you some info that's gonna rock your world."

A cocky grin lifted the corner of Ashe's mouth. Drily, he said, "I can't wait to hear it."

Jax licked his lips. "Yeah, well, why don't you buy me a drink and then we can have our little talk."

Oh, now that was just funny. Was this idiot really stupid enough to try and milk him?

Reaching over the table and snagging the junkie's scrawny wrist in a lightning-quick move, Ashe applied enough pressure to let him know he was done getting dicked around.

"Hey, man, ease off," Jax wheezed. "I'm just the messenger."

"Then deliver your damn message and get the hell out of here," Ashe demanded in a low, deadly rasp.

"All right, okay." Jax's eyes shot from side to side, as if he was having trouble deciding where to look. "All I know is that there's a woman eating dinner at an Italian place called something like Zizzi over on James Street. It's only a few blocks from here. She's wearing a green sweater, sitting out on the patio. She'll give you the location."

"What location?" he sneered, using his other hand to grip the vamp's chin, forcing him to hold his stare. "What the hell are you talking about? You were meant to give me information about the Sabin family!"

Jax's throat worked as he swallowed. "Look, don't hurt me, okay. The guy—"

"What guy?"

"I don't know, man." Jax was practically whining, his scent steeped in panic and fear. "He was one of us, you know. Brownish hair, Desch-gray eyes. He found me at a bar around the corner, described what you look like, then told me that if I wanted to earn a grand, all I had to do was come in here and tell you that the woman in the green sweater can give you Juliana Sabin's location. He said to hurry. To get your ass moving *now*."

Juliana's location? That didn't make any sense. He already knew her location. She was bound within the Wasteland with the rest of her family, and that's where the little criminal would remain.

With a grunt of disgust, Ashe released the guy's wrist and moved to his feet. He threw a twenty-pound note on the table to cover his drinks and headed through the crowd, out into the bitter evening. The wintry winds whipped around his ears and neck like a ghostly caress, but he didn't feel its chill, his body seething with heat. Christ, just the thought of Juliana had him so twisted up inside he felt like a knot.

Shoving one hand through his hair, he started down the crowded sidewalk, barely noticing the people who scrambled to get out of his way, while he recalled the way he'd spent the past year comparing every woman he met with the mysterious little vamp. Even when he was bedding another woman, it was Juliana's face he'd see in his mind. Her slim, strong body he'd imagine spread out beneath him. Her pale, slender throat he pictured driving his fangs into, deep and hard and thick, until her blood was flowing in a sweet, blistering rush over his tongue and his hips were slamming against hers, demanding she give him everything she had. Every stubborn, breathtaking, infuriating part of her.

Strange, that he could want her so badly, and

yet have never actually touched her with anything more than a brief, fleeting contact. But then, he and the exiled vampire had never hit it off, constantly butting heads and bickering over everything from the serious to the trivial.

She irritated the hell out of him, but Ashe couldn't argue the fact that she was a beautiful woman. Her features were delicate but sensual, her looks accentuated by long, glossy hair that had a touch of curl to it, the color almost as dark as his. She wore it in a side part, so that one side swung over the edge of her face, allowing her to hide behind it when she wanted, like a shield. Though why a woman as beautiful as her would ever want to hide, he couldn't understand. She had the silvery gray eyes of all the Deschanel vampires, heavily lashed and complemented by sweeping brows. And her mouth was…well, incredible. Lush and pink and naturally sexy, it was the kind of mouth that made a man think about all the wicked things she could do with it. Which he had, *often*.

Given the level of Ashe's lust, his brother, Gideon, didn't understand why he didn't just bed her and get her out of his system, convict or not. But then, there was a lot that Gideon didn't know—such as the fact that the dark-haired little vampire had kick-started Ashe's Burning. And he sure as hell never planned on letting his brother find out.

He also never planned to lay a finger on Juliana. It was the only rational, intelligent thing he could do, because Ashe refused to get involved with a woman who was more than likely a criminal and a liar. He'd learned his lesson with an angel-faced, dishonest female early on in life, and it wasn't one he would ever forget.

He couldn't stomach liars and cheats—and what made the situation with Juliana even worse was that she adamantly refused to tell him why she and her family had been sentenced to the Wasteland. Not knowing what they'd done drove him mad. Every single damn thing about the woman drove him to a dangerous state of mind, which was why Ashe had vowed to stay the hell away from her.

And yet…he hadn't been able to make himself stop searching for an answer to her banishment, which was why he was currently prowling down a crowded London street, following directions from a drugged-out junkie he doubted would lead to anything more than further frustration and irritation on his part.

It took only a handful of minutes to make it down Colbert Road and onto James Street. The stylish restaurant Jax had described was easy to locate, its black awning flapping in the wind three buildings down on the opposite side of the road. As he made his way around the corner, keeping to his side of the street, Ashe narrowed his eyes, his height allowing him to scan the people who were sitting at the outside tables interspersed with tall patio heaters. He searched for a woman wearing a green sweater and spotted her almost instantly, the jade shade of the material catching his eye. She sat at one of the front tables, closest to the street, the soft glow of the outside lighting glinting off the mahogany fall of her hair. A strange sense of awareness prickled across the surface of his skin, his nostrils flaring as he tried to draw in the woman's scent. But there were too many other scents between them, a deluge of London taxis and passenger cars making their way down the street, while bundled-up city goers walked briskly down the sidewalks.

Oblivious to the fact she was being watched, the woman reached out and lifted her glass of red wine, something about the casual gesture making him swear under his breath, a horrible suspicion gaining momentum through his system, buzzing through his mind.

It can't be. No way in hell.

Ashe started walking a little faster, practically pushing people out of his way.

"Not fucking possible," he growled, willing the woman to turn around so that he could see her face. Then, as if acting on his silent command, she set the glass down with trembling fingers, her shoulders tensing as she slowly turned her head, looking back over her slender shoulder.

Shock hit him so hard and fast, he nearly stumbled over his own two feet.

Holy...shit.

With his heartbeat roaring in his ears and a torrent of curses slipping past his lips, Ashe found himself staring not at an informant...but directly into Juliana Sabin's wide, steel-gray eyes.

AT FIRST GLANCE, JULIANA thought her luck was too good to be true. Here she'd spent the past day searching for Ashe, and he suddenly appeared out of nowhere, her vision filled with six feet plus of hard, intense-looking male. His big, beautiful body stood out so easily from those around him, as if he were simply standing there on his own, instead of on a sidewalk surrounded by bustling people. One of the city's historic gas lamps flickered behind him, leaving his expression in shadow. But she could see the glowing silver of his eyes. Eyes that burned with a hot, angry glow.

Unable to hold his stare even from a distance, feeling as if he could see right into her, she quickly swept her gaze over the rest of him. He was dressed in a black sweater, leather jacket and jeans, his body long and lean and heavily muscled, his hair a rich sable-brown that looked as dark as a mink's pelt in the deepening twilight. He had it cut even shorter than the last time she'd seen him, back in the spring, which would have been too much for most men, but when you had a face like Ashe's, it didn't matter. In fact, the severe cut only accentuated the fact that his tall body and rugged face were…well, obscenely perfect.

His skin was a little darker than before, the lines of strain around his eyes a bit deeper. He'd either been working his ass off or partying a little too hard. Though she knew the second idea was possible, given his popularity with women, she had a feeling it'd been the first, his vibe a little too edgy for someone who had been kicking back and living wild. He looked hard and mean and tough, and her insides did a little rumba at the reality of having all that raw male aggression and intensity focused directly on her.

It was said among the clans that the complex nature of the Deschanel was a delicate balance between the light and dark aspects of the world, and Ashe Granger was a prime example. He was a thing of outrageous beauty, and yet…he was also a thing of sinister danger. The complex duality of his nature was a helpless allure to most women, and Juliana knew damn well that he never lacked for female companionship when he wanted it. She'd also been told, by his close friend Morgan

Scott, that none of the women who shared his bed ever meant anything to him, which wasn't surprising. Men like Ashe Granger weren't the type to settle down and fall in love. They enjoyed their variety—and she'd seen Ashe in action enough times at her family's compound to know he liked his sexual assortment of partners more than most. Which meant she would never be foolish enough to get tangled up with him, even if he didn't treat her like a criminal.

It was no secret that he didn't like her. But that didn't matter. All that mattered was finding a way to make the badass hunter believe her story, because she needed his help.

Once, she'd risked everything and lost, because she'd risked it on the wrong man. She had no guarantees that Ashe could be trusted, but she had to give him a shot. He was the one she'd been directed to find, and she was in too deep to pull back now. If he refused, she knew that Morgan and the other shape-shifters that Ashe worked with would do their best to help her. Or even Gideon, who would likely have the same important contacts that Ashe would, since he was a Förmyndare, as well. But her gut told her that it should be Ashe.

Juliana didn't foresee them having an easy time of it, but at least his natural animosity toward her would keep things on a professional level. One without any of the sexual advances she assumed would come from Gideon, whose flirtatious personality was so at odds with his brother's rough demeanor there were times when they seemed polar opposites.

Then again, she mused, noticing the way several women who'd walked past him were looking back over their shoulders, Ashe never seemed to have any trouble attracting and flirting with females of all species and ages. It was just her he treated like a leper.

And that's a good thing, she reminded herself, eyeing him as he waited impatiently on the opposite side of the road, the heavy traffic keeping him from immediately crossing. *I just need his help to save my family. Nothing more.*

It might have seemed like a long shot, considering the last time she'd seen him he'd said something along the lines of *I won't be coming back; have a nice life.* Even when spoken in the warm, husky blend of his Eastern European and British accent, the words had been painfully harsh. But while an ass, she also knew that Ashe Granger was a man who had committed his life to fighting against injustice and taking down criminals. He might not *want* to help her, but she had a feeling he'd be willing to do it for the rest of her family, so long as she could convince him that she was telling the truth.

She didn't want to have the coming conversation on the restaurant's patio, but she also didn't want him to think she was running. Since she'd already paid her bill for the first truly delicious meal she'd had in years, she hefted her backpack over her shoulder and moved to the entrance of a narrow, shadowed lane that ran along the side of the restaurant, and waited for him there.

Chewing on the corner of her lip, Juliana wondered how he'd found her. She'd come to London searching for him, just like the letter in the pack she'd found outside the secret exit from the Wasteland had told her to do. She'd spent the day making inquiries at hotels, only targeting those in a higher price range, knowing the vampire enjoyed his luxuries. The guy was loaded, which meant he didn't have to slum it unless necessary. After she'd finished her meal, she'd planned to continue her search, moving from Chelsea and into Kensington. But somehow, he'd found her… and he didn't look happy about it.

With that furious look burning in his silver eyes, she found herself thinking back to one of their last conversations, when he'd been staying with his friends at her family's compound in the Wasteland. Everyone was gathering in the dining hall for the evening meal, and she'd been about to enter the room, when Ashe had grabbed hold of her arm, pulling her farther along the stone-lined hallway.

She flinched at the hot feel of his skin and jerked out of his hold, fighting the urge to raise her hand and strike him across the face. The only thing that stopped her was the fact that her family and their friends weren't far away, and she didn't want to cause a scene.

"You're burning up," she muttered, rubbing the spot on her arm where his hot fingers had gripped her. "Who was it this time?"

He stared down at her through hooded eyes. "Who was what?" he asked in a deceptively lazy drawl.

"No adult, unmated male vampire runs as hot as you are without having gotten off!" Outrage shook her voice, the brittle words scraping her throat. "Did you think to come into my home and just sleep your way through my relatives?"

His tone was dismissive. "They're not all your relatives," he pointed out, crossing his muscular arms over his broad chest.

"The women who work here are under my protection! They don't deserve to get mauled by some oversexed Lothario!"

A husky laugh rumbled in his chest. "I don't force myself on women, Jules."

Her lip curled with derision. "Making them false promises is just as bad."

His eyes narrowed. "What the hell are you talking about?"

"You flash that perfect smile at them, rattling their brains, and they start thinking they have a chance with you. Not for sex, but for something more."

"I don't lead women on," he growled, finally getting irritated.

A bitter smile twisted her mouth. "Your kind always does. I doubt you even realize you're doing it. But I won't be left with a compound full of scorned, heartsick women when you're gone. I have enough to deal with!"

"You know what your problem is, Jules?" He stepped closer, pointing his finger right at her nose. "You need to get laid."

"Well, when I do, you can sure as hell bet it will be with someone more honorable than you!"

Fury darkened his eyes. "I was going to talk to you about the compound's defenses," he said in a low, carefully controlled voice, "but I won't waste your time."

Without another word, he turned and walked away, leaving her standing there in the hallway alone, her throat trembling with a ridiculous burn of tears.

When Juliana had looked for him after she'd sat through dinner with her family, barely managing any of her food, he was nowhere to be found.

She'd fought the urge to go knocking on doors, sniffing the hallways, searching for his scent. In truth, she didn't trust what she would do if she found him in another woman's bed. And she'd been furious at the way he'd kept interrogating everyone at the compound, determined to learn the reason for their banishment.

No one had told him, but his persistence had made her nervous. There were aspects of her past that she never wanted this man to learn. She had enough blood on her hands without adding his, as well. Not to mention the embarrassment she would feel if he knew just how foolish and naive she'd once been.

Now that she'd come to him for help, she would have to tread carefully with the truth to protect her secrets. She would do everything she could to protect him, but she couldn't afford to let her emotions get in the way of what was important. There were too many people counting on her, their lives in her hands.

As soon as the traffic broke, he started making his way toward her, his stride long and angry. And then he was standing right in front of her, so close she could see the shadow of beard stubble darkening his hard jaw. His incredible scent wrapped around her like a warm breeze, so good she wanted to drool. God, he was even more gorgeous than the last time she'd seen him, and he smelled like sin. Hot and musky and deliciously male. Her physical reaction to him was a little overwhelming, her body heating and tingling with a strange rush of warmth as he swept his silvery gaze over her. She fought the urge to cover her chest with her arms, the tight turtleneck sweater more revealing than anything he would have ever seen her wear in the Wasteland, where clothing tended to be bulky and dated. She was surprised he'd even recognized her in the jeans, sweater and battered leather boots.

Without uttering a single word, he reached down and snagged her wrist with one of his big, callused hands, dragging her deeper into the shadows of the narrow lane. Darkened shop fronts lined both sides of the cobblestone path, a few flickering neon signs that had been left glowing in their windows sending strange splashes of color across the thickening evening shadows. They quickly reached another narrow pedestrian cross street, and he turned right, dragging her deeper into the mazelike network of historic buildings, the sounds of traffic and chattering voices growing fainter. Juliana would have objected, if it weren't for the fact that she knew the conversation they were about to have would be best done away from listening ears. After all, she was now an escaped convict who would be on the run for her life as soon as her absence was discovered in the Wasteland. Since he was sure to say as much, the more privacy they had the better.

Moving so quickly she barely had time to gasp, he turned and snagged the pack from her shoulder, tossing it to the ground. Within the blink of an eye, he had her trapped against a brick section of wall, both hands locking around her wrists, pressing them flat on either side of her head, the submissive position sending a surge of panic through her veins. To make it worse, he pressed the long, tense length of his much larger body into hers, his muscles rippling and vibrating with power, and she could feel the heavy weight of an impressive erection pressing against her stomach as she tilted her head back to hold his stare. But he wasn't looking in her eyes. He was staring at her mouth with a kind of primal, savage intensity that made her heart pound so fiercely she thought it might burst from her chest.

When he finally spoke, his voice was low and guttural. "What the hell are you doing in London?"

Juliana swallowed, then licked her lips, ignoring his question so that she could ask one of her own. "How did you find me?"

It seemed difficult for him, but he managed to rip his gaze away from her mouth, locking it with hers. "You first."

"I'm here because of you. I...I came here to find you."

His dark brows drew together as he glared down at her, so close she could see the brighter flecks of silver within the darkening gray. "Why in God's name would you do that?"

She flinched under the raw force of his gaze, struggling to control the tremor in her voice. "Because I need your help."

His laugh was ugly and mean, as was the snide grin that lifted the corner of his mouth. "I'm a Förmyndare soldier and you're an escaped convict, lady. What makes you think I won't just haul your little ass back to the Wasteland, where it belongs?"

CHAPTER TWO

JULIANA LIFTED HER CHIN, refusing to let the angry vampire see how much his words terrified her. "I thought you were working as part of S.T.U.D. now."

"We call it Specs," he muttered, the scowl on his face making it clear that he didn't care for the nickname she'd used. He and his friends had recently formed a new cross-species hunting unit known as the Specialized Teams for a Unified Defense, or S.T.U.D. for short. She'd heard that Kellan Scott, an irrepressible Lycan with a warped sense of humor, was determined to spread the nickname, but Ashe obviously had different ideas.

"I might spend the majority of my time with Specs, but I'm still bound by my oath to the Förmyndares," he went on, forcing the words through his clenched teeth. "So you'd better start talking. Fast."

Though she knew it was ridiculous to push him,

considering her situation, she couldn't control the burst of frustration that had her shouting, "You can be such an ass, Granger! I'm sick of you treating me like a criminal!"

His grip on her wrists tightened, nostrils flaring as he drew in a sharp breath. "Have you given me any reason to think otherwise?"

"I've given you many! Did I or did I not help you and your friends in the Wasteland?"

His voice was so tight it snapped. "You did. But you've always refused to explain why you were there. That hardly inspires confidence or the desire to believe what you say, Juliana."

"Maybe I refuse to explain because it's none of your bloody business! Did you ever think of that?"

She could feel his own frustration being shaped into something ugly and raw, his voice little more than a growl as he said, "I have a right to know, damn it."

She blinked with shock, an angry retort dying on her lips. Breathlessly, she said, "What? Why? What could possibly give you such a right? Have you lost your mind?"

"Getting there," he muttered under his breath, his face suddenly closer. He stared so deep into her eyes, she could feel his warmth surging inside her, roiling like a molten sea of fire, sweeping through the cold hollows of her soul. "You have so many secrets," he said softly. "What are you so bloody afraid of? Why do I scent fear on you every time I get near you?"

"I'm not afraid of you," she argued, but the trembling of her voice said otherwise.

"You are," he countered, watching her with dark, hooded eyes. "And I want to know why. I want to know every goddamn secret you're keeping from me."

She recoiled, that sumptuous burn of heat dissipating as quickly as it came, leaving her even colder than before. She could never let him know the humiliating truth of her mistakes, or the full price that she'd paid for them. It was so much easier to accept his anger and frustration than to face his pity.

Closing her eyes, Juliana forced the argument back on topic. "I came here because I need your help, Ashe. My family's compound was attacked last week. There were serious casualties. I lost five cousins and one of my uncles." She lifted her lashes, imploring him to believe her. "And before you say it, no, it wasn't rogue vampires encroaching on our land. This was a professional hit, and more are coming. I need to put a stop to it."

His eyes darkened with disbelief. "How did you get out?"

"Within a few days of the attack, I received a package."

"From who?"

She shook her head. "That's just it. I don't know. It was left outside the gates of our compound, addressed to me. Inside I found detailed directions to a secret passage that isn't bound by the banishment spells that control the Wasteland's borders. That's how I was able to escape."

"If the Sabins are in danger, why didn't you bring anyone with you?" he asked, his tone heavy with skepticism.

"I wanted to, but I was warned that if I tried to bring anyone else, an alarm would be raised." She took a deep breath, choking back a groan at the way it pushed her breasts tighter against his chest. He didn't say anything, but his jaw looked harder, as if he was gritting his teeth, and he pulled back a few inches, putting more space between them while still keeping his grip on her wrists.

Feeling her face warm with a ridiculous blush, Juliana continued with her explanation. "When I made it past the boundaries of the Wasteland, I found the pack you just tossed on the ground waiting for me. It had money and clothes inside, as well as several travel documents with my picture and false names on them. It also contained a note telling me that our lives were in danger, and that you could help me. It said to look for you in London."

"Why would someone go to all that trouble to help you?"

Without his incredible heat pressed against her, she shivered even more from the cold, her teeth chattering as she answered his question. "Maybe because whoever it is knows that my family and I were imprisoned without just cause?"

"Were you?"

She lifted her chin again. "Yes. My family is innocent."

Very softly, he said, "Of what?"

She wet her lips, not wanting to lie to him. "Our supposed crime isn't important. What's important is the fact that my family's in danger."

Finally releasing his hold on her wrists, he took a step back, his hands shoved in his front pockets. It wasn't a casual stance, his muscles bulging, shoulders looking broader than ever. She'd never really understood how big he was until now, standing alone with him in this deserted lane, with no one else around.

"You want my help, you talk, Juliana. Otherwise I'll use my phone to place a call, and you'll have an escort back to prison before you can blink."

"Fine," she breathed out, knowing she would have to choose her words with care. He was too bloody smart for his own good, and she'd never been talented at deception. The best plan would be to stick as close to the truth as she could, without giving too much away.

His voice got harder. "Your seconds are ticking down, Juliana."

"All right." She closed her eyes, took another deep breath, then opened them as she said, "My parents were convicted of conspiring to bring down the Deschanel Council. Only it was a lie. But the one who made the claim convinced the Council otherwise, saying that our entire family was in on the plot."

"They had evidence?"

"No, nothing substantial," she told him, crossing her arms over her chest in an attempt to cover her breasts, sharply aware of the way his gaze kept sweeping over them. "Just this person's word against ours. The Council was divided about how to act, so they banished us instead of a formal execution."

He studied her through piercing eyes, his expression impossible to read. "It would take a powerful enemy to convince the Council to act without solid proof."

"Yes, it would."

When it became apparent she wasn't going to say anything more, he jerked his chin. "We'll get back to that. For now, I want to know what the hell you think I can do to help you."

"In addition to the information about you, the pack that was left for me also contained another letter. It said that if I brought proof of the assassination orders that have been taken out against my family before the Council, they'll be forced to overrule our sentence and free us, since the orders would be evidence of the original conspiracy against us."

His laugh was ragged. "That's a long shot if I ever heard one. And assassination orders are going to be damn hard to prove." Ashe knew, because he'd had experience with them before. The Assassin's League hadn't remained a powerful underground entity for centuries because they were careless or stupid. And their system was nearly flawless.

If you wanted someone taken out, an anonymous payment was deposited into one of the highly secure accounts administered by the League. The size of the sum deposited determined how many League assassins would vie for the job, and payment was based on a first-kill basis.

If enough money had been paid in on the Sabins' blood, they would soon have all the forces of hell coming after them. And the League was the perfect venue, making it nearly impossible to trace where the order had come from.

In order to prove her claim, Juliana would have to take something substantial to the Council. A solid piece of evidence, some kind of proof of monetary exchange with the Assassin's League, and it wouldn't be easy to get.

"Considering how flimsy the claims against us were," she said, "the Council would be grossly negligent not to take action."

Ashe responded with a masculine snort. "It wouldn't be the first time those ol' bastards were negligent, and it probably won't be the last."

"I realize that. But this is the only choice I've got, and I'm taking it."

"The only choice you've got," he murmured under his breath, as if he were merely voicing his thoughts out loud. She could practically see the wheels turning in his head as he crunched the details together, the raw intensity of his dark stare making her feel as if he could read her mind. "You know, I've always found it strange—the way you're so determined to take responsibility for your family."

Going on the defensive, she arched one of her brows. "Are you a sexist, Ashe? Do you find it odd that a woman can take a position of authority?"

"I have no trouble with the concept of a powerful woman," he replied, failing to rise to her taunting. "But that kind of responsibility usually comes with age." A slight frown settled between his brows. "Exactly how old are you, anyway?"

Feeling oddly as if she were walking into some kind of trap, but unable to find it, Juliana answered him truthfully. "I'll be twenty-eight this year."

It was impossible to miss his surprise, those beautiful eyes going wide with shock. "Twenty-eight? Jesus, for a Deschanel, you're practically a babe!"

Juliana resisted the impulse to roll her eyes. "I'm hardly a child, Ashe."

His low grunt said he didn't particularly agree. Then he surprised her with another odd question. "How is it that your family is so well-off at the compound?"

"What are you talking about?"

His gaze became sharper, his focus so intense she felt like a criminal undergoing interrogation. "I'm not blind, Juliana. You have guards in the Wasteland…a small contingent of servants. Yes, it's like living in medieval times, but you have a certain degree of protection, when you should have nothing at all. Who's responsible for that?"

"I… We don't know," she said with all honesty.

Sarcasm edged his words. "Just gifts from a benevolent benefactor?"

"I don't know," she said more forcefully, her own misgivings about their situation bleeding into her words. "I've always assumed it was arranged by someone on my mother's side of the family who felt sorry for us. But they aren't the ones helping me now. They're very reclusive. They would never be able to orchestrate something like

my escape. I doubt they even know what assassination orders are!"

Flicking a look toward the pack that was lying
by her feet, he asked, "Can I see these letters?"

Her shoulders fell. "I'm afraid not. There were
instructions to destroy them, so I did."

He gave a dry laugh as those pure gray eyes reconnected with hers. "Tell me, Jules. If your secret
champion told you to find me in London, why
didn't he or she tell you where I was staying?"

Her head was starting to pound with the mother
of all headaches. "I don't know the answer to that,
either. Maybe they didn't know."

He lifted one hand from his pocket, rubbing his
palm along the edge of his hard, stubble-covered
jaw. "Or maybe he or she wanted to be the one to
decide how we ran into each other. We were more
than likely being watched. Hell, they could still
be watching us now."

"What do you mean?"

"I was told to come to that restaurant to find
you."

Chills spread over the surface of her skin, her
already frayed nerves unraveling even more. She
couldn't shake the horrible suspicion that she was
just a pawn in a game being played out on a po-
litical chessboard, her family's well-being simply
some casualty of a power play. "Who was it?" she
asked, wishing she wasn't so afraid. And wishing

she were better at hiding it. The slight flare of his nostrils as he pulled in a deep breath told her that Ashe had caught the embarrassing emotion on her scent. Fear was bad enough—but she hoped to hell he couldn't detect the desire she was trying so hard to tamp down and ignore, fully aware this was neither the time nor the place…nor for that matter, the right man. Not unless she wanted to be made a fool of for the second time in her life.

"I don't know who it was," he finally said in response to her frantic question. "They sent some drugged-out vamp to relay the information to me."

Pushing her hair back from her face, she exhaled a trembling breath. "Someone is setting this up to help me, but I swear I don't know who. Or why? And why you? I mean, there are other Förmyndares with your connections. How did they connect us?"

He tried to conceal the flicker in his eyes by lowering his lashes, but she caught it. "What?" she demanded, fisting her hands at her sides. "Just tell me. What have you done?"

He ground his jaw so hard it looked painful. "I haven't done anything other than ask questions about your family's banishment."

Frustration flared through her system, potent and hot. "Damn it! You just can't leave well enough alone, can you?"

"I wanted answers!" he growled, his broad

shoulders bunching with tension as he glared down at her.

"Even if they put you in danger?"

Her words seemed to throw him a little, as if he hadn't expected her to care one way or another about his safety. Narrowing his eyes, he said, "I can handle whatever gets thrown at me, little girl. What I can't handle are lies."

She shoved that statement to the side, not wanting to think about it. "Well, it's obvious why they picked you to help me. God, Ashe, your stupid questions about my family could be what set this whole thing off!"

Derision darkened his expression. "That's a pretty big leap."

"Ha! You're stirring it up, making people question what happened nine years ago, and now they've decided to silence us!"

"And who exactly would 'they' be?"

"I can explain later." She cast an uneasy look at the darkening sky. "Right now, we need to get someplace safe. I don't like wandering the streets once the sun goes down. I was warned to be careful. If the assassins have any reason to suspect I'm no longer in the Wasteland, they'll be coming for me."

He turned his head to the side, lost in thought and pissed with her answer...or her lack of one. Anger radiated from his big body in powerful waves, a muscle pulsing in the hard line of his jaw as he stared into the thickening shadows.

"Ashe, please." She took a step toward him, touching the steely strength of his arm, his biceps impossibly hard beneath the soft leather of his jacket. "We need to get moving."

"You're assuming I believe what you've told me," he bit out, the expression in his hooded eyes impossible to read as he slowly brought his gaze back to hers. "But I don't. There are too many damn holes in your story. I don't believe in mysterious benefactors, and I don't buy that you're just caught up in some conspiracy about your family. You're too involved in this, Juliana. There's something about you that stands out. It's why you carry so much guilt on your shoulders. Why you practically run that damn compound, working yourself to the bone to make sure that your family is as safe and as well cared for as they can be."

She blinked up at him, too unnerved by his insight to argue his words. Instead, she latched onto one of the only bits of truth she could give him. "Ashe, no matter how this came about, the truth is that I do need your help," she said, rubbing her hands over her arms to ward off the growing chill of the evening. "And, I hate to admit it, but I probably would have come to you anyway. Even without the letter I found in the pack."

"Why? It's no secret that we don't get along."

She couldn't disagree with the statement, since it was true. She'd always been wary of the sexy vamp because of how badly she wanted him, while at the same time despising the way he lived his life, moving indiscriminately from one woman to another. It reminded her too much of another man she'd once known, and in this case, the adage of "once burned, twice shy" was a perfect fit.

And as for Ashe…well, she wasn't exactly sure why he disliked her so intensely, aside from the fact that she was a convicted criminal. That definitely seemed to have put her on his shit list, whether she was innocent or not.

"That's true," she finally murmured. "But I'm not looking for someone to hang out with and be my pal. What I need is someone who can help me."

Frustration coated his words. "I want to know what you're up against. You'd better at least give me a name."

"Fine." Her breath shuddered past her lips. "If you must know, it was the Delacourts."

Shock registered in his wide eyes with a look of instant recognition. "Raphe Delacourt?"

She wasn't surprised he knew the name. Raphe Delacourt was a legendary crime lord who ruled the Deschanel underworld with a crafty intellect and bone-chilling ruthlessness…aided by lofty connections within the vampire hierarchy that protected him from the vampire Council's laws.

"Yes," she rasped, an unmistakable catch in her voice that she hoped he'd put down to fear. "Raphe...and his mother." Lenora Delacourt was a longstanding member of the Deschanel Council. One who, with her son's help, had managed to retain her position of power every time some crusading idealist tried to get rid of her. "Nine years ago, Raphe had her under his thumb, forcing her to follow his orders. As far as I know, he still does."

"I don't suppose you have any proof?"

She shook her head again. "The letter warned me that assassination orders had been purchased against my family by the Delacourts, but it was only a piece of paper. As for actual evidence, no, I don't have any."

"Of course not," he mocked. A sarcastic smile twisted across his firm, masculine lips.

Bristling, she said, "Look, my family is living on borrowed time. Either agree to help me or don't. But don't waste my time."

He moved a bit closer, his voice dropping to little more than a whisper. "And what will you do if I refuse?"

Hoping he couldn't tell how badly his words affected her, Juliana scrounged up every ounce of bravado she could find. "Then I'll find someone who *can* help me. You're not the only Förmyndare I know."

"But I *am* the one you came to first," he murmured, arching one dark brow. "Which was either incredibly smart…or incredibly stupid."

Her spine stacked up with indignation. "I'm not an idiot. I know what I'm doing."

"Like hell. You don't have a clue what you're doing," he snarled, all traces of his lazy arrogance vanishing beneath a rise of hard, biting fury. "Do you have any idea how foolish it was for you to sit out on that restaurant patio? You drew the eye of every damn male who walked by!"

"That's ridiculous," she scoffed.

"It's the bloody truth, you blind little fool. I'd be willing to bet there are Förmyndares already out searching for you."

"Not yet. Our compound isn't scheduled for our quarterly check for another week. No one knows I'm missing."

"You'd better hope to hell they don't," he ground out, coming even closer.

Craning her head back so that she could hold his stare, she said, "If I *am* being hunted, it won't be by your colleagues. It'll be by the same people who are trying to kill my family!"

A deep, shuddering breath shook his chest as his gaze moved slowly over her face, settling on her parted lips for several heart-pounding seconds before lifting back to her eyes. She wanted to look away, but she couldn't. She was trapped, caught in the raw, primitive power of his stare, the force of emotion burning in the stormy depths of his eyes nearly making her gasp.

"I swear to God," he warned in a tone that was low and dark and uncomfortably delicious. "If you're lying to me, I'm going to drag your little ass back to that hellhole myself."

"I'm not lying. Please, just bel—"

"Shut up." One arm suddenly snaked around her waist like a steel band, crushing her against his body, while his other hand covered her mouth. She had no idea what was happening, but the leather of his jacket was wonderfully soft beneath her hands as they flattened against his chest, the smell of his skin outdoorsy and fresh, sending an unwanted surge of hunger through her veins, desire pooling low and deep in her belly.

Panicked by her reaction, Juliana had shoved his hand away from her mouth and drawn in a deep breath, preparing to tell him to get the hell away from her, when he slapped it over her mouth even harder. *"Quiet,"* he snapped, staring into the thick shadows that darkened the far end of the narrow lane. "Something's coming," he breathed out so softly, she could barely hear him.

Some*thing*…not someone.

Within seconds, there was a musky scent in

the air, like a primal predator closing in, the cold breeze bringing a stronger whiff of the scent as it surged around them, blowing against her face. Her blood chilled, a different kind of fear quickly spiking through her system, sending her pulse racing.

Ashe's jaw hardened, and she knew he could detect every shuddering beat of her terror. His eyes drifted closed for a moment as he pulled in a slow breath, his brow furrowed with a deep frown, as if he was carrying on some kind of troubling internal debate. Then he exhaled with a sharp huff, lifted his dark lashes and looked her right in the eye.

Their faces were close enough that she could feel the warmth of his breath against her cheek. "Whatever happens, stay behind me."

She blinked, hope soaring, almost afraid to believe he wasn't going to leave her to deal with the threat on her own.

"Thank—"

He cut her off before she could finish. "Don't thank me too soon," he growled in a low voice, turning so that his back was to her. "We haven't made it out of here yet."

"What do you think it is?" Juliana asked, releasing the talons at the tips of her fingers as Ashe did the same, her fangs dropping with a burn of heat as she prepared to do whatever she could to help him.

There was a surge of movement before he could answer, five hulking, fur-covered bodies prowling into the flickering glow of a neon sign. Werewolves. Big, ugly, nasty ones.

And the monsters looked hungry.

CHAPTER THREE

IT WAS FIVE AGAINST TWO. Actually five against one, since he didn't plan on letting Juliana get involved in the fight. Not the best of odds, but Ashe had faced worse. Much worse. And he couldn't discount the connection he felt to this woman. She might be his worst nightmare, but there was no question that he'd fight to the death before he let these bastards get their hands on her.

He was careful to keep Juliana between his back and one of the storefronts as the Lycans surrounded them in a semicircle, each one standing over seven feet tall, with razor-sharp claws and deadly, fang-filled jaws. Ashe spoke to the one who had taken center position. "Who the hell sent you?"

"We have no quarrel with you, vampire." The beast's voice was thick and guttural, the words strangely rounded by the muzzled shape of his mouth. "We only want some playtime with the pretty little criminal."

Rage unlike anything he'd ever known scalded through Ashe's veins as the Lycan's intent bled over his face. The wolf planned on killing Juliana, but not until after he'd forced himself on her. "On whose authority?" Ashe demanded. "Did the Council send you?"

"Call it a private contract," the Lycan replied, his slick black lips lifting on one side in a wolfish smile.

"Shit," he cursed under his breath, realization sinking in.

"What?" Juliana whispered, pressing closer against him. Her sexy scent wrapped around him like a warm spill of sunshine, and he could feel the soft pressure of her breasts against his back, even through the layers of their clothing. With a tense, silent laugh, Ashe wondered how sick it made him to be taking in such prurient details when they were in mortal danger. If he were Catholic, there'd no doubt be a confessional with his name on it.

Answering her question, he said, "I've heard of these bastards before. They're a rogue group of shifters who work for a premium price in the Assassin's League. They specialize in vampire killings." The details he'd heard were a hell of a lot more gruesome than that, but he didn't see the point in scaring her.

The Lycan standing in the center spoke again. "If you don't want to be left headless in the street, vamp, then you need to get moving."

It was common knowledge among the clans that the most effective way to kill a Deschanel vampire was to behead him, and Ashe had no doubt these particular assassins had done their fair share of decapitations.

Flexing his talons at his sides, Ashe centered his body with a deep breath, his muscles loose but ready, knowing exactly what to do when the time came. "I'm afraid that isn't going to happen," he said in a low drawl, sensing they wouldn't wait long to launch their attack.

Because he'd anticipated he'd be patted down before gaining entrance to the club where he'd met Jax, he'd left his weapons back in his hotel room in Kensington. That meant he had to fight with his body, but Ashe had trained for years to handle situations like these.

Of course, he didn't usually have a female clutching his back, needing protection. And not just any female—but *his* female. The fact that he had no intention of ever permanently bonding with her made no difference to the more feral, primitive aspects of his nature. His woman was in danger, and no way in hell was he going to allow these furry-skinned fucks to harm her.

"Stay behind me," he threw over his shoulder, while keeping his attention on the wolves.

"No. I can help," she said unsteadily, clearly afraid, but brave enough not to cower.

"Just stay the hell back!" he barked, hoping she would listen to him as he engaged the first shifter who reached him, the creature coming in hard and fast. The wolf swiped with his long, curved claws, ripping through the side of Ashe's leather jacket. Reacting quickly, he slashed his talons across the beast's face, drawing a spray of blood, then delivered a punishing sidekick to his groin that sent the wolf reeling back, sprawling over the damp asphalt. A second and third Lycan immediately rushed him, while a fourth tried to make his way around the group, to Juliana. With the little vamp shouting for him to be careful, Ashe broke one's neck as he dodged the other's claws, then powered a crunching kick to the Lycan's jaw. Pivoting to keep her behind him, he faced off against the remaining two, while the first shifter started to regain his feet.

"You're good, pretty boy," the wolf on his left snarled. "But you can't take on all of us."

Before Ashe could knock back the Lycan on his right, the assassin reached out and made a grab for Juliana, catching a fistful of her sweater.

She cursed as she struck out at him, catching him on the shoulder with her talons. Spinning, Ashe slammed a kick into the side of the shifter's knee, sending the bones popping out the other side. The Lycan crumpled to the ground, howling in pain, as Ashe turned and faced off against the others.

Time to finish this shit, he thought savagely, his fury rising as he scented the sweet spill of Juliana's blood in the air. The shifter with the mangled knee had sliced her skin with his claws, and molten fury poured through Ashe's system, so powerful and hot he felt like he could have taken on twenty of these sons of bitches.

Unleashing the full force of his rage, he went on the offensive, fighting more viciously, more brutally, than he ever had before.

As the last Lycan slumped to the ground, Ashe rolled his shoulders and took another deep breath, while retracting his talons. He could hear Juliana panting behind him, but wasn't ready to turn and face her, too much adrenaline still pumping through his system. Instead, he cast a quick look over the nearby storefronts, spotting a small hardware store and heading toward it. Using his elbow to bust the window, he ignored the blaring alarm that filled the night and quickly grabbed lighter fluid and matches. Normally, he would have called in for a Förmyndare cleanup crew to deal with the bodies, but he couldn't risk creating any links between himself and the fallen assassins. Not if he intended to help Juliana. And not when he still wasn't sure exactly what they were dealing with.

Working quickly, Ashe doused the bodies, which had already returned to their human forms, then set them on fire. Using the black powder that he kept in a hidden pocket inside his jacket, he poured some on each body, the compound increasing the heat of the fire to the point the bodies were almost instantly charred.

"I hear sirens," Juliana murmured behind him.

Satisfied that he'd done all he could, Ashe snatched up her pack and grasped her delicate wrist, dragging her along behind him, while she thanked him several times for saving her life. He moved fast, but she managed to keep up as they snaked their way through the city, putting distance between themselves and the dead Lycans. When they finally reached a quiet, residential square with a tree-filled park in its center, he pulled her into the wooded shelter of the trees.

Releasing his hold on her wrist, Ashe mentally braced himself, working to get a grip on his anger as he turned to face her inside the shadowy bower.

Her gaze darted around the silent park, before locking with his. "Those Lycans weren't here to take me back. They were here to kill me. It's already starting."

He wanted to argue, but the denial burned in

his throat, followed quickly by another fiery rush of frustration. He'd fallen into a trap, caught between the past and the present, its jaws biting into his flesh with tearing force, making it impossible to escape.

"Do you believe me now?" she demanded, wetting her lips.

With a feral growl rumbling in his chest, Ashe dropped her pack and turned away from her, reaching out with both arms and bracing his hands on the thick trunk of the nearest towering willow tree, the swaying fall of leaves blocking them from the outside world. Screwing his eyes shut, he ran through every possible scenario in his mind, hating each of them with equal intensity. He was damned if he did, and damned if he didn't. No middle ground, no easy way out, and he choked back the urge to punch his fist against the chilled bark.

Yeah, he could fob her off on one of his friends. But could he really stomach sending her off alone with another man? And then there was her accusation that it was quite possibly *his* investigation into her family's banishment that had triggered the assassination orders in the first place, if someone was honestly trying to keep the case from being looked at too closely.

If she was telling him the truth, her story about the Delacourts made sense. There weren't many families wealthy enough to fund assassination orders on a family the size of the Sabins, especially when that family was banished to the Wasteland—a dangerous place even for a deadly assassin to travel—but the Delacourts were one of the few. He could buy that part of it.

But what bothered him was Juliana's version of events, as if she were merely a two-bit player in a larger family drama. It didn't feel right in his gut. She was too...involved. Too much a part of it. And he hadn't missed that catch to her voice when she'd said Raphe Delacourt's name.

Then there was the pack and the letters. Something about the whole setup made his instincts scream caution.

There were a lot of unknowns, and he had no idea about how it was all gonna play out. The only thing he was sure of was that he would pay for getting involved. It would no doubt cost him in blood, sweat and his God-given sanity.

Which means I'm an idiot if I go through with this.

Behind him, Juliana's voice was sharp with impatience. "I'm assuming that was the proof you needed. Those weren't Förmyndares charged with returning me to the Wasteland. Those bastards intended to kill me. You're going to help me, Ashe. You have to."

He didn't bother to argue with her assertion,

though he wanted to. Badly. The alternative was a bitter pill to swallow, because he was about to agree to work with the one woman on earth he'd vowed to avoid. It was going to be worse than hell for his mind…and far too close to torture for his body.

What am I doing? Can't turn my back on her, but can't be near her and not touch her.

That wasn't some kind of melodramatic bullshit. It was just pure, simple fact. Which meant he needed a new bloody plan, and he needed it *fast*.

The first time Ashe had ever set eyes on Juliana Sabin, the hairs on his arms stood on end from the shock that jittered through his system. The blast of warmth from the Burning hadn't even hit him yet, but he'd been floored. There was just something about the way she moved…the way she looked at him that had caught his attention. And once caught, he hadn't been able to shake loose of the hold.

And the more time he spent with her, his list of questions about the mysterious vamp just continued to grow.

Raine McConnell, a friend and psychic who was married to a human friend of Ashe's, had refused to "psychically" spy on Juliana for him when he'd asked for any information she could give him, claiming it was a matter of principle. Considering the current situation, Ashe won-

dered what the psychic would say now. He'd have
called and asked her for some help—begged for
it even—but the couple had taken off to some
remote island in the Pacific for a luxury vacation
and couldn't be reached by phone.

Some guys just had all the luck. His buddy
Seth was going to be wallowing the days away
in sexual bliss with his woman, while Ashe dealt
with this mess. And no matter what he did, he
wouldn't be able to shake the Burning with a
simple cure or reversal anytime soon. He was juic-
ing up with a concoction meant to ease the symptoms, but the results had been minimal. And as
for a way to put an end to it…nothing, so far.

He'd keep looking, just like the others who had
searched before him. As time moved on and their
numbers dwindled, more males of his race committed to women without Burning for them, but it
was a risky move. If you never found the woman
who set you on fire, then you had a shot at happiness. But once you Burned, you were caught…
trapped…and driven to possess. The instinct could
push you to do painful, gut-wrenching things, like
breaking the heart of a woman you loved, and
more than a few families had been shattered as a
result.

But Ashe wasn't going to let the failure of
others stop him. He *would* keep searching until
he finally found what he needed and broke the

Burning. Then he'd be able to get back to the life he'd had before.

Yeah, that'll be great. Running back to an existence full of one-night stands that was getting old...and boring. Like watching the same sitcom episode over and over, until you knew it by heart. No laughter. No surprises. Just the same old scenes droning on...and on.

Choking the words off with a thick curse, Ashe rubbed a hand over his gritty eyes. He refused to acknowledge that niggling voice whispering mundane bullshit in the back of his mind. Nothing good could come from it. He *had* to get his life back, because a life with Juliana Sabin was *not* something he could live with.

Not now. Not ever.

It infuriated him that he was being manipulated by the supernatural phenomenon, as if fate itself were plucking the strings of his life for a laugh. But even worse was the fact that he'd always found Juliana—a woman who, given his past, should have made him cold—too fascinating to ignore. Instead, he'd found himself watching her, thinking about her, working to puzzle out her contradictions too many times to count. She was so strong, and yet vulnerable. Brave, but with big gray eyes that burned with fear.

And, God, but she had the sexiest mouth he'd ever seen.

"Ashe, we need to get out of here."

Exhaling a ragged breath, he finally turned to face her again. His muscles ached as he ran his gaze over her body, tension and misery and hunger twining together in an unbreakable knot that would eventually break him down. It was a fact he needed to face as an absolute given, like the rising of the sun and the corruption of power. Until then, he'd just have to do the best he could with what he had, and hope to hell he didn't go too far.

Since he knew he wouldn't be able to keep his gaze off the creamy swell of flesh revealed by her torn sweater, the Lycan's claws having caught her just above her left breast, he slipped off his leather jacket and held it out to her, silently amused by the way she cautiously crept closer, as if wary of what he would do. A sudden thought struck like a hammer in his brain, lust punching his gut so strongly he nearly dropped to his knees.

Did her hesitation mean she felt the same searing pull that he did? He knew the Burning didn't affect the females of his species in the same way that it did the males, but it was rumored that there were some women who experienced a nearly irresistible need to be close to the man fate had chosen for them.

Something inside him started to splinter and crack, a force growing and rushing beneath his skin, gaining momentum with the raging strength of a storm. His hands shook at his sides. Sweat slipped down the hollow of his spine. He could feel each heavy pulse of his blood pumping through his veins.

Was she aching as badly as he was? Did she feel the same grinding, relentless pull?

Goddamn it. Knowing she might be feeling even a fraction of the need twisting through him was too much, shattering his control. Unable to stop himself, Ashe reached out and snagged a handful of her sweater, quickly pulling and pinning her between his body and the willow, his fist jammed right against the hammering beat of her heart.

She gasped and started to tell him to go to hell, but he cut her off, taking her mouth in a blistering kiss that was anything but soft. Hard and brutal and flavored with anger, it was more punishment than pleasure—until she moaned.

Their eyes shot open at the same time, rough breaths soughing together, and from one instant to the next, everything changed.

With a hoarse curse on his lips, Ashe shuddered against her. The night felt warmer, the air heavier…richer, as it pressed in on them. Lust spilled through his veins in a thick, decadent slide, more potent than any narcotic as it poured through his system. His tongue flicked against the velvety softness of her lower lip, coaxing her to accept him…to kiss him back. She shivered, blinking, then relented, her lips parting with a sigh…inviting him in, and he couldn't resist, sliding his tongue against hers in an explicit kiss that was wet and deep and hungry.

"Damn it," he gasped, breathing the words into her mouth as the heat in his body turned molten and thick. *"It's too good."*

Lush. Sweet. Delicious. God, she was everything he'd known she would be, his hands shaking as he drank in the taste of her.

Drugged by the pleasure, Ashe kissed her harder, deeper, his hands tangling in her thick, silken hair as he crowded against her feminine little body, fighting to get closer. He needed to stop, to pull away, but he couldn't do either. It was like standing at the edge of a towering cliff, with a violent wind rushing against your face while frothing waves crashed against the jagged rocks below, knowing damn well that your next move would change your life. You could either soar over the edge of that cliff and suffer the consequences, or step back. Could take the step backward to safety…or the one so dangerous it could change you forever.

Nothing in their situation was different. He still didn't trust her, and despite what she said about choosing him regardless of the letter she'd claimed to find, Ashe knew she was only there with him because someone else had manipulated the situation. Someone who might be helping her...or who might well be the enemy, considering how quickly those Lycans had found her. Juliana might need his help, but she didn't trust him any more than he trusted her. Hell, she didn't even like him. They were a bad mistake just waiting to happen. But maybe...maybe he'd been going about the whole thing in the wrong way. Maybe he should just get his fill while he had the chance.

Are you mad? What kind of screwed-up plan is that? What if it's so good you can't walk away?

It was a risk, yeah. But what were his alternatives?

Screw it, he decided, tearing his mouth from hers, grabbing her pack and dragging her along behind him as he quickly headed out of the park, her delicate wrist gripped in his hand once again. If he was going to be in hell, he might as well give himself a taste of what he was suffering for.

After all, what was the point in suffering if you never took the time to enjoy the sin?

IT TOOK NO MORE THAN ten minutes to reach the swanky, historic hotel where Ashe had been staying for the past week. But they didn't make it any farther than the elevator before he choked out a graveled curse, dropped the pack again, then immediately reached over and pushed the stop button, bringing the elevator to a standstill. A quick jab with his fist broke the dark lens of the camera in the upper right corner of the lift, a yank of the wires deftly severing the camera's connection. He knew for a fact, after having studied the hotel's security during his stay, that the on-the-clock guards always retreated to the break room at this time of the evening for their dinner and sports highlights on television, leaving the cameras unattended. By the time they realized the camera had been disabled, he and Juliana would be long gone.

"Why did you do that?" she whispered unsteadily, backing into a far corner of the elevator as he turned toward her. Her eyes were rapidly flashing between shock and fear, but her scent was pure, mouthwatering desire, making him crazed.

Crowding against her, Ashe pinned her into the corner, his hands braced on the mirrored walls he avoided with his eyes, not wanting to face the raging lust he knew he'd see carved into his features at that precise moment. "I need this again," he grated, lowering his head and taking her mouth in another raw, dominating kiss as she gasped against his lips, her hands flattening against his chest. He turned his head to the side, going at her from a deeper angle, needing *more*.

In the past, he'd never cared all that much about kissing, figuring there were better things he and a woman could be doing with their mouths when they were alone together—but he couldn't get enough of Juliana's soft lips. Could *not* get his fill. They were so smooth, so lush, the inside of her mouth so sweet and addictive.

Considering the location, he might have had a chance in hell of finding control, if hers hadn't started to slip. But suddenly she was kissing him back, making sexy little sounds in the back of her throat that drove him over the edge. Having to touch her, Ashe slipped his hands inside the jacket, onto her hips, his fingers gripping her tight. Sweat dampened the roots of his hair as he ran his hands up the sides of her body, then back down, wanting to touch her everywhere at once. Needing it so badly the hunger was like a physical thing in his body, punching against his skin... destroying his reason.

Before he even knew what he was doing, his shaking fingers were working open the button on her jeans, then jerking down the zipper. She cried out as he quickly shoved a hand into the front of her panties, the sharp sound becoming a breathless moan when he cupped her warm sex in his palm and gave a predatory growl. Her delicate hands were on the sides of his neck, clutching him to her, her tongue sliding against his in a way that made his blood boil. Heat poured off him in blistering, sweltering waves as he shoved two thick fingers inside the slick, narrow opening of her body, stretching tender tissues, surprised by how perfect and small she felt. By how tightly she gripped him.

"I knew," he groaned, nipping her mouth with his teeth as he pushed his fingers deeper into that hot, melting honey. "I fucking knew you were going to feel like this."

He also knew that if he didn't pull back, right now, he was going to nail her sweet little ass to that elevator wall, hard and fast and rough. But he couldn't do it. Couldn't pull away. Hell, he didn't even want to. She was drenching his hand, her plush, cushiony sheath clamping down on him as he pulled back his fingers, then thrust them deep into that tight, wet heat again, his thumb settling against the swollen knot of her clit in a firm, relentless rhythm. She arched against him, tearing her mouth from his as she gulped in air, her head falling back against the mirrored corner as he worked her with his fingers, going harder… deeper, his actions borne not from decades of practiced seductions, but a wrenching desperation to punish her with pleasure, needing her to feel the same biting need that he did. He wanted her to burn with it. Wanted her to feel empty and hollow every single time she looked at him, aching to have him inside her.

Slowly, as if her body was heavy with sensation, she lifted those long lashes, locking her hazy, passion-thick gaze with his. Then she shocked the hell out of him by lowering her eyes…and putting her hands on the top button of his fly.

Ashe made a sound unlike any he'd ever made before—half growl, half sob—his cock so hard he thought be might go off at the merest brush of her fingers.

Gritting his teeth, he managed to choke out three rough, guttural words. *"I won't stop."*

It was a warning—one she didn't heed as she caught her lower lip in her teeth and continued on with the buttons, the task a difficult one given the size of the heavy erection caught beneath the denim. And then she was pushing the front of his boxers lower, his body jerking with a hard shudder as she wrapped her cool fingers around him in a firm, eager hold.

Overwhelmed by the sensation of finally having his woman's hands on him, Ashe forgot how to breathe, his heart pumping in his chest to a hard, hammering beat.

With his pulse roaring in his ears, he barely heard the small, choked sound that slipped past her kiss-swollen lips as she got her first good look at his shaft. He could sense her apprehension as she took in his size and the hard proof of just how badly he wanted her—but she didn't pull away. Instead, she gripped him tighter, the feel of her soft hand better than any sex he'd had in...damn, he couldn't even remember. He was too experienced, too damn jaded, to be pushed to the edge by something as tame as a hand job, but apparently his body failed to recall that particular fact, because he was on the verge of exploding.

As she continued to stroke him, Ashe had to lock his knees to keep them from buckling. He rubbed her clit with more pressure as he pumped his fingers into her, their gazes locked on the erotic movement of their hands. Needing to feel her come, unable to wait for it, Ashe shook the sweat out of his eyes and hooked his fingers forward, finding the sweet spot deep inside her that sent her crashing over the edge. She kept using her hand to pump his shaft as she came in a hard, wet rush, the feel and scent of her so sweet it nearly killed him. Lowering his head, Ashe captured her husky cries with his mouth, feeding on the sexy sounds until he knew he couldn't hold back.

"Shit," he snarled, drawing back his head so he could see her face, his fingers still working inside her. "You'd better stop. *Now.*"

Instead of releasing him, she blushed as she stroked him faster, silently daring him to follow through.

Ashe had often wondered what kind of lover Juliana would be, the question occupying his mind well into the night on too many occasions to count. Tentative and shy? Or fearless and bold? But she was neither. Instead, she was a heady blend of the two, the unusual, unfamiliar combination driving him outta his mind.

"I mean it," he growled. "You're pushing me."

"Then prove it," she whispered, flicking another shy glance down at his cock, and that was it. Gritting his teeth, Ashe came so hard it was almost more pain than pleasure, the sensation so intense it felt like being turned inside out.

He didn't know how much time had passed when he finally leaned forward and pressed his damp forehead against hers, sucking air into his burning lungs while waves of pleasure continued to course through him. Reluctantly taking his hand from between her legs, loving the way her body fought to hold on to him, he stroked her hip with his damp fingers, waiting for a sense of ease to come. For his head to clear. But it didn't happen.

Damn it, he was still hard as a spike, shaking with another violent surge of lust. And he knew she felt the same. They were both starved for more. Desperate and aching for it.

"We're both Deschanel," he suddenly grunted, curving his hands in the back of her panties and pushing them down with her jeans. Then he curved his hands over her ass again and hoisted her up, pushing between her thighs. Their species couldn't carry sexually transmitted diseases, which meant they didn't need protection. "We don't need a condom," he muttered, rubbing his lips across her temple as he notched himself against her small opening, needing to shove himself inside her like he'd never needed anything in his entire life.

She shivered in response to the husky words, then immediately stiffened, tension snapping through her body so fast she cracked her head on the mirror as she reared back. "Oh, God. *Wait! Stop!*"

"Stop?" Ashe held his breath, praying he'd heard her wrong. Despite the warning he'd given her about not stopping, he'd never forced himself on a woman, and he wasn't about to start now.

"Please," she whispered, turning her face to the side, her chest lifting with the panting force of her breaths, her hands pushing against his shoulders. "I can't…"

Shit. Shit. *Shit.* It almost killed him, but he somehow managed to dredge up enough strength to set her on her feet and pull away, taking a step back.

She trembled with nerves, eyes lowered as she yanked up her panties and jeans, fumbling them closed. "We have…we have to stop this *now,* before something happens."

Despite his discomfort, a wry, gritty laugh

burst from Ashe's throat. "You came so hard you screamed, Jules. I'd hardly say that's nothing," he pointed out with a taunting smile, irritated as hell that she'd chickened out on him…but even more so because she was trying to act as if nothing had even happened between them.

She glared up at him. "You know what I mean."

"Yeah, I do," he murmured, reaching out and rubbing his thumb over the front of her sweater, right over the tight tip of her breast, her nipple swollen and sensitive. He did it partly to remind her that she enjoyed his touch, but mostly because he couldn't stop himself. He wanted that tight little nipple in his mouth, on his tongue. Wanted her stripped bare and under him, and he wanted it now. "But there isn't any point in pretending we don't want it."

"Isn't there?" she demanded, knocking his hand away.

Ashe lifted his gaze back to her eyes. "Not when I know it's going to happen." And it would. He didn't doubt it. And maybe that was the only logical answer to the problem. Not touching her hadn't worked. It'd only had him running around in circles and chasing his tail for months now, while suffering in a world of pain. So he'd take the opposite approach and gorge himself on her until he'd worked the Burn down to a dull, mellow glow. One he could live with when they parted ways, getting on with their lives.

True, he'd never heard of anything like that working before. But then, he'd never heard of anyone trying, either.

Juliana, however, was still looking at him as if he'd grown two heads. "I asked for your help, Ashe. Not… I didn't ask for sex. You…you don't even *like* me."

"Parts of me seem to like you just fine," he offered drily, shoving himself back into his jeans, the task not an easy one, given that he was still painfully hard.

"This is ridiculous. Are you going to help me or not?"

"I'm an idiot, but yeah, I'm going to help you." He looked right at her. "And you're going to help me, too. Think of it as your contribution to my mental stability."

"I don't think—"

"You don't have to think, Jules." Ashe watched her from beneath his lashes as he reached out and pressed the stop button for the second time, the elevator making a low hum as it once again started its slow ascent. His voice remained hard, determined, implacable—because no way in hell did he plan on letting her change his mind. "All you have to do is lie down and enjoy it."

CHAPTER FOUR

JULIANA COULDN'T BELIEVE what she'd just heard. She'd known he was arrogant, but this was over the top even for Ashe. She'd never been so pissed, and so turned on, in her entire life. Who the hell did he think he was?

She'd held her tongue as they made their way from the elevator to his room, but the second the door closed behind him and he flipped the lock, she asked, "Are you actually saying that you'll only help me if I sleep with you? Have sex with you?"

"It's not a one-sided deal, Jules. I'll let you have sex with me, too," he drawled with his typical warped sense of humor. "But, yeah, that's my offer."

Juliana didn't think she'd ever been more shocked. Not even when the man she had thought loved her had proved that he…well, that he didn't.

"Your *offer*," she repeated, her voice shaking

with anger. "What you're offering turns me into a whore."

His mouth flattened into a hard, tense line as he crossed the room to her. "Don't look at it like that," he said gruffly, tossing her pack onto the room's small sofa.

"How else am I supposed to look at it?"

Something that almost looked like desperation flared in his eyes, though she knew she must be reading him wrong. Projecting her own foolish fantasies onto him. Ashe Granger wasn't desperate for her. This was just some kind of power play on his part. One she was ridiculously tempted to fall for, especially now that she knew just how incredible it was to fool around with him. She'd imagined it so many times, but reality had been much more intense than any of her fantasies. Hotter…richer…more painfully intimate.

She knew that for as long as she lived, she'd never forget how he'd looked when he'd come in her hand. His gorgeous face tight with pleasure, tendons standing out in his neck, all those incredible muscles in his body rigid and straining. He'd been the most beautiful, masculine, breathtaking thing she'd ever seen, and she was more terrified of him than ever—because now she knew exactly what she was missing.

"I want to help you," he said with rough impatience, pulling her from her dangerous thoughts, "but I can't if I'm thinking about nailing you twenty-four bloody hours a day."

She could only imagine what her expression looked like at that moment. "So I sleep with you instead? To what? Give you peace of mind?"

He shoved his fingers through the short strands of his hair in a purely male gesture of frustration. "Nothing about this is perfect, but it's the reality of the situation. So we have to face it."

"Yeah, well, your idea of reality is ugly," she shot back, flinging the words at him.

His reply was soft. "I'm sorry, but I can't do anything to change that."

Her head dropped back on her shoulders as she stared up at the ceiling, trying so hard not to cry. She had a vague impression of the room around her, of warm colors and classy antiques, but Ashe took too much of her focus for anything more substantial than that. Knowing she had to get a handle on the situation before it got out of hand, Juliana finally forced her gaze back to his. "Look…I know you're probably still jacked up from the fight, but that's—" she licked her lips, fighting to make her voice stronger "—just adrenaline. If you'd…if you'd just take a moment to calm down, you'll realize that you don't really want to have sex with me."

A kind of stunned disbelief flared in his eyes, and he seemed to choose his next words with care.

"Yeah, you usually irritate the hell out of me," he said, his deep voice gritty and thick. "But what ever gave you the impression I didn't want to fuck you?"

"What gave me the impression?" Her laugh sounded hysterical. "Gee, I don't know. Maybe the fact that you screwed your way through the women who work at my compound, shoving it right in my face? God, you even slept with my cousin Arianna, one of the most self-centered, vindictive women I've ever known. She despises me!"

He went very still, watching her like a hawk. "What makes you think I slept with Arianna?"

Her breath trembled past her lips. "Because I saw you making out with her at the compound the last time you were there."

"You were spying on me?"

Instead of answering him, she asked, "Have you even considered the fact that I don't want to sleep with you?"

His eyes went cold and hard. "That's a damn lie."

"How would you know?" she demanded hotly. "You can't read my mind!"

He gave another ugly, gritty laugh. "Are you forgetting that I was there in that elevator with you, Jules? You were already so ripe for another orgasm, you'd have come the second I got inside you."

"And you know women's bodies well enough to determine that with nothing but your hand?" Her voice was veering toward what could only be described as shrill.

"You're damn right I do!"

"You're so arrogant it's not even funny!" she shouted, fisting her hands at her sides as she fought the urge to slap him.

"And this isn't a damn joke," he snarled, the muscle pulsing in his jaw a testament to his mounting anger. "I'm the one on the edge over you. That's not arrogance, Juliana. It's fucking desperation!"

There was that word again...*desperation*. It was so powerful...so compelling. Especially to a hopeless romantic like herself who never learned.

It was truly terrifying, how badly she wanted to believe him.

Between her sharp, panting breaths, she somehow managed to ask, "Why, Ashe? I mean...why me?"

"I wish to hell I knew," he muttered, rubbing his hand over his mouth, the stormy silver of his eyes barely visible through the thick fringe of his lashes as he glared at her.

"Don't be flippant," she snapped, trembling with emotion. "Just tell me the truth!"

He made a sharp, impatient gesture with his hand. "I could tell you how beautiful you are, but you already know that. But it's more than your looks. Something about you…I can't explain it. Call it chemistry. Call it whatever the hell you want to. All I know is that I've wanted to be buried inside you since the moment I first set eyes on you."

"You hid it well," she murmured warily, knowing she'd be an idiot to believe him.

His stare drilled into hers. "Yeah, well, I'm not the only one good at hiding things."

She did her best to ignore the guilt that slithered through her insides at his quiet words, but didn't succeed. "I'm being as honest with you as I can, Ashe."

"As you can, huh?" His gaze slid toward the massive window that nearly took up the entire far wall of the small sitting room, where the historic skyline of London sprawled out in meandering lines, the majestic dome of St. Paul's rising in the distance. "The reason I never acted on the attraction before," he said after a moment, hands shoved deep in his front pockets, "is because I didn't plan on doing anything about it. Seemed like a…like a bad idea for a lot of reasons. But that's no longer a realistic option if we're going to be stuck together." His gaze reconnected with hers, deep and dark and piercing, his voice even rougher than before. "If there was a chance in hell I could keep my hands off you, I would. But I know my limits."

Oh, man, he was good. There was so much hunger in his rough voice, etched into the rugged planes of his handsome face, she could feel her body readying itself in response, just as desperate as *he'd* claimed to be. But this was…God, it was so risky. She knew exactly how much danger she was courting. How much pain. Men like Ashe Granger might be gorgeous, but they were like triple-chocolate-fudge cake. You knew it was bad for you, but you craved it anyway. And a nibble was never enough. Once you tasted it, you just wanted more…and more, until you paid for your hunger in pounds…and when it came to men, in mountains of heartache.

"Ashe, even if I wanted to say yes," she whispered, "I don't know how I could. I'm barely keeping it together as it is. I'm scared and worried and sick of being made to feel like I'm an inch tall. If I let you use me, it would be the final blow."

He came a little closer, stopping less than an arm's length away, his heat blasting against her like the burning warmth of a sun. "I'm not trying to cut you down to size. But it doesn't change the facts. If I'm helping you do this, I don't need to waste time worrying about when I'll be able to touch you," he explained in a husky rasp, curling his fingers under her chin. "I'll need to know it's a given. That I can have my fix whenever I need it."

She gave a shaky laugh as he put his hands on her waist, pulling her against his body. "Whenever, huh? I'm on a deadline, Ashe. I need to get to the bottom of this, and fast." She placed her hands on his chest, her mouth watering at the feel of his firm, cut muscles beneath the soft cashmere of the sweater. "I can't…I can't just wallow the days away in bed with you, no matter how good you are."

He touched his lips to her temple. "I'm damn good," he rumbled sexily, his voice like a dark caress against her skin, seducing her senses. "And we'll find the time."

Juliana closed her eyes, knowing she was going to regret this as much as she enjoyed it. "Ashe, this is so crazy. I know I'm partly responsible for what happened in the elevator. I…I kissed you back, and I…I touched you. But what you're asking…it isn't smart."

"Fuck smart." His breath was warm against her ear, his tongue flicking teasingly inside the sensitive shell. "I know it isn't easy giving in. We don't have a lot of…trust between us. But I give you my word that by the time I'm done with you, you won't regret saying yes."

Oh, ouch. As she lifted her lashes, a strange kind of pain pierced her heart, reminding her of just how foolish this was. Softly…and a little wryly, she said, "But you will be done with me, huh?"

He pulled back just enough that he could see her eyes, his gaze dark and thoughtful. She sensed he was going to try to offer some kind of explanation, then stopped himself. Instead, he simply said, "Let's deal with that when we get there."

Knowing she couldn't allow this man any leverage—that she would only end up destroyed if she did—Juliana forced herself to see the situation for the cold, harsh exchange that it was. "I don't know why you're bothering to put on the moves." Her voice was brisk, her hands no longer spread over his chest but curled into tight fists. "This isn't about seduction or pleasure. You just want to nail me."

"Don't." The low word vibrated with angry frustration. "If all I wanted was to screw, I could already be doing it. There were at least twenty women back in that club where I met with the vamp tonight who would have been willing to say yes. Hell, they'd have been *eager* to say it. But I wasn't interested, because you're the only woman I want right now." He raised one hand to her face, tucking a strand of her hair behind her ear, then rubbed his thumb across her cheek, the tender gestures so at odds with his guttural tone. "I need to have you under me, Jules. I need it badly enough to make an ass of myself by pushing you into this. And yeah, I know it's a shitty thing to do. But I'm doing it anyway."

She blinked, utterly dazed. They were hardly the most romantic words she had ever heard, but there was no mistaking the urgent hunger roughening their edges. Or the raw desire she could see burning in his beautiful eyes. "When you say things like that, it's so confusing."

"Then we should stop talking and start—"

She placed her fingers over his mouth, muffling his words. "Fine, I...I accept," she whispered, her heart beating so hard and fast that it hurt. "But I...I have a condition."

He jerked his chin at her, waiting for her to name it, his silver eyes glittering with triumph.

Oh, God, what am I doing?

She hoped she was agreeing simply because she'd missed the intimacy of sex, as well as the pleasure—and not because she had some foolish hope of him falling madly in love with her. She knew better than to wish for that kind of miracle.

As long as she kept her head on straight, and didn't let her heart get any silly notions, she could enjoy his offer for exactly what it was: a purely physical exchange based on mutual attraction, without any messy emotional attachments. Not exactly cold...just not the kind of thing a girl could pin her hopes on.

The key was to simply stay grounded in reality, and to accept him for what he was: a gorgeous, ruthless womanizer who would walk away from her when he was done, without ever looking back. She couldn't make anything of the way he touched her, just like she couldn't make too much of the way he'd fought to protect her from the Lycans. That was just Ashe being Ashe, and she'd be a fool to take any of it personally.

Promising herself that she wouldn't forget any of that, Juliana finally lowered her hand from his mouth. "My condition is this—no feeding while we're...together. I won't take your vein, and you won't take mine."

Though his expression remained guarded, the rigid set of his shoulders hinted at a powerful re-action to her words, as did the tightness around his eyes. But he merely said, "Why?"

"It's too...intimate. I just...we need to keep things purely physical, and feeding for our kind during sex is meant to be very emotional."

"Meant to be?" he questioned, a sudden sharp-ness in his gaze that hadn't been there before. "Are you telling me you've never done that before?"

She shook her head, acutely aware that she was blushing again.

He kept his eyes on her face, studying her care-fully, looking for God only knew what. Several heartbeats later, he said, "All right. I accept the condition. Anything else?"

Another quick shake of her head, while her pulse roared in her ears. "No, that's it. Nothing else."

So much heat flared in his eyes, they glowed with a primal, metallic light. "So we're agreed?" he asked in a low voice, his arm curving around her lower back, as if he was afraid she would suddenly try to slip away from him.

Juliana nodded, and somehow found the strength to give him the words he was waiting to hear. "We're agreed."

It was happening again. That same jittery, twitchy feeling Ashe got whenever she was close, his heart thumping like an engine, his lungs tight, skin tingling. It drove him mad, the way he couldn't control it. What made it even worse was how controlled she seemed. How collected. If he was going to fall apart, he bloody well wanted her to fall apart with him.

Yeah, she'd agreed to his insane demand, but she wasn't happy about it. There was a belligerent tilt to her chin that made him feel as if she was slipping farther out of his reach, even as his hands were pressing her closer to his body.

And then he caught the telltale richness of her scent, and with a piercing jolt of relief, he knew she was with him. She might not like being backed into a corner, but she couldn't disguise her body's craving any more than he could, the heady scent of her desire making him so hard he literally pulsed with need, hunger burning in every cell of his body.

Wondering for the hundredth time if he was losing his mind, Ashe swept her up in his arms and carried her into the other room, where a massive king-size bed sprawled in the middle of a thick Persian rug in deep, soothing shades of blue, green and cream. But he wasn't soothed. He was falling off the deep end, playing fast and loose with his sanity.

"What are you doing?" she gasped, clutching his shoulders.

He shook his head. "I don't want to talk. I just want to strip you out of these clothes, lay you down on the bed, and get you under my mouth."

"What?"

"You heard me."

Her blush spread over the surface of her skin like a grass fire, turning her rosy and pink. "This is ridiculous. We don't have time for this *now*."

A ragged burst of laughter shook his chest as he lowered her to her feet. "Who knows how much time we have?" he muttered, pushing his jacket off her shoulders. "You're a wanted woman, Jules. Danger breathing down the back of your neck, hard and focused. If I want to get my fill of you, I had better do it fast, before some new threat sinks its teeth into us and I end up dying trying to save your life."

She flinched, blinking up at him. "Please... don't say that."

The sincerity of those quiet words hit him right in the chest, confusing the hell out of him.

Her hands gripped his arms. "I mean it, Ashe. I don't want anything to happen to you."

Before he'd even decided how to respond, he heard himself saying, "Then stop trying to push me away."

She must have read the determination on his face, because she was the one who took a deep breath and reached for the hem of her torn sweater, pulling it over her head. As she let the sweater fall to the floor, Ashe flexed his hands at his sides, his pulse hammering at the sight of the black satin bra propping up the creamy swells of her breasts. The scratches on her shoulder and upper chest were already fading, thanks to the rapid healing genes of their species. Only a few faint lines remained from her run-in with the Lycan.

Even so, he still wanted to rip the bastard to shreds all over again for causing her pain.

"Get it off," he grunted, jerking his chin at the bra. He felt like a bloody caveman, ready to drag his knuckles and pound his chest, demanding her submission, but there was no help for it.

Her head fell forward as she reached behind her back, undoing the clasp, her long hair streaming over her shoulders. A second later, the black satin fell to the floor, and hunger tore through him. He stared, hard, his ragged breathing sounding loud in the heavy quiet of the room. Her breasts weren't the largest he'd ever seen, but he didn't give a damn. What they were was impossibly beautiful…graceful, like the rest of her body. Perfectly curved and full and pale, her nipples small and pink, already pulled tight with need. A blatant temptation he couldn't resist.

Putting his hands on her rib cage, Ashe lifted her off the floor, bringing those succulent breasts to his mouth. His heart pounded as he pressed a soft kiss to the healing scratches, then lowered his head and hungrily tongued one small, velvety nipple, rubbing and licking at it. His breathing quickened as she arched her back and made a needy sound deep in her throat, her nails digging into his shoulders. He couldn't get enough of the way she tasted, moving to her other breast with a soft growl, licking and sucking until her nipple was like a plump, ripe berry on his tongue, driving him wild. He wanted to devour her. Lick every sumptuous inch of her firm little body from head to toe, as if he could somehow imprint himself on her with the ravenous demands of his mouth.

Needing more of her—needing *all* of her—Ashe gave a final lick to both nipples, taking a moment to enjoy how they looked all shiny and wet from his mouth, their color darker...deeper than before. Then he tossed her back into the middle of the bed, a gasp of shock spilling from her lips as she bounced there once...twice.

Leaning over the side of the mattress, he quickly tugged off her boots and jeans, then fisted his hand in the front of her black panties and gave a hard yank, wrenching them off in shreds. She cried out, her eyes huge in the blushing warmth of her face, lips parted with her increasingly fast breaths as she tried to cover herself.

He could scent the embarrassment simmering beneath her desire, her shyness yet another surprise that he hadn't expected. One that made the corner of his mouth twitch with a smile.

"Uh-uh. Spread your legs and pull your knees out at your sides," he told her, his low voice filled with need and lust and things he didn't want to think about. To even acknowledge. "I need to see you, Jules. All of you."

"I...uh..." The fiery blush on her cheeks spread, sweeping over her pale skin, her body vibrating at a high frequency, making him wonder how much time had passed since she'd last been with a man. He knew better than to hope for more than a few months, at the most. She was too beautiful, too sensual. Hell, the guards who worked for her family probably did their best to get her into bed as often as they could.

Shoving the infuriating thought aside, Ashe ripped off his sweater and followed her down onto the dark blue bedding. He'd wanted this woman for so long, and now he had her naked and laid out before him, her pale skin gleaming like a pearl against the stretch of midnight-blue beneath her. He couldn't believe it was even better than he'd imagined.

"Don't be shy," he coaxed in a low murmur, crawling over her and placing a kiss against her trembling fingers. The searing heat in his veins burned hotter, her warm, sensual scent making his mouth water. "Come on, Jules. I want to see what you've been hiding from me for so long."

With a deep breath, she pulled her hands away. Then she slowly exhaled, and relaxed the muscles in her thighs, inching them apart. "That's it," he groaned, running his tongue over the sensitive tip of a fang as he caught his first glimpse of her thick, slippery folds, his heart pounding to a brutal, painful rhythm. Struggling for control, Ashe rubbed a thumb over the pale, soft skin of her inner thigh, thinking it was a good thing she'd made that stipulation about no feeding. He wanted her blood—wanted the feel and the warmth of it sitting in his mouth—his fangs already aching with the need to feel that pale skin giving way beneath them. But he had no doubt the taste of it would push him too far.

But there were other things he could get his mouth on, and he was done waiting.

Wedging his body between her slender thighs, he pushed them wide, his eyes burning as he ran his gaze over that most lush, intimate part of her. It made his chest hurt just to look at her, she was so pretty and pink and delicate.

He exhaled in an audible rush. "Been waiting for this," he rasped, his voice sounding drugged to his own ears as he ran two fingers through her juicy folds, getting them nice and wet. Then he lifted the fingers to his lips and sucked them into his mouth, desperate for the taste of her.

Bright splotches of color burned across the tops of her cheekbones as she stared at him down the quivering length of her body. "What…?" she whispered, studying his expression. "What are you thinking?"

Pulling his fingers from his mouth, he shot her a slow smile, loving the way he could now scent her on his lips. "I'm thinking you taste as sinful as you look." *That you taste like mine.*

Her blush somehow got even brighter. "Um… thanks."

"My pleasure." He swiped his tongue over his lower lip. "Literally. I could lick your sweet little pu—"

"Okay," Juliana gasped, waving her hands in his face. "I get it! No reason to go into detail."

The smile on his lips made her breath catch, his deep voice almost tender as he said, "I didn't think it was possible, but your blush just keeps getting brighter."

"I'm embarrassed!"

"Don't be." He braced himself on his elbows, his rugged face so close to her sex she could feel the humid warmth of his breath. She felt too exposed, her head spinning, her mind unable to come to grips with how she'd ended up in this situation. An hour ago, she'd have bet her life on the fact that she'd never so much as allow Ashe Granger to kiss her—and now she was naked on a bed in his hotel room, with his mouth only inches from her sex, as vulnerable and exposed as a woman could be.

She should have been slapping his face and telling him to shove his manipulative "deal" up his ass. But she couldn't, because she needed this as badly as he'd claimed to need it. Even though she knew her heart and her pride were going to pay for the pleasure later, she had to have it. Had to have at least this much of him, an insatiable craving twisting through her body with so much force she couldn't focus or latch onto a thought.

Then she couldn't think at all as he used his thumbs to spread her open, a thick, hungry sound slipping from his lips as he leaned forward and put his mouth on her.

Ohmygod...

She could feel the liquid rush of pleasure pooling between her thighs as he licked her, the rough, primal sounds he made telling her just how much he enjoyed what he was doing. Hunger speared through her body with such explosive force she jerked open, arms and legs sprawled wide in sexual abandon, her body given over completely to her senses as the breathtaking sensations pulsed and swelled within her.

Her mind spun, shock warring with a need that was too powerful to control. He'd only just started and already she was losing it, writhing and arching beneath him, acting like someone she didn't even recognize.

"Just do it! *Please,*" she begged, her head tossing from side to side as she planted her feet against the mattress and pushed up, pumping against his greedy, devastating mouth. She felt as if she were going to shatter into a million pieces if he didn't hurry up and push her over the edge. *"Go faster! Please!"*

"No way in hell," he muttered, doing something

insanely wicked with his tongue. "I want this to last."

Pushing her trembling hands into his short, dark hair, Juliana realized that she'd never expected it to be like this. Never expected he would pleasure her this way as a part of their deal, instead of simply seeking his own relief as quickly as he could.

Obviously, she'd been wrong. As he flicked a smoldering look up at her face from beneath his lashes, his gorgeous features stamped with raw, brutal hunger, it was clear he didn't plan on rushing any part of the experience. Apparently determined to prove his point, the intoxicating strokes of his tongue became slower...deeper, forcing her to accept the stunning fact that he was savoring every part of her, getting off on the intimate act as strongly as she was.

And, God, was she getting off.

She could have come within seconds, and he knew it. But he deliberately kept the blinding, shattering release just out of her reach, gentling her whenever she got too close, which made the sensations grow and swell, until she was crying and gasping, her nails digging into his broad, muscular shoulders hard enough to draw blood.

In a low, silken whisper, he asked her, "You ready to come now, Jules?"

"Damn you, you're being such a bastard," she

snapped, her voice cracking, shaking with emotion. "Just do it!"

His low laugh rumbled against her flesh, and she could feel his slow, wicked smile.

"I love it when you get bossy," he told her, closing his mouth over her clit and softly sucking, just as he shoved two thick fingers back inside her, twisting them hard and deep. She arched as if she'd been electrocuted, her plush sex clamping down around him in a deliciously warm, wet hold. He pulled his fingers back, thrusting them in again, and she broke, screaming and pulsing as the mother of all orgasms stormed through her.

"That's so perfect," he growled, nearly following her over that blinding, crashing edge.

Minutes later, when he finally lifted his head, another harsh growl vibrated in Ashe's throat as he stared up at her, the feral part of his nature recognizing her for exactly what she was: the most stunning, mouthwatering, addictive woman he'd ever known. Her face was dewy and pink, soft tendrils of silky hair stuck to her temples and her cheeks, her mouth puffy and red from the bite of her teeth. Her gray eyes were heavy and lambent, hazy with satisfaction—but he could see the shock simmering in their stormy depths. The pink tip of her tongue darted across her lower lip, a kind of shy half smile curving her beautiful mouth as she stared back at him.

"Wow. I'm, um, normally not that…out of control," Juliana panted, still struggling to catch her breath.

A sin-tipped smile touched his mouth, making him too gorgeous to be real. "You don't hear me complaining, do you?"

Shaking her head, she thought he looked like some kind of breathtaking, ancient virility god as he braced his arms on either side of her hips and lowered his head again, giving a playful lick to her navel.

"To be honest, I loved it," he murmured in a dark, husky rumble, crawling over her a little higher, lapping his clever tongue against the tender underside of her breast. "There's nothing in the world better than having a woman melt all over you."

Oh…damn.

That easily, the warm, mellow glow slipping through her veins started to cool. She shivered, the chilled air in the room suddenly brushing over her skin like icy prickles of disappointment. She felt the ridiculous sting of tears burning at the backs of her eyes and wanted to die, the idea of crying in front of this man even more humiliating than the exceptional way he'd just handled her body. "So, um, any woman would do, huh?"

He went still, as if just realizing what he'd said. Then he slowly lifted his head and looked her in the eye, his stare deep and searching. "I wish it were that simple," he finally said in a low voice that was rough around the edges. "Fucking has always felt good. I'll be the first to admit it. But being like this with you…I don't—" He gave a hard, frustrated shake of his head. "I don't have a frame of reference for this kind of thing."

"What kind of thing?"

Several heavy seconds of silence passed before he blew out a sharp breath and rolled to his back beside her, his dark gaze focused on the ceiling. "Never mind," he muttered.

"Never mind?" She made a choked sound of disgust as she sat up, scrambling to cover as much of her body as she could with the soft green throw draped over a corner of the bed. "That's so like a man. God forbid one of you ever actually talked about his emotions!"

CHAPTER FIVE

ASHE TURNED HIS HEAD toward her, staring at the elegant line of her spine, wondering what the hell it was that she wanted from him. "What do you want me to say, Jules?"

"I don't know." Looking back at him over her shoulder, she brushed away the tears that were tracking down her cheeks. "I just…I can't separate emotions from sex. I thought that I could, but I'm not…I'm not like you."

"I don't mind if you get emotional and cry," he told her, his voice thick as he stared at the moisture glistening on her long lashes, her gray eyes luminous and bright. "A few tears aren't going to scare me away."

"Well, good for you!" she snapped, and he knew he was in deep shit when even that waspish tone of hers turned him on. He might not trust her, but their physical chemistry was as explosive as he'd always suspected it would be. Hell, it was even stronger.

His gaze traveled down the thick, shiny fall of her hair, over the pale curve of her hip, then the smooth length of her thigh. She was so delicate, but strong. Deliciously soft, but with a backbone of steel. A dangerous, potentially lethal combination, seeing as how it appealed to the predatory warrior in him on every level.

Reaching down to rearrange his aching shaft, Ashe felt the hunger moving through his body like a sinuous living thing, the beast prowling for a way to get what it wanted. So clearly, he could see himself grabbing hold of Juliana, rolling her beneath him and shoving himself inside her. Working his way in deeper...and deeper, until he'd made her take every inch of him. Then he'd fuck her until neither one of them could remember their damn names. Until he couldn't even remember why he couldn't just take what he wanted and bite— *No! Don't even go there.*

He gave his head a hard shake, clearing his thoughts. Christ, what the hell was he doing? Her bloody life was in danger, and here he was thinking with his dick again, same as he'd been doing for the past hour.

He was an idiot.

Sitting up beside her, he started to get off the bed, only to find himself leaning toward her instead, his mouth suddenly buried in the sensual curve of her neck and shoulder, his tongue seeking out the throbbing rhythm of her pulse. Her skin was exquisitely soft beneath his lips, his fangs burning with the need to sink into her tender flesh again...and again, until he'd marked the hell out of her.

Her breath caught, but she didn't push him away. "Are we...are we going to have sex now?" she asked, sounding adorably belligerent, but aroused.

Forcing himself to draw back, Ashe ran a hand over his tingling mouth, trying to figure out what had just happened...to put his chaotic thoughts in order. Even if it weren't for the danger bearing down on her, he knew this wasn't the time. There was too much at stake to push things too far before he could handle them, his control as shaky as a wet dog that'd been left out in the cold.

"Well?" she pressed.

His voice was little more than a croak, his throat tight and hot. "Not yet."

She pulled at the throw, trying to conceal the damp, sweet-smelling curls between her thighs, her tone almost hopeful as she said, "You've changed your mind?"

"Hardly," he snorted, making himself roll off the mattress and back to his feet. Watching her from the corner of his eye, he headed around to the other side of the bed. With a grimace, he reached down and rearranged his cock again, the thick shaft pulsing with pain, his blood running hot not only from the Burning, but from the sight of Juliana sitting there on the rumpled bedding, so tempting he could feel the serum throbbing in his fangs.

A serum that if injected into her bloodstream would bind them together forever, like a preternatural marriage that could never be undone.

Insane, how badly half of him wanted to push that serum into her veins, while the other half violently recoiled at the thought of permanently bonding with a woman who, for all he knew, could be a scheming little liar. Just because he wanted to believe her didn't mean that what she'd told him was the truth. Sex was one thing…but he couldn't afford to give her more than that.

"I haven't changed my mind." He snagged his sweater off the floor and pulled it on. "But I know my own limits. Once I get inside you, I'm going to be focused on nothing but how good it feels. Before that happens, I need you someplace where I don't have to worry about someone tracking us down. Someplace that's completely safe."

"Completely safe?" Her laugh was brittle. "Do places like that actually exist?"

He flicked her a shuttered look from beneath

his lashes. "I'll keep you protected while we get to the bottom of this. I won't turn my back on you."

"But you won't trust me, either, will you? Which is why you called off our—" she flushed, gesturing toward the bed "—whatever you want to call this."

"I'm pleading the Fifth," he muttered, knowing that Gideon would call him a chickenshit coward for still holding out on her, but this wasn't cowardice. This was pure goddamn self-preservation. If he was going to bed her, he needed to know he was in complete, absolute control of himself.

A quick glance down at his trembling hand told Ashe that, at the moment, he wasn't even close.

Closing his unsteady hand into a hard fist, he shoved his other hand through his hair. "Come on. Get cleaned up and let's get out of here."

"Where are we going?" she asked, sliding to the edge of the bed. When she stood up, she took the throw with her, the soft fabric draping over the feminine curves of her body as she clutched it against her chest.

She looked impossibly young at that moment, reminding him of that glaring gap in their ages. Feeling like a lecherous old man, Ashe forced his gaze away from all that rosy skin and tumbling hair, and walked into the other room as he answered her question. "We're heading someplace they won't expect to find us."

She followed after him, lingering in the doorway. "Can I have a little more than that?"

"You've heard of the Pinero Dominguez?" he asked, opening the small safe that sat on the top shelf of a coat closet.

"Of course." She'd answered with a slight hesitation, sounding as if she was wondering if he could actually be serious. "It's a kind of underground information and hideout network for criminals that runs through France and Northern Italy. It was named after its founder, a famous Spanish vampire who made a fortune sailing as a pirate several hundred years ago."

"That's right," he murmured, focused on emptying the safe and putting what he needed in his pockets. The rest he would put in a bag and store in a locker at the St. Pancras train station. Grabbing the worn leather backpack he'd left at the bottom of the closet, he said, "We're going to use some of their establishments to hide out in while getting to the bottom of those assassination orders."

He could feel her gaze against the side of his face as he set the pack on the small coffee table and started gathering his things from around the room, but he didn't dare look at her. Not yet. His control was already too thin as it was. One more glimpse of her clutching that throw against the front of her naked body and he'd have her on the floor, his cock buried a mile inside her, before she even realized he'd crossed the room.

"I told you that a passport had been left in the pack for me," she said. "But won't it be dangerous to use public transportation right now?"

"No more dangerous than it was for you to come over from Norway."

From the edge of his vision, he caught the way her gaze slid to the floor, her lower lip caught in her teeth. "I didn't actually use public transportation," she admitted, flicking him a quick glance to gauge his reaction. "I hitched some rides, then hid onboard a cargo ship that was crossing the Channel. I think they were, um, some kind of black-market smugglers."

"Christ," he breathed out, a dark scowl settling over his face as he stopped what he was doing and stalked toward her. He was too angry now to be worried about falling on her like a sex-starved maniac. He wanted to wring her bloody neck! "Are you out of your goddamn mind? What do you think would have happened to you if you'd been found?"

She shrugged. "The crew were all human. I could have handled myself."

"One female vampire against how many men?" A cold sweat slipped along his spine, his insides twisting with a nauseating burst of fear at the thought of her in such a dangerous situation.

"They would have been armed, Juliana. You'd have been raped before you could down five of them!"

"But I wasn't," she pointed out, her reasonable tone only making him angrier, "because I'm not stupid. I stayed hidden until it was safe to make my way off the boat."

Telling himself to calm the hell down, Ashe stalked away from her, heading toward the window. He took a deep breath and scrubbed his hands down his face, then shoved them into his pockets. He was having a hard enough time trying not to think about how much danger she was in, and the Lycan attack they'd been through that night, knowing it could push him into some seriously risky territory. One where he stopped fighting and simply acted on his more primal, visceral instincts—instincts that would have him marking her, bonding with her, before he even knew what hit him…his male ego fooling him into believing she would be so much safer if she were *his*. But knowing she'd taken such a ridiculous risk with her safety just pushed him that much closer to the edge.

Did the foolish woman have a death wish? Didn't she know it would destroy him if anything happened to her? Didn't she know that— *Whoa! Wait a minute…*

What the hell was he thinking? Of course she

didn't know. How could she, when he'd never given her a clue about how he felt before to-night? And even now, he was putting it all down to simple animal lust, refusing to tell her about the Burning. Refusing to let her know that even though he didn't trust her, he still thought she was the most beautiful, alluring, fascinating woman he'd ever known.

Completely oblivious to the intimate direction of his thoughts, she asked him another question about their coming trip. "Instead of the Pinero Dominguez, why can't we simply stay at one of your family's nesting grounds?"

Nesting grounds were sprawling castlelike communities where Deschanel families often lived for protection, the compounds protected by spells that made them invisible to the outside world. Most families had only one, but the Grangers were wealthy enough to have several smaller grounds, in addition to the main compound where he and Gideon had been raised, before their parents had passed away.

"If they discover I'm helping you, the nesting grounds will be the first place they look," he told her, turning away from the window. "But the P.D. won't even make their list. The last thing anyone in the Pinero Dominquez would do is harbor an escaped convict. They wouldn't risk drawing any Förmyndares onto their territory."

"But will it be safe?"

"Let me worry about that." He picked up the pack that held all her belongings from the sofa and tossed it to her, jerking his chin toward the bathroom behind her. The sooner her delectable little body was covered in clothes, the sooner he could start thinking straight again. "Do whatever you need to get ready," he told her, forcing himself to turn his attention back to his bag. "But hurry. If we're lucky, we can make all the necessary arrangements and be on the late train to Paris tonight."

BY ELEVEN, THEY WERE on the Eurostar, heading through an underground tunnel beneath the English Channel on a high-speed train that would take them to the Gare du Nord in Paris. Ashe had surprised her with a forged passport of his own when they'd cleared customs, explaining that everyone on his Specs team carried several forged passports with them in the event of an emergency. He'd used one tonight because he didn't want his name showing up on any government records. He obviously knew how far Raphe Delacourt's reach could extend, and wasn't taking any chances.

Despite the late hour, the train car was brimming with a group of British schoolkids on a foreign studies field trip, the lack of privacy no doubt a good thing, since it made any fooling around impossible. Juliana sat huddled inside Ashe's leather jacket, her eyes closed, trying her best to ignore him as he sat beside her, his head tilted back on the headrest, his eyes closed. But it wasn't easy. She'd been caught up in the powerful, sensual web he'd spun back in London, and now she couldn't shake herself free. Every move he made seemed laden with sensual overtones, his scent rich and deep and musky, making her mouth water every time she drew in a breath.

Thanks to the bagged human blood he'd offered her before they'd left his hotel room, the hunger that had been gnawing at her stomach had eased, so she didn't need to worry about feeding. The blood would also enable her to walk in the sunlight for a few days, thanks to a Deschanel vampire's ability to assume certain traits of those species they drank from.

So with those concerns taken care of, she was left to worry about other things, her family's safety residing at the top of the long, depressing list. And because of the spells that made the use of technology impossible in the Wasteland, she couldn't even borrow Ashe's cell phone to call and check on them.

For her family's sake, she would endure the emotional strain being around Ashe put her through, knowing she owed them that and so much more. More than she could ever repay...but she was willing to die trying.

And if she was honest with herself, she knew there was a damn good chance it would come to that.

Though she trusted Ashe to do everything he could to keep her safe—despite the tension between them, he was obviously one of those rare breed of men who would always protect those who needed it—she didn't have much faith that she'd survive the coming days. It made her ache for the life she'd never been given a chance to live. The one with a loving husband and children, a family to call her own. But she could accept her fate, as long as she managed to help her family escape the Wasteland, righting the wrongs that had been done to them. And as long as Ashe was able to walk away from this ordeal unscathed, which was why she would take her darker secrets to the grave with her, where they belonged.

A little more than two hours after leaving London, they arrived in Paris. Even in the middle of the night, the magnificent city was ablaze with lights. It had always been one of Juliana's favorite places in the world, and she'd spent most of her summers there while growing up. She'd even planned to move into a flat near the Musée d'Orsay after she'd finished her studies—but then she'd met Raphe Delacourt, and all her plans had changed. A few short months later, she'd been banished to the Wasteland, believing she'd never see Paris again.

Though she was nervous at the thought of using the Pinero Dominguez as their hideout, she was privately thrilled that Ashe had brought her to this particular city.

They grabbed one of the private taxis loitering at the curb near the front of the station, sliding into the backseat together. It all felt strangely intimate, almost as if they were simply two starry-eyed lovers arriving for a romantic weekend in the City of Lights, when the truth couldn't have been further from the truth. Ashe seemed determined to pretend she wasn't even there, only speaking to her when necessary, his dark gaze focused out his window, a muscle pulsing every now and then in the rigid set of his jaw. So she spent the time staring lovingly at the city as it passed by her window…and stealing greedy glances at him from the corner of her eye, a small smile touching her lips when she noticed how long and thick his eyelashes were. If he was anything like her brother, he'd probably hated them when he was younger, thinking they were too feminine-looking. But they were perfect for him now, adding another touch of devastating sexuality to a face that was all perfect, masculine angles. A rugged, utterly male face that was too gorgeous for its own good, making her feel like a homely little waif as she sat beside him.

It took nearly twenty minutes to reach the antiquated streets of Saint-Germain, one of the oldest districts in Paris, and Ashe instructed the driver to leave them in the middle of a long street of quaint little shops and cafés. Draping her pack over her shoulder, Juliana looked up and down the moonlit street. "This is where we're going?" she asked doubtfully, the appealing neighborhood so far from what she'd imagined for the Pinero Dominguez she wanted to laugh at herself.

"Not quite," Ashe drawled with a lopsided smile. "We still have a little ways to go."

They headed down the cobbled sidewalk, turning into a narrow walkway situated between a boutique and a bookstore. At the far end of the walkway there was an ivy-covered gate, and behind that, a simple black door, the modern keypad on the lock strangely at odds with the historic surroundings. Ashe keyed a number into the pad, and a second later there was a metallic click, like a lock disengaging. He opened the door, telling her to follow behind him, then started down what appeared to be a long, crumbling flight of stone stairs. Chewing nervously on her lower lip, Juliana closed the door behind her, and made her way down.

At the bottom, a long, dimly lit tunnel stretched

out before them, raucous laughter and music spilling from several open doorways, the faded signs hanging above them impossible to read.

"This is more what I had in mind," she whispered, wishing she could reach out and take his hand, her nerves squirming like a handful of eels in her belly.

"Just stay close to me," he murmured, pulling his pack higher on his shoulder. "We've got a ways to walk."

"It's a good thing I'm not claustrophobic," she muttered a few minutes later, the ceiling so low in several places that Ashe had to hunch down to keep from hitting his head on the rough stones. They walked for what must have been about fifteen minutes, going deeper into the noisy underground tunnel, until Ashe finally stopped in front of what appeared to be some sort of biker bar or nightclub.

Juliana stared at the blacked-out windows lining the bar's front, the neon sign hanging above the closed door flickering too rapidly for her to read what it said. All she could make out was the shape of a topless blonde with fangs and a tail straddling what appeared to be some sort of motorcycle. "Um, wow."

Ashe pushed his hands into his pockets. "I know it's not much to look at," he said, "but a friend of mine owns it." His tone was wry, as if he knew just how horrified she was by the thought of going inside, half-expecting there to be strippers dancing on the tables. "I need his help to start our search," he went on, "and he'll be willing to give us a room for the night. Plus, the security is better than anything else we'll find."

"Are you sure Raphe won't think to send assassins here?" She scrunched her nose as she looked up at him. "I mean, this is a criminal underground network, and he's one of the biggest vampire criminals in existence."

His chest shook with a grim laugh. "Trust me, Delacourt has no connection to the P.D. At least, not to any of the places we'll be staying."

"How do you know?"

He popped his jaw, the look of fury suddenly glittering in his eyes sending a shiver down her spine. "Because these people are friends of mine. Which means they despise the Delacourts as much as—" he broke off and ran his tongue over his teeth "—as much as most of the Förmyndares do."

She knew he'd been about to say as much as *he* did, but had stopped. For some reason, he didn't want her to know what his connection was to Raphe Delacourt, or even that he had one. But she had no doubt there was something between them. At this point, she was starting to think Ashe might hate the crime lord *almost* as much as she did.

"Not that it's any of my business," she murmured, arching one of her brows. "But isn't it a little strange…I mean a Förmyndare being friends with known criminals?"

Though his eyes still glinted with that hot, visceral glow, his expression softened, a cocky smile twitching on his lips. "I wouldn't call my friends criminals, per se. Gideon and I think of them more as law manipulators."

She gave a quiet snort.

"Seriously," he said with an easy shrug, "I'm not friendly with murderers or rapists or terrorists. These are good people. They just aren't happy with the current status quo, and they have their own ideas about how to bring about change."

"I'm surprised at you, Granger." Her tone was teasing. "From the sound of it, you're cronies with a bunch of revolutionaries!"

"Revolutionaries, huh?" His smile flashed as he reached for the door. "I'll have to pass that on to Knox. He'll get a kick out of it."

"Who's Knox?" she asked, following him inside the smoky interior, her eyes burning from the heavy veil of cigarette smoke lingering in the air.

"Knox is the guy who owns this place."

Only a few tables near the front were still occupied at this hour, the rest of the customers having already headed home. Ashe said something to the flirty blonde counting the money in the cash register, and a moment later a tall, auburn-haired man stalked through the doorway at the far end of the bar, a scowl twisting his sensual mouth as he looked toward Ashe. He was wearing black jeans and a black T-shirt, his arms covered in intricate tattoos, another one climbing up the right side of his throat. Despite being big and mean and some-what scary-looking, the male was undeniably at-tractive, an unmistakable air of wicked sexuality wrapping around his tall, muscular body as he paced toward them.

Juliana kept her voice low, knowing from the man's scent that he was some sort of shape-shifter, which meant his hearing would be exceptional. "Is it just me, or does he not look too happy to see you?"

"Ignore the scowl. It's his usual expression. Only time I've ever seen him smile is when he's got two women on him and he's in the middle of co—" He suddenly broke off, coughing into his fist, but she could see the smile he was trying to hide.

"Lovely," she drawled, lifting her brows. "You've brought me to one of your whoring bud-dies."

Instead of gloating, which she'd expected, Ashe slid her a considering gaze, his dark head cocked just a little to the side as he stared down at her.

Quietly, he said, "You really don't have a very high opinion of me, do you?"

Looking away, she exhaled an unsteady breath. "Let's just say I learned early on not to trust a beautiful face."

"Hmm," he said in a low tone. "You're not the only one who's learned that lesson."

Before she could ask him to elaborate on that telling statement, the tattooed shifter reached them. He kept the ferocious-looking scowl in place until he stood nearly nose to nose with Ashe. Then a huge grin split his face and he threw a long arm around Ashe's shoulders, whacking him on the back so hard it would have flattened a lesser man.

"It's been too long, you son of a bitch!" the shifter growled with genuine affection, giving Ashe another spine-cracking whack before pulling back and crossing his massive arms over his chest, his biceps straining the sleeves of his T-shirt in the same way she'd seen Ashe's do. She thought she'd caught a bit of an Irish accent in his craggy voice, but couldn't be sure.

"I wish this was just a friendly visit," Ashe said, "but I've got a problem I'm hoping you can help with."

The shifter slid an interested look toward Juliana, a wicked smile spreading over his handsome face. "No problem, boyo. I'll be happy to help out with the little filly any way I can."

Little filly?

Juliana blinked, while Ashe gave a husky laugh. "She's not the problem, you ass. And you're sure as hell not getting your sleazy hands on her."

"Damn," the giant drawled, giving her a playful wink before shifting his curious gaze back to Ashe, waiting for him to explain.

Placing his hand on her lower back in a strangely possessive gesture, Ashe first made the introductions, his voice dry. "Knox, this is Juliana, and you can stop leering at her anytime now. Juliana, this is Knox, criminal mastermind and unparalleled thief." At her wary expression, he added, "Don't worry. If anything, he's more of a modern-day Robin Hood, only without the tights. And the charm, for that matter."

"How…interesting."

Knox gave her a slow smile as he snatched her hand, placing a lingering kiss on her knuckles. "Aren't I just?" he drawled, before arching a dark brow at Ashe. "And I have more charm than you, you witless clod."

"God, don't start," he said with a heartfelt groan, jerking Juliana's hand out of Knox's grip… and keeping it in his own. "I can't take your shit tonight."

Knox narrowed his dark blue eyes. "Yeah, now

that you mention it, you do look like shit. There's something grim around your eyes."

Lowering his voice, Ashe said, "You're going to have that same grim look when I tell you we're searching for information on the Delacourts."

Knox whistled softly, then suggested they take the conversation to one of the tables in the back of the room, away from the staff, who were now cleaning up after what appeared to have been a rough, bacchanalian kind of night, several pieces of broken bar stools still littering the floor, as well as some racy lingerie hanging from the overhead light fixtures. At a signal from Knox, the blonde behind the bar brought them each a tall, icy bottle of beer. Knox took a long drink of the dark brew, then looked at Ashe. "What's your interest in the Delacourts?"

Ashe briefly explained the situation, relaying what Juliana had told him, and Knox listened with keen interest, his dark eyes sharp with intelligence. He didn't come right out and call her a liar, but she had the uncomfortable feeling that he thought there was more to the story than what she had shared, the same as Ashe did.

As he wrapped up his explanation, Ashe's deep voice took on a raw edge. "So we have reason to believe the Delacourts have taken out assassination orders against Juliana and her family in order to…keep the whole thing quiet."

Knox gave another soft whistle as he leaned back in his chair, lacing his fingers behind his head. "If anyone has the kind of money to fund an operation like that, especially when the targets are inside the Wasteland, it would be the Delacourts."

Sprawling sideways in his chair, Ashe thumped his knuckles against the scarred surface of the table. "That's what I was thinking. Raphe's drug money has given the family a substantial bankroll for the past decade."

A stunned sound slipped past her lips. "That long?"

"Easily," Knox replied, locking his dark gaze with hers. "Ashe could tell you more about it than I could, but Raphe got started when he was little more than a pup. You can guarantee that if it's illegal and it makes money, then he's got one of his sticky fingers in the pie."

"Wow." From the corner of her eye, she caught the intense way Ashe was looking at her, and quickly said, "I'm just surprised. I mean, I knew he was considered a criminal back then, but I'd always thought that until recently he was into more...um, gentlemanly crimes." Whatever those were.

"Gentlemanly crimes?" Knox gave a low laugh, flashing Ashe a smile. "I like this girl, Granger."

"If we can get back on topic," he muttered.

"Have you heard anything that could be useful to us?"

Knox lowered his arms, scrubbing one huge hand across the auburn stubble on his jaw. "Actually, there's a lot of talk going on about Raphe at the moment."

Ashe leaned forward, crossing his arms on the table. "What kind of talk?"

"His mama's always been powerful. You know that as well as I. But the rumor going around is that her son is forcing her to make some kind of monumental power play within the Council. One that will shake the foundations of clan society."

"Anything specific?"

"You know ol' Selingham?" Knox asked, reaching for his beer again.

Juliana was familiar with the name, recalling an old, decrepit vampire who had served on the Deschanel Council for centuries.

"I know him," Ashe replied with a nod, his voice getting rougher. "What happened?"

Knox tilted his bottle to his lips, taking a long swallow, then wiped the back of his wrist over his mouth. "He turned up dead a little over a week ago."

"Natural causes?"

Setting his bottle back down on the table, Knox snorted. "Hardly. He was supposedly mauled to death by a rogue Lycanthrope while at the Deschanel Court in Rome." The Deschanel courts were where all the high-ranking officials within the Deschanel clan lived and worked, as well as the Council. There were several official court compounds scattered across Europe, the court itself moving from one location to the next as the mood struck them.

Ashe's breath hissed through his teeth in response to Knox's news. "Like hell that would have happened. The courts have some of the most stringent security there is. No way could a rogue have gotten inside without it being a setup. Is there an investigation?"

"That's the thing," Knox murmured, shaking his head. "The whole case was apparently wrapped up within a few hours and judged a freak accident. One of those momentary lapses in security, if you can believe that bullshit."

"Christ," Ashe muttered, leaning back in his chair, his expression as dark as the look in his eyes. He had his hands fisted at his sides. "The Delacourts must have them by the balls."

"I'd say they're holding on tight, and any second now, they're going to just rip the damn things off," Knox drawled.

Flinching from the gruesome image his words put in her mind, Juliana looked at Ashe. "What does he mean?"

"He means they're going to destroy the Council," he grated, the lines of strain around his eyes and mouth getting deeper. "Then dissolve the Court...and put *themselves* in power."

CHAPTER SIX

SITTING AT A CORNER TABLE in Knox's bar the following afternoon, Ashe took a slow sip of his whiskey, his mind running over everything that had happened since he'd found Juliana…and everything that he'd learned. Someone was going to a hell of a lot of trouble to set this thing up, putting him and Juliana in league together, and he wanted to know why.

Even more than that, though, he wanted confirmation of who was behind the assassination orders against the Sabins…and Juliana herself. Was it really Raphe Delacourt, and if so, why go to the trouble of killing the family now? Was the bastard worried that someone in the Sabin family could pose a threat to him? And if so, then what was the threat? According to Juliana, no one had believed their claims nine years ago that Lenora's accusations were false. So why the fear that someone might believe them now? And was that someone the person who had plotted Juliana's escape from the Wasteland?

Or were they being deliberately steered off course? Was it some unknown enemy hiring the assassins, with some unknown grievance against her family?

Ashe didn't know the answers, and the questions were running his brain ragged. Not to mention the sexual hunger ripping through his insides that wouldn't ease up. He supposed there was more truth to the old saying *"no good deed goes unpunished"* than he'd ever actually realized. In trying to help the little vampire, he was putting himself through hell. Even Knox had noticed how much strain he was under, the shifter's crude teasing throughout the day his way of showing concern.

In the early hours of the morning, Ashe had left Juliana upstairs in the room Knox had given them, telling her to get some rest while she could. Knowing he needed to get things moving as quickly as possible, he'd put off sleep and spent the day working with Knox. They'd both met with various informants, setting up feelers across the underground networks that Knox moved in, hoping information would soon start trickling in.

There were still a lot of calls he needed to make, which meant he needed to concentrate, but he couldn't stop thinking about the female cuddling up in that bed upstairs by herself. Christ, where was his blasted control when he needed it?

For what must be the hundredth time, he wondered if it was possible that she felt the same need that he did. That same inexorable pull. Throughout the night, he'd caught the way she constantly watched him from the corner of her eye when she thought he wasn't paying attention. And then there was the way she'd reacted to him back in London. She'd been so hot she'd practically singed him. So responsive he'd just wanted to keep pushing her over that sweet, melting edge, feeling her come for him again and again, until he'd laid claim to every part of her.

He wished he knew what was going on in that stubborn head of hers. Hell, he wished he knew everything about her. And he wasn't above snooping to learn what he could. While she'd taken a quick shower after he'd walked her up to their room, Ashe had looked through the pack she carried with her. He knew money had been left for her in the pack, and that she'd used it to buy some things after her escape from the Wasteland. His mouth curved with a grim smile as he recalled the things he'd found. There'd been none of the frivolous cosmetics that so many women would have seen as a necessity. Instead, Juliana had purchased a couple of romance novels and several self-help books. The romance novels had been a surprise, simply because he hadn't expected her to be a romantic. He wondered if she read them back at the Sabin compound, and if so, why? Was it because she needed to escape into another world...or did she simply get lonely, even when surrounded by her relatives?

And don't forget the men who work for them.

He scowled, hating the thought of the brawny males, who had basically served under Juliana's command, servicing her in more intimate ways. And hating that he hated it.

Throwing off the irritating emotion, he focused his thoughts on the self-help books that he'd found, the titles suggesting they were about grief and guilt. He wished he knew exactly what she felt so guilty about. Did it have to do with her family's banishment? Despite how intensely he'd searched, he'd never been able to find anyone who could give him so much as a hint as to why the Sabin family was living in exile. There were no records of their punishment in the official Council documents, and no one in the Court had even been willing to discuss the case with him. Not even the old friends of his parents and grandparents, who had always been willing to help him and Gideon in their investigations when they needed it.

A sultry, feminine laugh suddenly drew him out of his reverie, and he looked toward the entrance of the bar, where Knox stood chatting with

Ashe's next appointment, the woman's gaze glittering with interest as she flirted with the auburn-haired shifter. He wasn't surprised by her reaction. Knox had the height and build of a soldier, and the air of dominance, as well. In the past, Ashe had seen women fawn over the guy's tattoos and shoulder-length auburn hair more times than he could count, and had heard dozens refer to the shifter's face as "wickedly sinful."

He wondered if Juliana had thought the same thing, another uncomfortable wave of jealousy biting him hard in the ass.

Choking back a sharp curse, he watched as the female—who was a powerful witch, as well as a scientist—eventually made her way over to his table, her shapely figure wrapped in brightly colored swaths of jewel-colored silks, her black hair falling in heavy waves to the small of her back. Her name was Sybil Le Fleur and she worked with a healer Ashe had met in the Wasteland named Gabby Reyker, a quirky little vamp with a talent for concocting antidotes and cures. Gabby was also friendly with Juliana, but then Jules was just one of those women who others found it difficult to dislike, her personality the kind that put others at ease. She was warm and caring, without being insincere and annoying.

At least, that's how she was with everyone

but Ashe. He didn't know whether he should feel special…or like a total jackass.

Ashe had contacted Gabby not long after his Burning had begun, swearing her to secrecy before asking for her help, though he wouldn't even tell Gabby the identity of the woman who'd started the change in his body. She'd told him the same thing that everyone else had, claiming that there was no cure for the infuriating phenomenon. But after he'd practically begged, she'd offered him a new concoction she'd been working on. She hadn't made any promises, but it'd been Gabby's belief that the special blend might lessen the effects of the Burning for him, and so he'd been taking it religiously every day.

"Before you think of running off with him," he advised Sybil, who was currently eyeing Knox's ass as he headed back to his office, "I should warn you that his longest relationship with a woman lasted little more than a half hour."

Sybil arched her brows as she settled her onyx gaze on him, sliding into one of the chairs at his table. "So Knox has a short attention span, hmm? Sounds like a typical guy."

With a snort, he said, "Women are just as bad, Syb. If not worse."

Her laugh was deep and throaty. "Gods, Ashe. Has anyone ever told you that you're a cynical ass?"

"Believe it or not, I get that a lot." Which wasn't entirely true. Over the past year, he'd actually done his part to ease several misunderstandings between his male friends and their women. Despite his own crap experiences, he'd seen enough happy couples among his friends and family to know that not all relationships sucked. He'd seen love and devotion and happiness. But that didn't mean he could ever take such a risk for himself simply because of the Burning.

Forcing his attention back to Sybil, he watched as she reached into a pocket in her silk pants and drew out a small glass vial filled with a clear liquid. "I know this isn't much," she said, passing the vial to him. "But it's all Gabby could make on such short notice."

"Tell her I'm going to need more," he said, slipping the vial into his pocket. "I'm going to double up on the doses because it isn't working."

The witch eyed him with the shrewd gaze of a scientist. "How do you know?"

His words rumbled in his throat like distant thunder. "I know because I still want to get inside the woman more than I want to breathe." Though both Gabby and Sybil knew that he wanted the concoction to reduce the effects of his Burning, neither woman knew the identity of the responsible female, and Ashe planned on keeping it that way. Which was why he'd warned Juliana to stay up in the room, and had forbidden Knox from mentioning her name to Sybil.

The witch studied him for a moment, her head cocked a bit to the side, her dark eyes swirling with shadows and light that could have made him dizzy if he stared at them for too long. Just when he was about to demand to know what the hell she was doing, she crossed her arms on the table and gave him a careful smile. "Ashe, have you ever considered that your attraction to this woman could be about more than just the Burning?"

Pushing his knuckles into his tired eyes, he growled what he knew was more than likely a lie and told her that it wasn't. Only, he said it a lot more colorfully.

"I wouldn't be so sure," she murmured. "After all, the whole purpose of the Burning is to bring two complementary forces together. It's meant to be fate's way of joining two vampires with his and her ideal mate."

"Not in all cases," he argued.

Sybil's smile was knowing. "There are always exceptions to a rule, Ashe. But you're a smart guy. I'm sure you'll figure it out."

With those frustrating words, she leaned over the small table and kissed his cheek, told him to give Knox her number, and then made her way out of the bar, leaving him feeling even edgier than before. Taking the vial she'd given him from his pocket, he twisted the cap off and downed two sips of the blend, hoping like hell that it worked.

Scrubbing his hands down his face, he drew in a couple of deep breaths, waiting to feel some relief. But it wasn't coming. He was just getting edgier…his tension mounting. The crowd in the bar was starting to pick up, the noise growing louder, grating on his nerves, so he used it as an excuse to do what he'd wanted to do ever since he'd come downstairs, and headed back up to see Juliana.

He opened the door to their room without knocking, and found her sitting with her legs crisscrossed in the middle of the bed, dressed in a T-shirt and jeans. Her long hair tumbled over her shoulders as she stared down at the dark duvet beneath her, completely lost in her thoughts.

"I asked Knox to send up some food for you in a little while," he said, drawing her gaze. He tried to keep his eyes on her face, but failed, his gaze dipping lower, lingering on the way the tight gray T-shirt cupped her breasts, the soft material clinging like a second skin. He knew damn well she wasn't wearing a bra, the shape of her nipples growing more distinct the longer he stared.

She muttered something under her breath, then crossed her arms over her chest in a nonverbal message he heard loud and clear.

Forcing his attention back on her face, he swal-

lowed the lump of lust in his throat and managed
to ask, "Are you hungry?"

"A LITTLE," JULIANA replied, watching him close
the door...and lock it. "Can we leave soon?" she
asked, her voice trembling with nerves at the idea
of being alone with him. "I'm not comfortable
here."

Which was true. She'd felt ready to come out of
her skin ever since she'd awakened from an erotic
dream almost two hours ago. One that had her
twisting on the bed, a throaty moan spilling from
her lips as a stunning orgasm had ripped through
her body. She'd felt destroyed, and that was only
from "imagining" sex with Ashe Granger. God
only knew what the real thing would do to her,
and she wasn't ready to find out yet, too worried
she'd do something unforgivably stupid, like fall
in love with the sexy vamp.

A much better plan was to get back on the road
and out of this room, away from the bed and the
disturbingly vivid memories of that dream.

"I told you this place is safe," he said, turning
and propping his shoulder against the door. He'd
obviously mistaken her nervous tension for fear.
"You don't need to worry. No one will find us
here."

"So I should just take your word for it?" she
drawled, knowing she sounded bitchy.

With a dark expression falling over his face, he started toward her. "Trust isn't negotiable in degrees. You either trust me or you don't, Juliana. There's no middle ground."

"And what about you?" she demanded, glaring at up him as he loomed over her from the side of the bed.

His voice was deceptively soft. "What about me?"

"Never mind," she muttered, sliding toward the opposite side of the queen-size mattress. She moved to her feet and started to pace barefoot on the hardwood floor, her arms crossed over her chest again, only sneaking glimpses at him from the corner of her eye. "Have you learned anything?"

Pushing his hands in his pockets, he answered her question. "A little. It sounds as if Raphe has been busy these past few months. In addition to destroying another South American cartel that had been giving him some heavy competition, he's also built four different high-security compounds across Europe. He's obviously gearing up for something, and it's making the Deschanel Court nervous as hell, not to mention the Council."

It was impossible to miss the derision in his tone whenever he said that particular vampire's name. Stopping in the center of the room, she slid him a curious stare. "Are you ever going to tell me what your connection is to Raphe Delacourt? Or am I meant to guess?"

"My connection?"

"Come on, Ashe. I'm not an idiot. Every time his name comes up, you look ready to rip out his throat. I have a right to know what your association is with him."

His tone was dry. "You're hardly one to lecture about keeping secrets."

"I've told you everything you need to know." Which was true. Mostly. Minus a few potentially deadly details.

Getting back on topic, she said, "It's obvious from listening to you and Knox that you have some kind of history with the Delacourts. I'd like to know what it is."

He walked over to the room's lone window, which looked down on the main floor of the bar, and braced his hands against the window frame, the masculine position doing incredible things to his broad, muscular shoulders and back. Staring out the tinted glass, he gave a tired, drawn-out sigh. "It's a long, boring story, Juliana."

She made a dry sound that could have almost passed for a laugh. "I've spent years trapped in the Wasteland, Ashe. At this point, you could recite the alphabet and I'd probably find it fascinating. So you needn't worry I'll be bored to tears."

His head fell forward, one hand rubbing over his eyes, then shoving back through his short hair. It was clear he was carrying on some kind of internal debate. She waited to see what he would decide, a spark of relief spreading through her insides when he braced his hand against the frame again and said, "Gideon and I have been trying to nail Raphe Delacourt for a long time now, but it isn't easy. Not when his mama sits on the Council, doing whatever he tells her to do, using her position of power to protect him."

"Lenora Delacourt adores him," she said in a low voice, picturing the lovely, raven-haired vampire in her mind. If ever a woman's angelic face had hidden a black soul, it was Lenora's. "She's the one who ordered my parents' execution."

He spun toward her, his expression one of grim surprise. "What do you mean their execution? I thought they died in the Wasteland."

Rolling her lips together, she said, "No. By the time the Council convicted my mother and father of conspiring against them, they were already dead. Lenora Delacourt's private guards had supposedly killed them by accident when they'd tried to resist arrest. But it was a lie." She took a deep breath, deciding she could go ahead and give him at least a little more information. "My parents were on their way to the Council with damaging information about the Delacourts when her guards attacked them. They both died at the scene."

His stare was dark and penetrating. "What kind of information? What did they have on the Delacourts?"

Juliana chose her words with care. "They were taking evidence to the Council that proved it was actually the Delacourts who intended to overthrow them."

He absorbed that with a quiet curse, then asked, "Did Lenora have the authorization to bring them in?"

"No. It was all a huge embarrassment for the Council. I mean, one of their own members making an illegal kill against two esteemed vampires. I think that's why the Council was so eager to believe Lenora's bullshit story about our quest for power and why they sentenced the entire family line. They wanted us somewhere we couldn't cause them any trouble."

As far as stories went, this one wasn't so far-fetched. Ashe had heard tales of the Council doing extraordinary things to save its ass. But he could tell there was more she wasn't telling him.

Still, she'd given him something, and he could do the same.

"Raphe Delacourt killed one of my cousins. His name was Sanders." Dropping into a nearby chair, he leaned forward, elbows braced on his parted knees, and locked his gaze with hers. "He was a punk of a kid," he admitted with a wry smile, "but he had a good heart. Gid and I tried hard to get him to join the Förmyndares, thinking a little discipline was all he needed to get his priorities straight. But he…" His voice trailed off as he felt the familiar burn of rage pouring through his system, and he blew out a rough breath before going on.

"But Raphe got his hands on him, instead, offering him a life that Sanders saw as an easy way out." His lip curled with a sneer. "Get rich quick, without having to work very hard for it. All the women and drink and drugs he could want. Gid and I started investigating Raphe, looking for a way to bring him down, without the authorization of the Förmyndares. We were still hoping to get Sanders out, hoping we could save him before he ended up serving time for the rest of his life."

He paused for a moment, wishing like hell that he had a bottle of whiskey with him. "It was a bad time for us," he finally forced out, lowering his gaze, watching his hands as he rubbed one thumb into the palm of the other. "Our family's main nesting ground had been hit at the start of the war last year, and we'd lost so many. Gid and I were willing to do anything to keep from losing Sanders, too. You name it, we tried it. We blackmailed, threatened, even took a shot at acting as if we'd switched sides, trying anything we could think of to take down Delacourt's operation.

"Hell, I'd have even taken out Delacourt myself," he growled, his hands slowly curling into fists, "but the bastard hides behind a damn battalion of private guards, as well as his mother's protection. In the end, nothing Gid and I did worked. Sanders just got sucked in deeper, and before we knew it, the kid we'd watched grow up was no longer even there. From what we were able to put together, it sounds as if Raphe killed him for becoming a liability to his operation. He'd become a hard user, and started making serious mistakes." Lifting his head, he stared into her dark eyes as he said, "We finally found his body toward the end of the summer."

"I'm sorry," she whispered, her soft voice rough with emotion. "I know what it's like to feel responsible for your family."

"Speaking of which," he grunted, clearing his throat as he moved to his feet, "I've made arrangements to have extra protection provided for your family at the Sabin compound. There's a unit from Specs on their way there now. They'll make sure that nothing happens to your family while we're getting to the bottom of those assassination orders."

She returned his stare with a look of complete

amazement, her eyes wide, breaths coming in rapid little puffs that made him think of sex. "I...I don't know what to say."

"You could thank me," he suggested, doing his best to appear easygoing and relaxed as he shoved his hands back in his pockets. "With a kiss."

"I could," she replied, looking as if she was trying to hold back a smile, her eyes shining with laughter and some deeper, vibrant emotion that made him want to do ridiculous things like grab hold of her and refuse to let go. "But I think I'll just say thank you, instead."

"You're a coldhearted woman," he proclaimed with a playful sigh. He was enjoying this easy banter with her, his chest actually feeling a little lighter after telling her about Sanders. In a softer voice, he added, "Cold and beautiful and cruel."

She snuffled a quiet laugh as she shook her head. "And you're too pretty for your own good, when you stop scowling and actually smile."

"Pretty?" A theatrical wince twisted his features. "Christ, you don't call a man pretty, Jules. Not ever. It's just...wrong."

Juliana raised her brows. "Oh, I'm sorry. Is that too feminine? Should I say something like 'ruggedly godlike' instead? Is that masculine enough for your fragile ego?"

"God, you're a smart-ass," he drawled, admiring her gutsy personality on so many levels.

Despite the strain she was under, she was never afraid to tease or argue or demand. She was the perfect combination of gentleness and strength, of mystery and directness, and it was worrying the hell out of him that he actually liked being around her as much as he did.

"A smart-ass, huh?" A sad smile hovered on her lips. "So my brother always says."

"Micah?"

"Yeah."

"How is he?" he asked, feeling like an ass for not having asked that particular question sooner. Micah Sabin suffered from a powerful vampire poison that affected his sanity, at times making him a violent, volatile danger, even to those he loved. When he was going through one of his bad spells, the Sabins often had to lock him up, since they couldn't bring themselves to kill him.

She ran her hands over her arms, her shoulders lifting in a weary shrug. "He's better. Worse. It all depends on the day, really."

"I'm sorry."

"Yeah." Her voice sounded thick with tears. "Me, too."

She looked so lost suddenly, it was all he could do not to walk over and take her into his arms, offering what comfort he could. Granted, after becoming a hard bastard at an early age, comfort had never really been one of his strong points. But it hadn't mattered. He hadn't felt the need to offer it for years, and damn it, he shouldn't be feeling it now. Not with Juliana.

Every single time he looked at her, loud, ear-shattering sirens bombarded his brain, as if a nuclear holocaust was bearing down on him. They were irritating as hell, but he figured he'd just keep ignoring the buggers and stick to his plan of getting as much of her as he could before it ended.

And, yeah, he knew what he sounded like. Some desperate junkie trying to justify his next fix. Stupid. Dangerous. And potentially lethal. But even knowing it, he couldn't stop. His plan might not be perfect, but it was the only one he had, and he was sticking with it. Hopefully Gabby's blend would be enough to prevent him from making the mother lode of all mistakes. And if it didn't…

No, he wouldn't think about that. He'd resist it with everything he had—even if it meant doing the unthinkable…and sending Gideon in to take his place.

Which meant he needed to start getting his fill, now, while he still had the chance.

"What are you doing?" she asked, a wary note edging into her voice as he sat down in the chair again and started taking off his boots and socks. Then he stood back up and pulled off the T-shirt he'd changed into earlier, dropping it on the floor, and reached for the top button on his fly.

"I'm getting ready for bed," he told her, his fingers sliding to the next button.

Her eyes went huge. "But this is *my* room."

He worked open another button. "Which is precisely why I'm here, and not in another one. I'm dead on my feet, but there's no way in hell I'll be able to sleep when I'm this wound up. So I plan on fucking you until we're both too exhausted to move, then grab a few hours of downtime before I do it again." He finished with the last button, the denim slouching low on his hips as he made his way toward her, saying, "And by that time, I reckon it'll be time to check back in with Knox."

She took a deep breath, looking as if she was trying very hard not to panic, while at the same time doing her best to rein in her temper. "I'll have sex with you, because that's what I agreed to. But I'm not…I won't sleep beside you."

His brows drew together in confusion as he reached the place where she stood, no more than a foot of space between them. "Why the hell not?"

"Because," she explained, wetting her lips, "that wasn't part of the agreement."

Shrugging his shoulders, he said, "I'm making the rules up as I go along."

Her nostrils flared, arms crossed so tight over her chest it was probably difficult for her to breathe. "How convenient for you!" she practically shouted, the panic in her words impossible to miss.

"You're not…afraid of me, are you?"

"No!"

A wave of relief, followed by a fresh burst of frustration. "Then what's the bloody problem?"

"Sleeping is like feeding," she argued. "It's too…too intimate."

"Then it's too damn bad you feel that way," he bit out in a hard voice, irritated as hell that he was apparently good enough to fuck, but not to share a bed with. "You should have made that stipulation last night, when we were negotiating, but you didn't. Now it's too damn late."

"That isn't fair!"

"Fair?" he growled, yanking her against his chest. "What isn't fair is spending the last year needing to be inside you so badly I can't see straight, and you turning your little nose up at me every time I got close to you!"

She craned her head back to gape up at him. "I did no such thing!"

"The hell you didn't," he groaned, suddenly covering her mouth with his in a kiss that was hot and angry and hard, flavored with raw, seething emotions that had him tearing away before he got lost in the storm.

Keeping his fingers locked around her arms, he stared her right in the eye, his chest rising and falling from the jagged force of his breaths. "I want you in a bed, Juliana. I want hours on top of you, under you, beside you. Hell, I want it all. And I want to be able to drift off, knowing that I can roll back over at any time and sink right back into you." His voice dropped even lower. "So stop arguing and get back on the damn bed."

"You know what your problem is? You're too accustomed to getting your own way."

Sliding his hands up to her shoulders, he gave her a cocky smile. "No harm in that."

"It's bad for your ego!" she fumed, thumping her fists against his chest.

"You're the only thing feeding my ego," he said, digging his hands in her hair to keep her from pulling away, his fingers shaping around her skull. "I touch you and you start coming," he growled, turning her head so that he could put the gravelly words in her ear, giving a quick nip to the delicate lobe. "Makes me feel like a god when you do that."

"A g-god?" she said with an angry burst of laughter, trembling so hard her teeth were chattering. "You're c-crazy!"

About you... He almost said the words out loud, but bit them back at the last second, knowing that was a bit of insanity he could never allow. Bad enough that she knew how much he wanted her physically. He had no intention of letting her know exactly how much he enjoyed the rest of her.

"I know this place isn't ideal," he told her, forcing himself to take a step back and let her go, giving himself a minute to get his head on straight, "but it's better than nothing. And I'll probably cause some kind of permanent damage to myself if we don't go ahead and get this over with."

Her spine stacked up to her full height, which still left her a good ten inches shorter than him. "Over with?" she choked, her gray eyes flashing with indignation. "I swear you're the most crass man I've ever known."

"You want some smooth-talking seduction," he muttered, rubbing a hand over his mouth, his heavy-lidded gaze lowering to her breasts, "you're going to have to let me take the bloody edge off first. I'm dying here, woman."

That was such a guy thing to say, Juliana almost laughed. But the husky sound was cut off as soon as he reached down and shucked his jeans, his tight black boxers doing little to hide his blatant, jaw-dropping erection. But then, the rest of his body was just as incredible. Tall and hard and dangerously powerful, he was all tough, ropy muscles and sinew bunched beneath dark, hair-dusted skin. So ruggedly gorgeous he could have made a freaking fortune as a model.

With a hard swallow, she tried to clear the husky note of lust from her throat. But it didn't work. "Ashe...I'm not sure this is smart."

"Like I told you before, fuck smart," he rasped, his rough tone the sexiest damn thing she'd ever heard. He lifted his hand, tipping her chin up with his fingers, while his other hand grabbed a fistful of her hair, dragging her closer. Then he lowered his head over hers, his mouth close enough for her to feel the sensual warmth of his breath. "You don't want me buried inside you, Jules, then you had better tell me now," he whispered, the bright, molten look in his eyes making her want impossible things. "Because in another thirty seconds, honey, it'll be too late."

CHAPTER SEVEN

JULIANA HAD EVERY INTENTION of telling the man no, even with that blasted agreement weighing between them. She knew she wasn't ready yet... that she had to find some way to bolster her defenses before letting him inside her. But when she opened her mouth, the words wouldn't come. All she could make was a soft, needy sound that made his silver eyes burn hot with triumph.

God, she was so easy it was embarrassing. After everything she'd been through, everything she and her loved ones had suffered, and she still couldn't turn her back on a beautiful face when it counted.

He wrapped her in his arms, his big hands hot and strong against her back, molding her against the front of his body as he took her mouth, claiming it, reminding her of exactly how perfect it felt to lose herself in him. To lose herself in this pulsing, deafening, shattering rush of sensation, everything warm and heavy with promise, like some kind of incandescent emotion thrumming through her veins. She couldn't put a name to it. All she could do was fall deeper into that blazing, blinding light as he thrust his tongue against hers in a kiss that was blatantly sexual. He held nothing back, his aggressive hunger like a physical entity wrapping around them, binding her in his spell. His arms tightened, lifting her off the ground, his delicious, devastating mouth never leaving hers as he turned and carried her to the foot of the bed.

She lost herself in the scorching depths of the kiss, drugged by the sensual pleasure, her heart pounding in deep, rhythmic beats as she felt him reach for the bottom of her shirt. He broke away only long enough to rip the shirt over her head, then took her mouth in another blistering kiss, his chest rubbing against her sensitive breasts, making them feel swollen and full, while his fingers started to work on her jeans. Within seconds, her jeans and panties were lying on the floor at her feet, and she was standing naked in his arms. His black boxers were the only thing that separated them.

"I can't get enough of your mouth," he groaned, kissing her with an almost visceral hunger, her breath coming in short, choppy bursts as she tried to keep up with him. She held on tight to his big shoulders, her knees shaking as his hands moved in bold sweeps over her breasts and hips, before curving around to squeeze her ass. "You need to get on the bed," he growled against her lips.

Breaking away from the kiss, Juliana struggled to catch her breath. "Can we turn off the lights first?"

His hands tightened on her hips, his bright gaze tracking down her body. "No way in hell."

She opened her mouth to argue, feelings of insecurity and shyness nipping at her heels, but then snapped it shut. They'd already argued enough for one day. If this was going to happen, and it sure as hell appeared that it was, she didn't want to remember acting like a shrew. For once, she wanted something amazing to look back on. Something hotter and more wicked than anything she'd ever read in a book. An incredible memory to keep her warm on a cold winter's night.

And if any man was capable of creating a memorable sexual moment, she knew it was this one.

"On the bed," he grunted, picking her up and tossing her into the middle of the mattress as if she weighed nothing.

"Damn it," she gasped, throwing her arms out as she stopped bouncing, her knees bent and spread in a way that was no doubt giving him a hell of a shot. Arching her brows at him, she asked, "What is it with you and tossing me onto things?"

"It gets you where I want you faster." His voice was low, his attention focused hard and tight on the tingling flesh between her thighs. Juliana started to snap them together, but he said, "Don't!"

She probably would have ignored him and closed her legs anyway, if he hadn't diverted her attention by reaching down and shoving his boxers over his hips, the soft cotton dropping to the floor. She was still blinking, trying to take in her first stunning encounter with his completely naked, mouthwatering body, when he said, "How do you take your birth control?"

"What?" she asked, distracted. But in her defense, it was hard to concentrate when his impressive erection kept stealing her attention. Then she thought about what he'd said, and her wide-eyed gaze locked with his, his expression taut with hard, masculine need.

"I was so wound up in London," he said roughly, "I didn't even think about the possibility of pregnancy." A wry, crooked smile kicked up the corner of his mouth, the crinkly lines at the corners of his eyes making him even sexier. "I guess you blew my mind. We're talking complete and total meltdown."

She opened her mouth, but couldn't think of a single thing to say.

There was an odd expression in his eyes that

she couldn't define, his tone turning almost tender. "Problem is," he said, settling on his knees on the foot of the bed, "I still don't want to wear a condom. I want to feel all those cushy little muscles inside you gripping my naked dick, without anything between us. But I can try to pull out if I need to. Just tell me now, so I can be ready."

"I… Uh, it's not a problem," she stammered, wondering what she was supposed to make of this. "We're covered. You don't need to…uh, pull out."

Juliana was afraid he would press her for details, but he accepted her words with a slow nod, his gaze sliding from her face, taking a slow sweep of her body. Still staring, he reached down and gripped his cock, fisting the heavy shaft in a brutal hold as he studied the flare of her hips, then the curve of her breasts, before dipping once again to the damp curls between her thighs. "God, Jules. You are so beautiful."

She smiled, her hands grabbing on to handfuls of the bedding as she watched him crawl toward her, his powerful muscles rippling beneath the tight stretch of his skin, making him look like a predator. Which he was. A mouthwatering, sexy, gorgeous one that she wanted to hate for making her want him so deeply, for the simple fact that he could never be hers.

But for the moment, Ashe Granger was in *her* bed, and she was going to enjoy the hell out of him, not expecting any more than this. Than these fleeting moments of pleasure.

Shoving any mood-killing thoughts of the future out of her mind, Juliana gave herself completely over to the moment. And to the man.

As if he sensed her silent surrender, he placed his hands on her ankles, the calluses on his palms scraping lightly against her flesh as he stroked his way up her legs, his thumbs rubbing against the inner curve of her thighs. Then his grip tightened, his gaze zeroed in hard and tight on her sex. He made a rough sound in his throat, then pushed her thighs wider. And even though she'd known what was coming, she still cried out when he leaned down and lashed his tongue over her clit.

She blinked, unable to believe that keening sound had come from her.

Tucking her chin into her chest, Juliana stared down at his dark head buried between her legs, his tongue doing some kind of fluttering tremolo that made it impossible to breathe. Pushing two thick fingers inside her, he twisted them deep as he kissed his way up over her belly, her ribs, until he'd taken one of her tight nipples into the scorching heat of his mouth.

"I need you," he groaned, his lips moving against her nipple while his fingers continued to move in slow thrusts, working against the tightness of her body. "So badly, Jules."

"Then take me," she whispered, running her hands over his powerful arms, the muscles so hard and thick they'd pushed his veins to the surface, her knees hugging his sides.

He lifted higher over her body and claimed her mouth again in a kiss that was deliciously wicked, his tongue tasting like her as he licked and stroked, scattering her rational thoughts like confetti. He moved one hand to the back of her neck, holding her still for the marauding pressure of his mouth, his other hand now curving around her thigh as he rolled his hips, rubbing the hot ridge of his cock against her sensitive folds. He was teasing her…drugging her, building her up until she was ready to scream for him to just do it already.

"Ashe, please!"

"You're tiny, baby, and I'm not." The words sounded as if they were ripped from his throat. "I'll try not to hurt you, but…"

"I don't care!" She dug her nails into his hard, sweat-slick shoulders, loving how strong he was. How big and beautiful and deadly. "I trust you." *At least in this bed…*

He hissed her name, a hard shudder moving through his powerful frame as he braced his weight on one arm. She lifted her head again, wanting a better view of what was about to happen. Breathing hard, he hooked his thumb at the base of his cock, pulling it away from his ridged abdomen. Another sharp, keening sound fell from her lips when he pushed that huge thing against her opening, her body burning as he pressed to gain entry.

"Ohmygod," she gasped, breathing hard, scared and excited and so turned-on she was pulsing against him. So drenched he was able to slip in a little deeper, until the tip of him was finally in, stretching her open, hugged tight by her body.

She swallowed, her gaze lifting, locking with his.

In that moment, she couldn't have looked away if her life depended on it.

THROUGH BURNING EYES, Ashe watched Juliana arch beneath him in sweet, feminine surrender, and nearly died. His heart was pounding so hard, he hoped to hell he wasn't in the middle of a heart attack. He'd never heard of a vampire having one before…but then, he figured these were extraordinary circumstances.

Then she wrapped her arms around him, her soft hands slipping down the sleek length of his spine, and he knew he had to act. Fast. Before she ripped what little control he had right out from under him.

Snagging her wrists, he pushed her arms over her head, pressing her wrists into the bedding, and held himself over her, her gorgeous breasts cushioned against his chest. Locking his jaw, Ashe watched the awareness burn in her eyes the moment he started pressing deeper inside, pushing himself into her. His hips rolled in blunt surges as he carefully worked himself in, inch by painstaking inch. She was hot and wet and incredibly tight, strangely so for a woman who wasn't a virgin, and he knew it had to hurt a little. Maybe even a lot.

"You okay?" he asked, holding still about halfway in. His muscles were tremoring, his body slick with sweat, his chest heaving as if he'd just finished a bloody marathon.

She licked her lips, her lashes fluttering as she focused her hazy gaze on his. "Yeah. But it was…a lot."

A breathless laugh shook his chest, the tenderness piercing through him creating an odd sensation when combined with the raw-edged lust. It made him want to press a gentle kiss to her lips, while screwing the ever-loving hell out of her. "I hate to tell you this, but we're, uh, only about halfway there."

Her eyes shot comically wide. "Half… You're kidding, right?"

"'Fraid not," he said as he laughed, rubbing his lips over hers, a goofy smile on his lips that he couldn't get rid of. "But, God, you're adorable."

"I'm glad you find this funny, but there isn't

any way that that thing…I mean, er, that *you* are getting all the way inside me."

"Just give it time," he soothed in a dark, rumbling drawl, rubbing his tongue across the cushy swell of her lower lip. He kissed her slow and deep, losing himself in the warm, pansy-soft texture of her mouth as he rubbed his chest against her tight nipples, giving her a chance to relax.

He was no doubt about to bust an artery, but he managed to wait until she was arching against him again before he started working deeper into her, the feel of her the most incredible thing he'd ever experienced. Dragging her wrists down to either side of her head, he raised himself on his arms and looked down as he pulled back. Then he drove back into her with more force, the thrust getting away from him, her sharp intake of air making him feel like a prick.

"How come you're so…tight?" he forced out through his gritted teeth, holding still inside her. He hoped to hell the conversation would give him a moment to get it together, letting her get used to him, before he went off the deep end and found himself pounding her into the mattress. If he hurt her, he was going to feel like seven kinds of shit and end up having to kick his own ass.

"What do you mean?" she whispered.

Ashe lifted his head, looking her right in the eye. "I mean, how long's it been?"

"Since what?" she asked, baffled.

His nostrils flared as he sucked in a sharp breath. "The last time you did this, Juliana. When was it?"

"Oh. Um, before the imprisonment."

Before the...? Holy Christ.

His voice was so rough, he sounded like he'd been crunching gravel. "Why?"

She pulled her lower lip through her teeth as her lashes lowered, concealing the look in her eyes. "I, um, just didn't feel that way about any of the men who worked for my family. And they're the only ones who've been available."

Something flipped over in his chest, and he found himself pushing into her a little deeper. "You should have told me. If I'd known, I'd have gone a bit longer on the foreplay. Given you a few orgasms first to make it a little easier."

A small smile touched her lips as she lifted her lashes, staring up at him with a luminous look of joy. "I'm not complaining."

He closed his eyes. "Shit, don't look at me like that." His voice was tight, strained. "I'm trying to hold it together here."

"There's no need for that," she murmured. "Go ahead and let go."

He cracked one eye open, giving her a dubious look.

Laughter bubbled up from her chest. "I promise. It's all good now. You're not hurting me. Just…do your thing."

"My thing, huh?" He was smiling as he lowered his head, running his tongue over her lip again, coaxing her to open for him. When she did, he slipped his tongue inside, licking as if he was starved for her flavor. Which he was. His head was already spinning from the provocative kiss when he pulled back his hips, then surged right back into her, working against the tight resistance of her body. It took a few hard, heavy lunges, but she finally gave way around him. The sensation was so electric it buzzed in every cell of his body, crackling in the air.

"Jesus…*God*…" he rambled hoarsely, his blood burning with such fiery heat, he was surprised steam wasn't rising from the surface of his skin. "I'm gonna take you so fucking hard, woman."

Juliana's breath caught at his words, the look of awe on her face no doubt one that would only feed his outrageous ego. She should have bitten her tongue, but as he pumped that thick, textured shaft back inside her, holding tight against her womb, she couldn't stop herself from saying, "I didn't think it was possible, but you feel even better than in my dream."

The hot, primal glow in eyes burned brighter. "You dreamed about me?"

She licked her lower lip, and gave a slow nod.

"This afternoon. Woke up…coming." *Just like I've done so many other times when dreaming about you.*

He ground against the moist cushion of her sex, sending sweet, shivering chills over the surface of her body. "Is that why you wanted to leave?" he asked. "Because of the dream?"

"Just shut up and kiss me," she gasped, lifting her head and nipping his bottom lip. Though she was the one who started it, he quickly took control of the kiss, ravaging her mouth with wicked, sliding thrusts of his tongue as his hips started increasing their tempo, his thick shaft pumping into her harder…deeper…faster. She tore her mouth away, gulping air as she writhed beneath him, his fingers tightening around her wrists to keep her in place.

She trembled, shaking, her skin suddenly too tight for the wild, terrifying emotions building inside her. She felt trapped, penetrated, her mind instinctively trying to fight it even as her body craved more.

It wasn't just his size or his strength destroying her defenses, battering through the walls she'd built to protect herself. It was everything. The things he said. The raw intensity of his gaze as he stared into her eyes, watching the pleasure push through her…filling her. It was even in the way he moved, the powerful muscles flexing so sinuously beneath the tight stretch of his skin. He made one of those rough, purely male sounds in his throat as he started moving even harder, faster, her back arching as she begged for more. She didn't know who this woman was who wanted to claw his back with her nails, her fangs heavy and sharp, mad with the need for his blood. "God, I want to bite you so badly," she cried out, her voice cracking at the end.

His own fangs flashed as he growled, his control slipping a little more. She could feel it in the hardness and speed of his strokes, the bed crashing against the wall loud enough to be heard downstairs in the bar. He was rougher than she ever would have imagined, but she loved it. Couldn't get enough of it.

"More," she gasped, staring up at him. His jaw hardened as he ground his teeth, his eyes glowing like a fire beneath the dark slash of his brows.

"You'd better be sure this is what you want."

"Do it," she snapped, so desperate she wanted to scream. "I want it all."

"It'll be rough," he warned, pushing up on his knees.

"I don't care. That's how I want it! I want everything you've got!"

He took her at her word, the hands that had been gripping her wrists suddenly behind her knees, folding her over. She looked down, loving what she saw, the explicit position leaving her sex tilted and exposed. He rammed himself into her with breathtaking thrusts, and she could see it all, the sound of their bodies coming together the most erotic thing she'd ever heard. She'd always been embarrassed when she'd accidentally wandered too close to one of the couples at the compound when they were having sex. With a vampire's hearing, it was difficult not to eavesdrop now and then. But there was nothing embarrassing about it now. The sounds were raw and earthy, the bed groaning as it slammed repeatedly into the wall, the low growls rumbling in his throat making her hotter. Making her need it even more.

Then he shifted over her, tilting her hips up even higher, his cock hitting so deep that it jerked a sharp cry from her chest that made him go still.

"I warned you," he growled, a muscle pulsing in the hard line of his jaw.

"Like I said before, I'm not complaining!" she shot back, using her arms for leverage as she pushed her hips up, pressing against him until not even a sliver of space existed between their bodies. Every thick, rigid inch of him was buried inside her, and she tightened her muscles, clamping down on him, his body shaking with a hard, muscular shudder as she said, "Now do it again."

He swore something guttural and hoarse as he pulled back halfway, then slammed back inside her, her body pulsing around him, bathing him in her juices. He made a thick, helpless sound, as if undone by her, and then they were going at it again, the rhythm as violent and frenzied as it'd been before. A secret smile bloomed inside her, melting and sweet. She loved that she'd been able to give him this. That he was finding pleasure in an act she'd feared might bore him…or worse. Her track record was hardly anything to inspire, but… maybe that hadn't been entirely her fault.

Lowering her gaze, Juliana watched the rippling of his abs as he moved, his thrusts so strong now they were shoving her up the bed. He used one hand to grip on to the headboard for leverage, crushing the wood in his grip, the muscles in his arm rigid beneath his golden skin. "Need you," he growled, looking at her as if he wanted to devour her, his fangs longer than she'd ever seen them. "Need every goddamn part of you."

She wanted to tell him that she needed him, too, but the words turned into a breathless cry as he shifted his body higher, rubbing against her at the perfect angle. She gasped, bracing her hands against the rock-solid wall of his chest, her back arching as the most devastating orgasm she could have imagined slammed into her, a thousand times more stunning than her dream. She screamed, thrashing, instinctively fighting the pleasure at first, it was so shocking, before giving in and embracing every part of it as it pulsed through her, surging like an unstoppable wave, the heat so extreme it was like burning at the center of a star.

"That's it," he ground out, his hips thrusting faster…and faster, until his own release had him growling and flinging his head back. Tendons stood out in his strong throat as he shuddered and pulsed, blasting heavy streams of heat inside her that went on…and on, until everything in her mind went heavy and silent and black.

"Christ," Ashe groaned under his breath, his body practically turning itself inside out as he pumped into her, the pleasure so extreme he wasn't sure if it was the best bloody thing he'd ever felt…or something that would kill him. When it finally eased, he carefully worked himself out of her sweet, clinging hold, then slumped onto his back beside her, one hand covering his eyes as he struggled to catch his breath. She rolled, snuggling into his side, and he tried to put his arm around her, but wasn't sure if he managed it. His body no longer felt like his own, his mind floating in a daze. He didn't know how long he drifted in that lazy sprawl, exhaustion weighing down on him, but when he suddenly opened his eyes, he was instantly awake, the memory of what had happened between them playing through his mind in vivid, heart-pounding detail.

Holy…living…hell.

Ashe couldn't wrap his mind around it. He'd had more than his fair share of sex in his lifetime, but he'd never experienced anything like what had happened between him and Juliana.

He knew he should turn tail and get the hell out of there, but the thought of leaving her alone left him cold inside. He didn't even want to think about how he'd feel if he knew he wasn't getting a piece of her again.

He'd probably made the biggest mistake of his life in thinking he could handle this, but it was too late to turn back now. All he could do was suck it up and make sure that he kept it together better next time. Surely he wouldn't be as blown away by the experience, now that he'd already had her. And despite how badly he'd wanted to drive his fangs into her, he'd managed to hold back. It would get easier. Feel more…normal. Right?

But as he tucked in his chin, watching her sleep beside him, Ashe knew that was just more bullshit talking. Her face rested on the curve of his biceps, so damn beautiful it made his chest hurt just to look at her. He could easily stay buried inside this woman for hours, days, and never get his fill. And it wasn't just the Burning making the experience into something that blew his mind. It was Jules, everything about her appealing to him so deeply, it was as if she'd been *made* for him.

And Jesus, there he went spouting romantic

nonsense again. He was starting to sound like Sybil! Definitely time to get the hell out of bed and back to work.

Smoothing his hand over her shoulder, he said, "Come on, Jules. It's time to get up."

"Hmm?" she moaned sleepily, snuggling closer against him.

A low laugh rumbled in his chest. "Out of bed, sleepyhead. I need to get you some food if I want you to keep up your energy."

She cracked open one eye, a delightful blush spreading across her cheeks as he reached over and cupped her breast, rubbing his thumb over her pink nipple. Unable to resist, he pushed her to her back and lowered his head, suckling that tender tip into his mouth, laving it with his tongue.

Wrapping her arms around his dark head, Juliana held Ashe to her breast, the poignant moment bringing tears to her eyes. Shivering waves of pleasure coursed over her sensitive skin at each slow, possessive lap of his tongue, the bed dipping as he shifted his weight, his mouth latching on to her other nipple, while his thumb stroked the one he'd left damp and aching. Her eyes slid closed, a sensual wave of lassitude pouring through her, melting her down, until she stiffened in alarm.

"What was that?" she whispered, certain she'd heard something that sounded like breaking glass coming from downstairs. There was another sharp sound, followed by a guttural shout, then definite sounds of fighting.

With a vicious curse, Ashe lunged out of bed and pulled on his jeans. He didn't even bother with a shirt or shoes as he headed bare-chested for the door. Pinning her with a sharp look over his shoulder, he barked, "Stay the hell in this room!"

It was a direct order, but as soon as the door slammed shut behind him, Juliana scrambled off the bed. She had no intention of hiding out like a coward when he might be facing God only knew what downstairs.

Dressing as quickly as she could, Juliana pulled on her jeans and T-shirt, then opened the door and crept barefoot into the hallway. The sounds of fighting were louder in the hall, the staircase at the far end leading down to the bar. Someone shouted something that sounded like *"Fucking assassins!"* but she couldn't tell who it was. Knox, maybe? As she neared the top of the stairs, she could see crazy shadows thrown against the wall, the sounds coming from below more animal than man. Something made a hissing catlike sound, the thick, musky scent in the air belonging to what must have been a cat-shifter of some sort.

Actually, it smelled like a *lot* of cat-shifters, and fear slithered down her spine.

Releasing the talons at the tips of her fingers,

she kept close to the wall as she started down the stairs, the open area of the bar coming into view on her right about halfway down. With her heart in her throat, she spotted Ashe fighting what looked like four leopard shifters near the entrance, the cats in their partially shifted forms. They stood on their hind legs, like a human, but were covered with spotted fur and had animal-shaped heads. It was terrifying, knowing Ashe was in danger, but it was also breathtaking to watch his sexy body in action, his chest gleaming as he punched and slashed, his muscles rippling beneath the dark sheen of his skin. The leopards were good, but Ashe was better, and he fought dirty as hell, which she kind of liked.

Shaking her head at her ridiculous fascination with the man, when she should have been scared out of her mind, Juliana scanned the rest of the room, catching sight of Knox in the middle of the floor, battling against another group of leopards. Knox had long claws at the tips of his fingers, and a vicious set of fangs, but she still couldn't figure out exactly what kind of shifter he was. Then he let out a bellowing, ear-shattering roar, the sound deep and guttural, reminding her of a furious bear. She knew the species' numbers were small, but would have been willing to bet her life's savings, if she had any, that Knox was a grizzly.

Though most of the patrons seemed to be making for the exit as quickly as possible, about ten to fifteen of them hung back to face off against the leopards. For a gang of assassins, it was a big one. Especially seeing as how leopards were known to be solitary creatures.

From the looks of things, they obviously had no problem fighting together when there was enough money on the line.

Torn between wanting to help with the fight and worried she'd just get in the way, Juliana tried to stay out of view, deciding she'd only intervene if Ashe or Knox needed her help. It would have been a sound plan, if one of the leopards Knox was fighting hadn't caught sight of her crouching on the stairs. He must have been shown her picture, because he immediately recognized her as his prey. With a sly smile, the shifter leaped across the ten feet separating them, clearing the railing to land on the steps just below her. She hissed, kicking out at him in a move that Micah had taught her, but he caught her ankle, his claws digging into her skin in a brutal, crushing hold.

She'd trained for combat, along with the rest of her family, the ability to fight a necessary skill if you wanted to survive in the Wasteland. But the assassin was so freaking strong, it was like trying to escape from a steel manacle. Kicking out with her free leg, Juliana landed a solid blow against his jaw, but it didn't even make him flinch. Accepting the fact that she would never be able to pull free, she flexed her talons. She was about to throw herself at him, clawing at his face and throat, prepared to fight with everything that she had, when the sound of gunshots ricocheted through the air. *Bam bam.*

Flicking a quick glance across the room, she spotted the blonde who had served them drinks the night before standing on the bar, a large automatic handgun in her hand. Bullets wouldn't kill the leopards, but they'd slow the assholes down enough that Ashe and Knox could quickly finish the job.

A wet gurgling sound drew Juliana's attention back to the shifter trapping her ankle, her bile rising at the spray of blood streaming from his throat, a bullet hole piercing his Adam's apple. His grip on her ankle grew lax as he slumped to the side, and she wasted no time pulling her leg free. Moving back to her feet, she was ready to heed Ashe's original command and get her ass back to the room, when she looked up and found two more of the shifters leaping toward her, the gunshot probably what had drawn their attention.

It had drawn Knox's, too, she realized, when he turned his head and spotted her on the stairs. "Ashe!" he roared, turning his back on the leopards he was fighting to throw himself at the ones leaping toward her. They crashed into a violent, snarling tangle of bodies at the foot of the stairs, Knox's deep voice booming louder as he shouted, "Get your damn woman out of here!"

Ashe swung around from his fight, the body of his last opponent falling to the floor. The instant he saw her, white-hot fury transformed his expression into a savage mask of rage. He roared for her to get the hell out of there as he started running toward her, but the other leopards were already closing in. The blonde continued firing shots, taking down one of the spotted shifters, but Juliana knew it was far past time to go. She turned, banging her knees against the next step as one of the leopards leaped past her, crouching on the stairs above her and blocking her escape. He smiled down at her, his expression gloating.

"Get down!" Knox growled, his big body suddenly sailing over her head as he slammed into the leopard. Since Knox and the leopard were blocking her escape up the stairs, she twisted back around, her eyes going wide as she watched Ashe cut his way through the remaining shifters. He looked like a wild animal, raw and lean, a deadly fire burning in his eyes as he fought to reach her. She'd never seen anything so magnificent, her heart pounding as she watched him tear his way through the leopards with deadly skill, the blonde's shots stopping those who tried to charge the stairs.

Though time seemed to move like a slow, sticky spill of molasses, Juliana knew the whole thing was actually finished within a matter of moments. Knox tossed the dead leopard over the banister, then followed him over, landing on his feet, just as Ashe shoved the last of the assassins to the floor. With his glittering gaze locked on her face, he came up the stairs, looking ready to throttle her.

"What part of stay the hell in the room didn't you understand?" he grated, wrapping his bloody hands around her arms and giving her a hard shake. "You could have been killed, you little idiot!"

"I know. I'm sorry. I just…I wanted to make sure you were okay. To help, if you needed it."

He still looked as if wanted to throttle her, but as he took a swift look down her body, she had the feeling he wanted to kiss her, too. But he didn't. He just pulled in a deep breath, then roughly exhaled, his body still vibing with tension. "I can see right through your shirt," he muttered, jerking his chin at her chest as he lowered his arms. "Get up the stairs. Now!"

She jumped, hurrying up the stairs, only distantly aware of him saying something to Knox, her mind finally assimilating what had just happened. A group of leopard shifters had come into Knox's bar to kill her. Her jaw started shaking as she headed into their room, Ashe right on her heels, closing the door with an angry click.

She stood trembling at the foot of the bed, numb with shock, while he went into the bathroom. He came out holding a towel, using it to wipe the blood off his face, chest and arms. She stared, relieved that most of the blood must have been from the leopards, and was not his own. He had a few scratches on his left arm and across his ribs, but nothing that wouldn't heal quickly.

Tossing the red-smeared towel on the floor, he went back into the bathroom and came out with a clean one. "Wipe off and get your shoes on," he told her, tossing her the towel. "We're getting the hell out of here."

"Are you okay to travel?" she asked, scanning his body for any injuries she might have missed.

His snort sounded hard and angry. "I've gone into battle a hell of a lot worse off than this. And those bastards coming after you are tenacious. We don't have time to wait around."

"Do you think Knox sold us out?" she asked, after wiping her face.

"I might have," he grunted, "if I hadn't seen the way he fought to protect you."

"Right," she whispered, wetting her lips. "I'm sorry. I just…I mean, how did they find us?"

He cut a sharp look toward the pack she'd left

sitting on the dresser. "I'm guessing there's a tracking device in that bag that was left for you."

"No, that isn't possible," she said, sitting down to pull on a pair of socks and her boots. "I told you on our way to the train station last night that I checked it carefully."

"Then it was one of the Lycans." He sat down on the edge of the bed to pull on his combat boots. "They must have tagged our clothing last night. Probably my jacket. And the leopards were able to pick up on the signal."

"What do we do?"

"Leave it here, along with everything else." He quickly pulled on a sweater. "Only things that go with us are what we're wearing. We'll stop in a store before catching our next train and ditch our clothes for some new stuff."

"What about the bodies downstairs?" She had a feeling his friend wasn't going to be happy about having his bar wrecked...and even less so if they left such a disgusting mess behind.

"Don't worry about them," Ashe said, stuffing his wallet, passport and cell phone in his pockets. "Knox will take care of them."

"But shouldn't we help? It doesn't seem right to—"

"Jules, focus!" She jumped at the drill sergeant tone of his voice, his rage-edged energy all but blasting against her as he reached for the door.

"We can talk about this shit later," he barked, the impatient look on his face telling her to get a move on. "Right now, I just want your ass as far from this place as we can get it."

Grabbing her passport from her bag, Juliana quickly followed him out the door, hoping that wherever they were headed, the nightmares from her past wouldn't be able to find them.

CHAPTER EIGHT

IT TOOK THEM FOUR HARD HOURS of traveling before they arrived at their next destination, a rough-looking nightclub near the seaside in one of the less refined areas of Nice. Since the leopards had found them at Knox's bar, a place well-known for being part of the Pinero Dominguez, Ashe had decided they needed to change tactics. Knox had suggested this particular club, which was run by a friend of his. A Lycan friend who catered to an inhuman clientele, but with everything kept aboveboard, which was why he hadn't been made an official member of the P.D.

A wry smile twisted Juliana's lips as she stood on the sidewalk, watching the way the fading sunlight glinted off the club's neon sign. Instead of Knox's half-dressed biker babe, this one showed a woman bending over at the waist in a red thong, her lips pursed as she blew a kiss back over her shoulder. "Gee, Granger," she drawled. "You really know how to impress a girl."

"It might not look like much," he murmured, "but you won't mind."

"Oh, yeah? Why's that?" she asked, the briny scent of the Mediterranean filling her nose.

He shot her a cocky grin. "Because I'll keep you coming so hard, you won't be able to see straight."

She couldn't help but laugh, relieved to finally see him lightening up a bit. He'd been so pissed at her for leaving the room during the fight at Knox's, she was worried they'd just spend the rest of the day arguing. But he obviously had other ideas, and Juliana found her body responding with a warm wave of desire, apparently liking those ideas just fine.

Yes, she was afraid to trust him—that hadn't changed—but she could still enjoy him. God only knew she'd liked what they'd done so far.

With their new bags draped over their shoulders, the things they'd bought that day stashed inside, they made their way into the club. From behind the bar, a surly old guy with a crew cut and a scowl told Ashe that Knox had booked them a room. Some kind of construction work was taking place in the middle of the floor, several workmen using saws and hammers to repair a giant hole in the floorboards. Juliana snuffled a soft laugh under her breath, wondering just how rough this place got.

Ashe chatted to the guy behind the bar for a few minutes, questioning him about the exits and potential escape routes, and then they headed up to their room. The second he closed the door behind him, sealing them in a small sitting room, he flicked the lock and slid her a glittering, heavy-lidded look. "If you don't want those new duds of yours in shreds, get them off. Right now."

It wasn't the most romantic come-on Juliana had ever heard, but she'd have been lying if she'd said she didn't think the raw hunger roughening his voice wasn't sexy as hell. It burned in his eyes with a wild, feral glow, his long, muscular body seeming even bigger as he came toward her, rippling with power and strength. "Don't you need to get some rest first?" she asked, reaching down to pull off her new boots.

"Waste of time," he replied in a low voice, stopping to toss his new leather jacket aside and pull off his shirt. "I still have an adrenaline hard-on from that fight and it isn't going away anytime soon."

"Not that I'm complaining, but I didn't think you'd want to have sex again today." She pulled her jacket off, then her sweater, liking the hungry way he stared at her body. "Aren't you still unhappy with me for what happened?"

Pulling her long hair over her shoulder, Juliana watched a hard, sexy smile twist the corner of his mouth. "Welcome to the world of the male animal," he said with an amused snort. "You might drive me crazy, but I still want you."

Then he herded her into the small bedroom, and their jeans hit the floor at the same time, followed by their underwear and her bra. He reached out, probably intending to toss her into the middle of the bed again, but Juliana held up her hand, warning him to stay back. "Before we…uh, hit the sheets, I need to shower first. Think this place has any hot water?"

"Let's find out together," he said, grabbing her wrist and pulling her along behind him into the even smaller but thankfully clean bathroom. There was a tub with a white shower curtain against one wall, and he leaned down, turning the knobs to get the shower running.

Enjoying the spectacular view of his ass, Juliana chewed on the corner of her lip…and tried not to feel nervous about something that most women her age would have done many times already. "Are you, um, taking one with me?"

Something in her tone must have given her away, because he had a curious look in his eyes when he turned around. "Never done it in a shower before?"

She shook her head. "I'm afraid not."

"Don't worry," he murmured, his deep voice stroking across her senses as he reached out and pulled her against his hard, surprisingly warm chest, the feverish heat of his skin making her jump. "You'll enjoy it."

"It'll be nice to feel clean again," she stated with a dreamy kind of sigh, her head tilting to the side as if it had just grown too heavy for her neck, while he pressed a warm kiss to the sensitive skin beneath her ear.

"And here I was planning on making you like it dirty," he said with a wicked drawl, and she could feel his smile as he ran his firm lips along the edge of her jaw.

Feeling guilty for enjoying herself so much, considering the circumstances, Juliana suddenly felt as if she should put up at least a little resistance, instead of just falling right back into his arms. "You've already had me once today, Ashe. Shouldn't we save this for later and spend some more time on the investigation?"

Despite the relief she felt at the knowledge that her family would soon have the protection of a Specs team, their lives would continue to be in danger until Ashe and his contacts had managed to get to the bottom of those assassination orders.

Steam was starting to fill the small bathroom as he trailed his lips down the side of her throat. "Knox and I have already made all the necessary calls to get things moving. So right now, we need to just lay low for a while and give it time." He drew back his head, looking her right in the eye, his hands sliding down her back to curve over her bottom, pulling her tighter against his body…and his rampant erection. "And as for already having had you once today, I'll say this. I could have you ten times over, and it wouldn't be enough. I could stay inside you for days on end, and it still wouldn't…" He broke off, shaking his head with a dry laugh. "Just quit dragging your feet and get in the damn shower."

"Wait! I want to know what you were going to say."

"I wasn't going to say anything," he muttered, moving aside and giving her a little smack on her backside. "Now get in. We've talked enough."

"Ashe, that's so rude," she complained, sliding him a narrow look. "I'm not some puppet you can just—*mmphh*."

His sudden kiss cut off the rest of her words as he curled one big hand around the back of her neck and yanked her against his mouth—which was fine, since she could no longer remember what she was going to say anyway. She was lost in his rich taste, undone by the provocative way his tongue tangled with hers, his free hand covering her breast, his thumb rubbing across her tender nipple. Her head spun, senses buzzing as he maneuvered her into the shower, under the hot spray of the water, his mouth never leaving hers. He tasted hot and deep and addictive, and she couldn't get enough.

"I know you're not a puppet," he growled, when they both had to come up for air. "If you were, you'd do what the hell I tell you to do."

"You know, that arrogant mouth of yours really pisses me off sometimes," she said breathlessly, reaching between them and wrapping her fingers around his long, beautiful cock. Her hand wasn't anywhere big enough to close around all of him, his size sending a dark thrill through her body.

"Yeah, I can tell just how much you hate me," he groaned, his chest shaking with a gritty laugh as he shaped her breasts with his hands, his mouth already moving lower. Before the moan could even work its way from her throat, he'd lifted her higher, closing his lips around a sensitive nipple, his tongue swirling with lazy strokes over the hard tip, as if he were licking at something delicious. It was the same way he licked her between her legs, the dual assault of reality and memory making Juliana cry out. She pumped her hand along his thick shaft, wanting to make him feel this same blinding need, and knew she'd succeeded when he tore his mouth away with a serrated growl.

The next thing Juliana knew, he had her braced against the back wall of the shower, one hand under her bottom, the other tangled in the back of her wet hair, holding her in place as he took her mouth with what seemed to be an urgent, desperate craving, and claimed her body in the same way. His cock found her soft notch, his first thick thrust so hard and deep it shoved the air up out of her lungs, her thoughts fracturing beneath the violent surge of sensation. Steam billowed around them, her arms wrapped tight around his shoulders, while the slapping sounds of their bodies coming together filled the air.

He was relentless in his possession, hammering at her, the pumping rhythm of his body inside hers the most incredible thing she'd ever felt. He kept his eyes locked tight on hers, his expression a mesmerizing blend of hunger and lust and need, as if she was the only woman in the world he wanted to be like this with.

It scared the ever-loving hell out of her, how badly she wanted that to be true.

"I wish I could read your mind." She watched glistening drops of water bead on his long eyelashes, his face so rugged and beautiful. "I wish I could know what you're thinking."

"I'm thinking I can't get enough of you," he said, his fingers tightening in her hair.

"I can't...I can't get enough of you, either."

He made a rough sound deep in his chest, suddenly kissing her again as if he wanted to crawl inside her. Trembling, Juliana rubbed her tongue against his…only seconds away from crashing over that blinding edge, when he ripped his mouth from hers and pulled out, the tight clench of her body resisting him to the very end.

"What are you doing?" she gasped, feeling empty and aching without him inside her, her legs quivering from the loss as he set her back on her feet.

"I thought it might ease up," he growled, his deep voice thick with frustration as he turned her around, placing her hands against the wall, "but I just keep wanting you even more."

He didn't sound happy about that particular admission, but then she wouldn't expect him to. She knew exactly what it felt like to have the needs of your body overthrow the logic of your mind. Neither of them was comfortable with this…whatever this *thing* was burning between them, their lack of trust too great to ignore. But they were both caught up in it, unable to stop. She was just thankful that she wasn't the only one who felt that way. That she wasn't in this alone.

"You ever done it this way?" His lips were against her ear, his hands molding over her hips as he pulled her back tighter against him, his cock burning against the curve of her bottom.

Juliana shook her head from side to side, her muscles straining as she stretched up on the tips of her toes, trying to make it easier for him. She needed him so badly she was ready to scream.

"Then this'll be two firsts for you," he said, suddenly burying himself back inside her with a solid, bone-jarring thrust.

Her eyes closed, teeth sinking into her lower lip almost hard enough to draw blood. The feeling of penetration was deeper this way, each thick lunge pushing raw sounds up from her chest, her hands curling into tight fists against the damp surface of the wall.

It didn't take long before her body gave way around him, taking every inch of him, his rough groans and the biting grip of his hands as he pounded into her only driving her closer to that breathtaking edge. Then he reached around to her front, using two fingers to rub at her clit, his other arm banding across her torso, his thumb and fore-finger rolling her nipple. Within moments she was coming, the thrashing, shattering wave of ecstasy so intense she screamed, his mouth latching on to the side of her arched throat as the thick cries kept spilling…and spilling. She was going to have what her favorite aunt called a "love bite" there on her neck. Either that, or two deep puncture wounds from his fangs, if he gave in to his hunger and bit her.

Ohmygod…

Juliana could feel his need to do just that roiling through him, his tongue rubbing against the rushing beat of her pulse. She was strangely disappointed when he ripped his mouth away with a low, guttural snarl just as his own release slammed through him, his thrusts so powerful they nearly drove her toes off the bottom of the tub.

Struggling to catch her breath, she rested her forehead against the wall, wanting to laugh at herself for being upset he hadn't made the bite. After all, she was the one who'd stipulated the no-feeding policy between them during sex, knowing it was an intimacy that would only make her feelings for the sexy vampire more complicated than they already were. But…that didn't mean she wasn't tempted to know what it would be like to have him buried deep inside her, those long fangs piercing her flesh, while he took her blood into his body. Just like she wanted to take his. Her own fangs were heavy in her mouth, tingling with sensation, so sensitive she probably could have come again just from having them stroked.

Ashe was pressing a warm kiss to her shoulder, his body still joined intimately with hers, when she heard someone knock on the outer door to their room. "Who do you think that is?" she asked, still sounding a little breathless.

"Don't worry," he rasped, carefully disengaging their bodies. "I called Gideon while I was buying the tickets at the train station today. It's gonna be him."

She turned and leaned her back against the wall, her legs too wobbly to risk standing. "How did he get here so fast?"

"He just wrapped up a case in Marseilles." He squirted some of the liquid soap that was sitting on the edge of the tub into his hand, then quickly lathered up. Juliana was pretty sure her mouth was hanging open, the sight of him soaping up that tough, muscular body the most erotic thing she'd ever seen.

Another round of knocking came from the other room, and with one more possessive look that swept over her from head to toe, Ashe rinsed off and climbed out of the tub, wrapping a white towel around his hips.

Peeking around the edge of the shower curtain, Juliana said, "Okay. I'll just, um, finish my shower while you guys are talking." She knew her face was burning with embarrassment, since it was going to be obvious to Gideon Granger just what she and his brother had been doing together. The fun-loving vamp was probably going to have a blast teasing her about it.

As if reading her mind, Ashe shot her a quick smile. "Don't worry," he said. "I'll make him behave." Then he shut the bathroom door behind him.

Pulling the curtain closed, Juliana dunked her head under the spray, praying the hot water would last a little longer…and that the brothers' conversation would be a fast one.

PULLING ON A NEW PAIR of jeans and a T-shirt, Ashe called out, "On my way." He was still buttoning up his jeans when he walked into the sitting room, making sure to close the bedroom door behind him. He didn't want his brother catching a glimpse of Juliana while she was getting dressed, her bag now waiting for her on the foot of the bed, so that she wouldn't have to come out in a towel. He'd never been the possessive or even the jealous type before, but here it was. Just the thought of another man seeing too much of her pale skin made him want to inflict bodily harm.

In fact, any foolish hopes Ashe might have possessed that taking her would ease some of his pain had now been officially laid to rest. If anything, the two mind-blowing bouts of sex had simply cranked his hunger even higher.

Of course, it was a mistake he planned on making again. As in, as soon as he got Gideon's sorry ass back on the road.

The second he opened the door, Gideon took one look at him and shook his head. "What the hell happened to you?" he demanded, his accent more Scandinavian than Ashe's, since that's where he'd spent the majority of his time when he was younger. "You look like shit."

"Thanks," he remarked drily, noting that Gideon's dark hair was even longer than the last time he'd seen him, the tips nearly touching his shoulders. Ashe didn't know how his brother could stand to wear his hair so long, his own dark locks cropped close to his scalp, where it couldn't get in his way. "Now get your ass inside."

Gideon made his way into the room, and Ashe shut the door behind him, making sure to flick the lock. Then he crossed his arms over his chest, leaned his back against the door and locked his gaze with Gid's. "I didn't want to go into too many details over the phone, but I called you here for a reason."

Slipping the small pack on his shoulder onto the table at the end of the sofa, Gideon said, "I brought the blood you asked for." Then he pushed his hands into the pockets of his jeans, his silver eyes burning with curiosity as he waited to hear what was going on.

Knowing the easiest thing to do was just get it out there, Ashe said, "I'm here with Juliana. She'll be out soon. She's just taking a shower."

Gideon's gaze shot to Ashe's damp hair, and his brows started rising. "Let me get this straight. We're talking about Juliana Sabin, right?"

Aware of every muscle in his body going rigid

with tension, Ashe nodded. "She escaped from the Wasteland."

Gideon's brows went even higher, the look of shock on his face one that Ashe would have thought was funny as hell, if the situation weren't so serious.

"I'm helping her—"

"You're *helping* her?" Gideon croaked, cutting him off. "I thought you hated her! Isn't that what you've been trying to convince me of for nearly a year now?"

Wincing, Ashe lifted one hand and rubbed at the knots of tension in the back of his neck. "I don't hate her," he grunted, flicking a quick glance toward the door to the bedroom, hoping she'd stay in the shower long enough that he could get all this said in privacy. "She's in trouble. The whole family is."

He quickly relayed the story to Gideon, telling him everything that had happened up to their arrival in Nice—minus the sex, of course. He knew Gideon could read him too well not to have guessed it had happened, but that didn't mean he had any intention of discussing it with him.

"So what do you need me to do?" his brother asked, a sly smile already kicking up the corner of his mouth. "Am I meant to hold your hand for support? Keep you two from talking trash to each other?"

Ashe took a hard swallow, biting back the sharp retort burning in his throat. It was no secret that he and the little vampire didn't get along. But that didn't mean he was going to take any of Gideon's bullshit about it. "If you could act like a mature adult for a minute, I'll explain what it is that I need from you."

Gideon snickered, but listened as Ashe detailed what he wanted. When he was done, Ashe asked, "How long do you think it'll take you?"

"Hopefully only a day or two, at the most, to make all the initial contacts. I'll head over to the airport and grab a flight out as soon as I leave here," Gideon murmured, something in his tone telling Ashe that he wasn't going to like what came next. Gideon had been watching him too closely the entire time he'd been talking, studying his expression, and God only knew what he was thinking now. Bracing himself, Ashe ground his jaw as he listened to his brother say, "You know what you need to do, man."

"God, this should be good," he drawled with a heavy dose of sarcasm. "My little brother is going to give me advice. Come on, Gid. Slam me with your words of wisdom. Make my brain hurt from the force of your brilliance."

Instead of rising to the bait, Gid just shook his head and said, "You're an insufferable ass at times, you know that?"

Ashe opened his mouth, ready to tell him to go to hell, when Gideon quietly said, "She's the one, isn't she?"

Despite the heat raging through his veins, he felt a cold sweat slip down his spine. "She who?"

Gideon narrowed his eyes. "Don't play dumb, Ashe. It just makes you look like an asshole."

"I'm not doing this with you." His voice vibrated with raw frustration. "So leave it alone."

Unfortunately, his younger brother had never been good at following orders. "Damn wimp," Gideon muttered, his words thick with disgust.

Pushing off from the door, Ashe fisted his hands at his sides. "What is it with you?"

"What the hell do you think?" Gideon snarled, throwing his hands up in the air. "I'm pissed. You've got what we all want and you're throwing it away like a pathetic jackass. Why wouldn't I be pissed?"

Shock slammed through him with the stunning force of a bullet. "You know?" He rubbed a shaky hand over his mouth, seeing the truth glinting in his brother's eyes. "About the Burning?"

Gideon ran his tongue over his teeth. "Yeah, I know. I might not be as slick as you, but I'm not a moron. It took me a while, but I finally figured it out. Your current situation just confirms it." His voice dropped to a guttural rasp. "And if you walk away from her, then you don't deserve her."

A bitter sound tore from Ashe's chest. "So what's the answer, Gid? You think I ought to shack up with the criminal?"

"She's not a criminal," Gideon shot back. "Anyone who's met her knows that."

The shower turned off, which meant they only had moments before Juliana appeared, and Ashe pinned Gideon with a dark look. "Juliana doesn't know about the Burning," he said, keeping his voice low. "And I plan to keep it that way."

"I won't say anything to her," Gideon murmured, taking a step closer. "But I've got more to say to you. Not that you deserve it, mind you, but I love you and I don't want to see you screw this up."

Ashe choked back a curse, knowing damn well he wasn't going to like what was coming.

"Don't get me wrong," Gideon said, shaking his head again. "I'm still pissed at you. I mean, I can't believe you didn't tell me. Talk about a low blow. Why don't you just cut my heart out? I'll probably be emotionally scarred after this."

"You're a dumbass. And I didn't tell you about it because it isn't important."

Gideon's eyes went wide. "Isn't important? Are you out of your freaking mind? Nothing in your life will *ever* be more important than this. Do you even have any idea what you're in for? I've heard that orgasms between Burning mates only get more intense as the years go by. How can it not matter? This woman was *made* for you, Ashe. Have you really thought about what that means?"

He sucked in a deep breath for patience, his jaw clenched so tight it ached. "It doesn't matter, because I'm not going to claim her. Somehow, I'm going to find a way to have it undone."

Gideon grabbed him by the arm. "Undone?"

He jerked his arm free, glaring. "You heard me."

His brother shoved one hand back through his hair, his gaze even more troubled than before. "Ashe, this isn't like a tattoo you change your mind about, forking out a bunch of dough to have the damn thing lasered off. You don't just have something like this *un*done. That's not the way it works."

"How do we know for sure?" His quiet voice lashed with frustration. "Yeah, some have tried it. But how do we know the answer isn't just waiting to be uncovered?"

"Because it's a part of your DNA," Gideon said, his calm tone grating on Ashe's nerves. "And if we've learned anything fighting the battles we've fought, it's that one does not dick with the rules of nature. I've heard you say that again and again, Ashe."

"This is different," he muttered, rolling his

shoulder. "It might take years, but I'll figure out a way. I'm not stopping until I do."

"You fucking hypocrite," Gideon said softly, narrowing his eyes. "You're just chickening out, unwilling to man up. I cannot believe you're pussying out!"

"I'm only going to say this once, so—"

"Is it because of that banishment crap?" Gideon demanded, cutting him off. "You really think she's some kind of evil bitch maniac who's going to destroy your life?"

"No. I don't think she's evil. I also don't think she's a maniac or a bitch." Yes, he still believed she was keeping secrets from him, but he also believed Juliana was a good person. No matter the real story behind her banishment, he knew it wouldn't be because she'd ever hurt anyone.

"Then what the hell's the problem?"

"It's…complicated."

Gideon studied his pained expression and held up his hands. "Okay, all right, man. Just…promise me you'll think about it. I hate to see you screwing this up."

"SCREWING WHAT UP?" Juliana asked, coming into the room. She hadn't been able to hear what they were saying, their voices too quiet, but she could feel the tension crackling in the air. "What are you talking about?"

"Nothing important," Ashe murmured. "Let it go, Jules."

"Hmm. Giving orders again, Ashe?" She knew he was keeping something from her, and as hypocritical as it made her, she couldn't stand it. "I'm not one of your groupies, you know, willing to do whatever you say."

"Much to his disappointment, I'm sure," Gideon murmured, earning him a warning glare from his brother. The two were strikingly similar in appearance, with huge, muscular bodies, sable hair and silvery eyes. Strong, striking bone structure, softened only by the sensual shape of their mouths. But the resemblance was often missed at first glance because of the difference in their expressions. While Gideon Granger was usually smiling, Ashe was more…intense. Not somber, just…private.

As if sensing this was an opportune time to change the subject, Gideon looked at his brother and said, "On top of having every assassin within the League gunning for that kill money, the Förmyndares are going to be tracking her down the second they realize she's missing. I'll put in some calls and see what I can find out for you."

"Thanks," Ashe rasped, looking exhausted as he dropped down onto the room's short sofa.

Leaning his backside against the narrow desk wedged against the opposite wall, Gideon crossed his arms over his chest. "Are you going to tell the rest of the guys what you're up to?"

She knew Gideon was asking about the Specs team both brothers were now a part of, and she waited to hear his answer.

Bracing his elbows on his spread knees, Ashe said, "I talked to Kierland while we were at Knox's and arranged for one of the other teams to go into the Wasteland to provide protection detail for the Sabins. But I asked him not to tell the others yet. I want them involved in this as little as possible. They've already been through enough."

"They're going to be pissed when they find out you left them outta the action," Gideon predicted.

A grin tugged at Ashe's lips. "Naw. They'll be okay. They're too busy trying to procreate with their new wives to want to fight." After finally defeating an ancient evil that had tried to destroy the world, the other guys in their Specs team had gotten married back during the summer and were enjoying some much needed downtime.

Gideon laughed under his breath. "True. But they'd want to have your back."

"They can bitch me out about it later," he said, and even though Juliana had slid her gaze toward Gideon, she could feel Ashe's stare as it raked over her body, her cheeks flushing as she realized the crazy man was checking her out right in front of his brother.

Noticing the color in her cheeks, Gideon shot her a quick wink, and then pushed away from the desk, saying, "I guess I'll get out of your hair, then."

Juliana was about to ask where he was going, when Ashe moved back to his feet and said, "Don't take no for an answer. I want to have a viable option in case this all goes to shit and we can't get the Council to overthrow the ruling."

"What viable option?" she asked.

It was Gideon who answered her question. "I'm going to visit the Court and talk to some old friends of our parents. See if I can convince them to give us their support."

Her stunned gaze shot to Ashe. "But what did you mean about an option?"

Pushing his hands in his pockets, he said, "I'm not as confident as that mysterious benefactor of yours that the Council will be willing to over-turn their decision, no matter how strong our evidence is. It all depends on how deep Lenora has her claws in them. They'll either have the guts to stand against her, or they'll fold. And if that happens, I think she'll push for execution. So the smartest thing to do is to have a viable escape plan set up for your family to get them out and into hiding."

She drew an unsteady breath. "You're going to break them out of the Wasteland?"

With a shrug, he said, "If it comes to that."

Gideon gave a low laugh. "And to think everyone always thought *I'd* be the one who became an outlaw."

Hoping she wasn't about to make a fool of herself in front of Gideon, Juliana caught Ashe's gaze. "When you were talking about getting the Council to overthrow the ruling, you said 'we.' Does that... I mean, are you planning on going before the Council *with* me?"

He looked irritated by her question, but he gave her an answer. "I am."

She blinked, wetting her lips, unable to believe what she'd just heard...and what it implied. She'd assumed that if they got lucky enough and found what they needed, Ashe would wish her good luck and send her on her way. The idea that he would stand by her side was almost too sweet to bear.

"Ashe, does this...does this mean that you think we're innocent?"

"It doesn't matter what I think." His tone was gruff. "What matters is making sure you don't end up in that hellhole again."

"Well, it might not matter to you, but it matters to me," she told him. "I want you to believe that you're doing the right thing."

His gaze was so intense, it was like a physical

touch. "Then I guess you're just going to have to find some way to prove it to me."

She knew exactly what he was saying. That he wanted her to trust him and share the secrets she was keeping. But it wasn't a matter of trust. It was a matter of his safety. If things went wrong, and she and her family had to run, the less Ashe knew about the Delacourts the better.

Softly, she said, "What about taking it on faith?"

His voice got rougher. "I can't do that."

"You mean you won't," she said, thinking the man could give lessons on stubborn. "But it still means a lot to me that you're willing to stand by my side. It means…more than I can say."

He looked like he wanted to grab her and kiss her, but since they weren't alone, he simply responded with one of those scorching looks and an arrogant nod. They didn't say anything more on the subject, and Gideon headed out not long after, promising to be in touch as soon as he had some news for them.

"Where are we going now?" she asked when Ashe closed the door behind his brother and told her they were heading out.

"I thought we could grab some dinner. There's a café behind the club. Nothing fancy, but we should be able to find something decent to eat there."

"Aren't you worried that we'll be seen?"

"I don't think anyone can track us here that quickly. But I'll make sure we get a table in the back."

She ran a hand self-consciously through her damp hair, then glanced down at her jeans and simple gray sweater. "I'm not really dressed for dinner."

"Don't worry. You don't need fancy clothes or makeup," he said in a low voice. "You look beautiful without them."

Stunned, Juliana lifted her gaze to his, and felt something turn over in her chest.

He'd told her she was beautiful before, but that had been during sex, so it didn't count. And at any rate, she knew she was average. That wasn't false modesty—it was just a simple truth.

But when Ashe Granger looked at her with that dark, smoldering look on his face, Juliana not only felt pretty…she felt like the most beautiful woman on earth.

CHAPTER NINE

UNLIKE THE CLUB WHERE THEY were staying, the café had a certain charm that soothed Juliana's nerves, the dim lighting giving it a cozy atmosphere. And the food was exceptional. Ashe ordered a steak and fries, while she had opted for a chicken sandwich and salad. There was an awkward moment when they'd first walked inside the café and ran into a tall redhead Ashe knew. Her name was Lacey, and it didn't take a genius to figure out that the two had a history, the female vamp's gray eyes shooting daggers at Juliana as she gave Ashe a hug goodbye before leaving with a group of her girlfriends.

After that, the conversation had been awkward as they'd eaten their food, the tension between them too thick to ignore, but they managed to talk about his friends in the Specs team he'd joined and how they were all getting on. The stories of their weddings had made Juliana ridiculously weepy, though she did her best not to let it show. Last thing she needed was for this man to think she was looking for her own happily-ever-after. Which she wasn't. She knew better than to dream for something that could never be hers.

She'd made her mistakes, and she was willing to pay the price for them. She just didn't want her family to continue to pay, as well. She even held out hope for poor Micah, whose ravaged mind had caused him to inflict so much pain on others. She was prepared to accept those sins as her own, knowing Micah's life would have taken a much different course if they hadn't been banished. He would have eventually found his mate, the woman who would hold his heart and start his Burning, and they would have had a beautiful life together, raising a family and growing old with each other.

Reaching for her wineglass, she looked at Ashe and asked, "Have you ever watched any of the males in your family go through the Burning?"

He choked on the whiskey he was swallowing, his eyes watering as he coughed. "What the hell made you think of that?" he wheezed, still struggling to catch his breath.

She waited until the waiter had cleared their plates, then shrugged one shoulder. "I was just thinking of Micah and all the things he's missed out on."

He made a noncommittal sound under his breath.

"Well, have you?" she asked, after taking a sip of her wine.

Stiffly, he said, "Just an uncle."

She set her glass down, watching the tip of her finger as she ran it around the fragile rim. "It's strange, isn't it? How the female isn't always as compelled as the male. Why do you think that is?"

"Maybe to add some sanity to the process," he offered in a wry drawl.

She lifted her laughing eyes back to his face. "You're very cynical, aren't you?"

His tone got drier. "I've been hearing that a lot lately," he said, leaning back in his chair, "but I prefer to think of it as realistic."

Crossing her arms on the table, she leaned forward, studying him in the golden candlelight. "You don't have a very high opinion of women, Ashe. I can't help but think there's a story in there somewhere."

"No story," he said in a low voice. "I just don't like the idea of my future being decided for me."

"Hmm. I can understand that. Having one's life decided for them…no, that's not something I would wish on another person." She took another sip of her wine, staring into the burgundy depths of the glass. "Perhaps they should find some way to inoculate against it, like a vaccine. I mean, who is fate to decide who our hearts should belong to?"

"Hearts aren't always involved," he muttered, looking uneasy again. He downed another swallow of whiskey, his voice tight as he said, "The purpose of the Burning is to simply promote the prosperity of our species."

She couldn't stop a whimsical smile from curling her lips. "Still, it would be more romantic to marry or bond for love. I mean, if two life spans are going to be synced so that one isn't left behind without the other, it would be nice if those hundred years together were filled with love, rather than passion alone."

"Why are you unmarried?"

This time she was the one who coughed, nearly spewing the sip of wine she'd just taken over the table. "What?"

"Why haven't you settled down yet?" he pressed, his expression giving nothing away. But there was a fire burning in his eyes, the hot glow making her shiver. "Despite being banished, there are often soldiers and hunters traveling through the Wasteland. I doubt my friends and I were the only ones you ever came into contact with."

She exhaled a slow breath, suddenly wishing she'd never started this uncomfortable conversation. "I suppose the simplest answer is that I haven't caused any man to…um, go through the change."

"So? A lot of couples marry nowadays without it."

"That's true," she murmured, her fingers fiddling nervously with the stem of her wineglass. Forcing a tight smile, she said, "I, uh, guess I'm just not the marrying type. Too much of a romantic, really. I would want a man who would be faithful to me, and from what I've seen, there aren't many of those around."

"You don't have a very high opinion of men," he told her, giving her back a similar version of her earlier words.

The smile curving her lips turned wry. "No, I don't. But I appreciate what you've done."

"And what's that?" he rasped, the sexual tone of his voice impossible to miss. Heat flooded her cheeks as she realized how her words might be interpreted, as if she were appreciative of the orgasms he'd given her. Which she was. But she didn't plan on telling the blasted man that! He was already arrogant enough.

Taking a deep breath, she forced herself to hold his sensual gaze. "I mean that I appreciate what you're doing with the investigation. All the contacts you have searching for information. The way you've already protected me from two assassination attempts. And for what you're willing to do for my family to keep them safe." She coughed again, trying to clear the husky note from her voice. "I can't...I can't tell you how much that means to me, Ashe."

She couldn't be sure, but it almost looked as if he flinched. From one instant to the next, the heat in his gaze became banked, his sensual tone now clipped. "I'm willing to help you because you need it, Juliana. Just don't think it means anything."

She blinked. "Meaning?"

With an awkward roll of his shoulder, he muttered, "There could never be anything more between us. An...affair is all I can offer you."

An embarrassed flush swept over Juliana's face, while a cold, mortified feeling sank into the pit of her stomach. She felt dizzy and nauseous, but she held on to her temper, forcing out what she hoped sounded like a calm, rational response. "I don't believe I asked for anything from you, other than your help. I certainly didn't ask to sleep with you." Her control started to slip, her throat quivering, but she struggled to keep her voice soft, mindful of the other tables as she said, "I didn't even want you to touch me in the first place."

"That's a lie and you know it," he quietly argued. "But I didn't mean to be insulting. I just want there to be clarity between us."

"Oh, don't worry." She pulled in a shudder-

ing breath, so mad she wanted to cry. "I understand men like you completely, Ashe. You'll never
commit yourself to one woman because you're too
blasted in love with your endless variety."

"No. The reason I'll never commit," he ground
out, forcing the words through his gritted teeth,
"is because I could never trust a woman to give
me the same kind of honesty and commitment that
she'd expect from me."

Juliana shook her head, unable to believe what
she'd just heard. "Wait a minute. You can't throw
that argument back in my face."

He worked his jaw. "Why not? You think it
only works for women?"

Taken aback, she asked, "What exactly are you
saying?"

He looked uncomfortable as hell, but he didn't
back down. "I'm saying that it's not always the
woman who gets her heart trampled. That it's not
always the man who lies and destroys trust and
strays."

She shook her head again, dazed. "You honestly
think any woman you chose would stray from a
man like you?"

His eyes narrowed, his gaze so intense she
could feel its heat pulsing against her face. The
noisy chatter surrounding them in the bustling
café faded into the background, the air thick with

sudden awareness, crackling with tension. "What do you mean, a man like me?"

She arched a brow. "Come on, Ashe. You've seen a mirror. It can't come as a surprise that you're gorgeous."

"And you're beautiful." His rough tone made it clear that he wasn't just saying it to be nice. He actually believed it, and Juliana felt her icy anger begin to thaw.

"Not really, but it's nice of you to say so. And it's different for women. Looks fade." She slid him a slight smile. "Even for our kind."

"True," he agreed. Then he shocked the hell out of her by saying, "But when two people are in love, it doesn't matter."

"I have a hard time picturing a man like you in love," she murmured. "Though I imagine hundreds of women have been in love with you over the years."

"They've loved certain parts of me, but that's all," he replied, and she could tell by the tight grin that worked its way across his mouth which "parts" he was referring to. Then she caught the gleam of some dark emotion in his eyes, and a slow, thick wave of shock moved through her, leaving her blinking back at him. In that moment, she realized a stunning truth. For all his arrogance and attitude, Ashe Granger didn't think he was someone who could be loved.

God, all this time she'd been judging him…
unfairly. He didn't sleep around because he was
heartless. He kept away from intimate relationships because he didn't believe they were something he could ever have.

"Who was she?" she asked.

He flicked her a shuttered look from beneath
his lashes, his jaw tight. "Who was who?"

"The woman who betrayed you. Did she sleep
with someone you knew?"

He didn't respond right away, his attention
focused inward. She could see the muscle ticking in his cheek, just below his right eye, his jaw
clenched so hard it looked painful. She was about
to prompt him for an answer, unable to just let it
go, when he blew out a rough breath and said, "It
wasn't just a someone. She slept with men that I
knew, as well as men that I didn't."

"I'm sorry, Ashe. That sucks."

He downed the rest of his whiskey in one hard
swallow. "It gets worse," he said, setting the glass
back on the table.

"How could it get worse than that?" she whispered, her chest hurting at the pain she could see
on his beautiful face. He looked haunted as he
pushed his chair back from the table. He sat with
his elbows braced on his spread knees, his head
turned to the side, gaze focused on a patch of floor
between their table and the wall.

After a long, tense silence, he said, "She wasn't who I thought she was."

Juliana waited, sensing that he had more to say. He just needed time to figure out how to say it.

The moments slowly ticked by, weighted with grief and unwanted memories, and then he quietly said, "Gretchen was a young vampire whose family had arranged her marriage to a wealthy male who was much older than her. I had just started working as a Förmyndare and was sent to investigate when her husband was found murdered." Lines crinkled at the corners of his eyes as he winced. "She was young and beautiful, and I was cocky enough to think she fell in love with me at first sight. We started an affair, and I was also stupid enough to ask her for an explanation when my investigation kept leading back to her."

Wetting her lips, Juliana said, "I have a feeling this isn't going to end well."

She watched a flat smile twist the corner of his mouth. "You could say that," he murmured. "She confessed that she'd killed him, but claimed that she hadn't had any choice. Said that her husband had been abusive and that she'd killed him in self-defense." He turned his head, locking those piercing, storm-dark eyes with hers. "Then she pleaded with me to help her hide, while I searched for a way to clear her name. I was able to accomplish the first, but not the second. Instead, I eventually proved that she was nothing but a two-bit liar. She'd offed the old guy for his money, and his valet had helped her. The two of them had been lovers all along. As it turned out, there weren't many men she knew that she hadn't slept with."

"What happened?" she whispered, her throat tight with emotion.

"She ran, confident that I wouldn't have the heart to go after her."

"But you did." It wasn't a question. She could see the truth written in the grim lines of his expression.

He nodded slowly. "I didn't have a choice. I'd let her manipulate me, and because of that, she'd almost gotten away with murder. It was up to me to set it right." He leaned back in his chair again with a tired sigh, rubbing a hand roughly over his mouth, before saying, "It took a long time, but I finally tracked them down."

"Where is she now?"

He stared back, unrelenting. "She's dead."

"Oh, God."

His voice was raw. "By the time I caught up with her, she'd killed several more times. Claimed she'd gotten a taste for it. She tried to kill me. I killed her first."

"I'm sorry," she said hoarsely, finally understanding why it was so difficult for him to put his trust in her. He'd been scarred inside as deeply as she had, suffering that same soul-sucking pain. The kind that made you feel broken and raw and bleeding.

Staring at his stark expression, a new flurry of emotions vibrated through her with a sweet, shocking warmth, but she fought them back, sensing the danger. No matter how incredible it would be to dream of being the woman that would change his views on the subject of love, the fact remained that Ashe Granger would be a hard man to reach, likely closing himself off from anyone who ever tried to get close to his heart. And he would almost certainly strike first, cheating before he could be cheated on, like a preemptive strike against the thing he most feared: being hurt by someone he desperately wanted to love him.

What a fascinating contradiction he was, and what a shallow bitch she felt like for projecting her past experiences with men onto him. In truth, she and Ashe were more alike than she could have ever realized.

And they were so wrong for each other, it was surprising they didn't repel like two opposing sides of a magnet. Bad enough when one person had trust issues, but when both parties were carrying the same scars it was a soap opera just waiting to happen.

The sudden clatter of plates breaking in the

café's kitchen made her jump, and she realized with a flush how long she'd been sitting there in the candlelight, simply staring at him, absorbed in her thoughts.

Clearing her throat, she held his dark stare as she said, "I'm not like her, Ashe. I'm not a criminal, and I'm not trying to con you. And before this is over, I'll have figured out some way to prove that to you."

"And then what, Jules? We'll settle down together, fucking like minks, and be a happy couple?" he drawled, his tone more mocking than serious.

"No," she answered honestly, shaking her head. "I would never expect that of you. And even if I did, I know it wouldn't be possible."

"And why's that?" he asked in a silky rasp, his dark brows lifting.

"Because even if I manage to change your mind about me, there's still one thing we'd never be able to get past."

His reply was soft. "And what's that?"

"The fact that while I might trust you with my life, Ashe…I could never learn to trust you with my heart. And you could never truly trust me with yours."

IRRITATED BY THE WAY the conversation had gone, Ashe suggested they stop in the club and have another drink before heading up to their room for the night. God only knew he needed the sleep, having only caught a handful of hours here and there since they'd left London, and it was starting to wear him down. Not to mention the constant worry about Juliana's safety and the way she kept stripping down his barriers, getting him to talk about things he knew were best left alone.

But he needed the drink more.

It was hell, treading his way through those emotional minefields with her. And yet, the more time he spent with Juliana, the clearer it became that he'd been more infatuated with Gretchen than in love with her. It'd made him angry when he'd realized what she truly was, but it hadn't destroyed him. He'd picked himself up and had gone on, more cynical and untrusting, yeah—but her loss hadn't torn out a part of his soul.

Juliana, on the other hand, was already ripping him to pieces, battering her way past the walls he used to close himself off. Walls he needed…that he wasn't willing to give up.

He didn't know why he'd told her about Gretchen, when he'd never shared that story with anyone before. But one thing was becoming crystal clear with every moment Ashe spent in Juliana Sabin's company: she was dangerous not only to his peace of mind, but to his entire bloody existence. And if he wasn't careful, he was going to find himself in a situation he couldn't get out of. Which meant he needed to start getting a handle on things now, before they slipped so far out of his reach he couldn't get them back again.

As she swung up onto a stool at a small table in the back of the nightclub's front room, he said, "It'll take forever if we wait for someone to take our order. I'll just go up to the bar. What do you want?"

She started to tell him, but a shape-shifter walking by diverted his attention, the guy's green eyes sweeping over Juliana with obvious appreciation. Ashe could feel his talons growing warm beneath the tips of his fingers, aching to slip their skin and tear into the shifter with an animalistic frenzy.

Giving the shifter a low growl and a glimpse of fang, Ashe was still watching the jackass to make sure he didn't look at Juliana again, when she reached over and touched his arm. "Ashe, did you hear me?"

Sucking in a sharp breath, he slid his gaze back to hers. "Sorry. What was that?"

"I'd like another glass of red wine, please. A Shiraz if they've got it."

"Don't go anywhere," he warned her, confident they hadn't been tracked to Nice, but not wanting to take any chances.

Despite the repairs that had been going on that

afternoon, the club was packed with people, most of whom he sensed were from the clans, which wasn't uncommon. Humans tended to be uncomfortable in a crowd of nonhumans, even if they didn't understand exactly why.

Finally making his way to the bar, Ashe ordered a glass of wine and a double whiskey, careful to keep one eye on Juliana. There was a strange sense of dread simmering inside him, as if he was about to make a colossal mistake. One that would have serious repercussions, ending in a shitload of regret.

"Here ya go, buddy." The bartender set two glasses before him, but Ashe couldn't unclench his hands from his sides to reach out and grab them, his fangs suddenly bursting into his mouth with a searing pulse of pain. A savage wave of hunger rolled through him so strongly it nearly brought him to his knees. Closing his eyes, he slumped against the hard edge of the bar, panting, struggling for control, when a cool hand reached out and touched his arm.

"You look hungry, Ashe."

Lifting his lashes, Ashe found himself staring into Lacey Denniver's gray eyes, her red hair gleaming in the smoky lights of the bar.

"What?" he croaked, his voice so thick it was barely recognizable. Panic flooded through his veins, while a primal fear pounded through his head. The fear that he'd made a critical mistake in thinking he could be near Juliana and control the Burning. He couldn't control shit, and if he didn't do something fast, he was going to charge through these people, throw her little ass over his shoulder, and take her someplace where he could do every raw, raunchy thing that he wanted to her, before thrusting his fangs into her tight flesh and claiming her as his own.

Then they'd both be screwed, and he'd have no one to blame but himself.

"I said you look hungry," Lacey murmured, edging so close that her breasts pressed against his arm, the sultry smile on her rouged lips telling him exactly what she was offering. "I normally don't encroach on another woman's date, but we're old…friends. And you look desperate, Ashe."

Desperate. Yeah, that was right. And terrified enough to take her up on her offer, knowing damn well it was going to rip Juliana away from him. She'd still need his help in finding proof of the assassination orders, but she would never let him touch her again. He knew that as well as he knew this was the perfect opportunity to set things between them on the right path.

Do it. Right now. Cut the fucking cord and save your ass, while you still have the chance.

Putting his arm around Lacey's waist, Ashe said the gruff words that would set Juliana Sabin forever out of his reach. "Let's get away from this crowd."

Ten minutes later, when he came back into the front room, Juliana was gone.

CHAPTER TEN

JULIANA COULDN'T BELIEVE she was standing outside in the chilly night air, talking to Josh Everett, the older brother of a childhood friend. She'd been on the verge of tears after watching Ashe and Lacey head into the club's back room together, his hand on the small of her back, and was just getting up to leave when she spotted Josh coming in the front entrance with a group of friends. She'd tried to turn before he recognized her, but hadn't been fast enough. He'd noticed her instantly, leaving his friends behind to catch up with her as she tried to make her way out the back exit.

At first Juliana was terrified Josh might say something that would reveal she was an escaped convict, but he'd seemed to know she didn't want to be spotted, angling his body so that his friends couldn't see her as they went out the back door together.

Staring up at his handsome face, she said, "Josh, I can't believe it's you. It's been so long."

Concern darkened his eyes. "Jules, I thought you were in the Wasteland. How did you—?"

She cut him off. "Please, don't ask anything about what I'm doing here," she pleaded, gripping his forearm and pulling him deeper into the shadowed walkway that ran between the nightclub and the café. "I don't want to put you in danger."

He looked like he wanted to argue, then changed his mind, probably sensing that it would just send her running. He pushed one hand through the light brown strands of his hair, the familiar gesture taking her back to the weekends she'd shared with his family. His sister Jackie had been her best friend since the age of six, and Juliana had grown up with a huge crush on Josh, who was older than her and Jackie by five years. She'd never told him, but she'd always suspected that he knew. He'd even asked her out when he'd moved back home after university, and she would have said yes, if it hadn't been for Raphe.

The years had been good to him, adding a maturity to his looks that probably had women chasing after him in droves, his athletic build one that any female would appreciate.

"Can we at least talk for a little while?" he asked, catching and squeezing her hand. "I know this is going to sound crazy, but I've…I've missed you. We all have."

Juliana knew she should say no and head back up to her room to confront Ashe when he returned. But…she just wasn't ready yet, her emotions still too shredded to face him. And that was assuming he even bothered to go back to their room tonight.

Knowing she needed a distraction, she gave Josh a wobbly smile. "I don't have much time, but…I'd like that. We could take a walk in the park across the street."

They headed toward the empty park, leaving the noise of the nightclub behind as they walked together down the winding path that cut through the sloping hills. The park spread out over several city blocks, the wintry trees softened by the twinkling white lights that had been strung through their boughs, creating a magical effect in the moonlit darkness.

Noticing her shiver, Josh slipped off his coat and wrapped it around her shoulders.

"Thanks," she murmured, keeping a careful eye on their surroundings. Ashe had bought her a knife when they'd gone shopping, and she was wearing the blade in a sheath on her calf. She felt better about being out in the open knowing she was armed, but didn't want to take any chances with Josh's safety.

"How's your family?" he asked, reaching down and taking her cold hand in his.

"Good. I mean, as good as can be expected," she told him, finding the entire situation surreal. For a moment, it had felt so good to simply walk beside him, as if she'd gone back in time and chosen a different path for her life, agreeing to go out with Josh instead of thinking she could handle a man like Raphe Delacourt. She'd been so stupid, and so many people had paid for her mistake.

And now she was putting Josh's life in danger by letting him be seen with her, just so she could keep from facing what had happened back in the club. God, did she never learn?

Yes, it had been like a knife in her heart, watching Ashe disappear with the busty redhead. But she'd known what the score was. She hadn't expected him to be exclusive—had known, when she'd accepted his deal, that he would sleep with other women. That's the only reason she'd accepted it in the first place, thinking she could satisfy her body's craving for him without risking her heart. After all, only an idiot would fall in love with a man who was as promiscuous as Ashe Granger.

It's just too bad I didn't realize I fit into that embarrassing category before we left London.

She flinched, shoving that painful thought into

the back of her mind, unable to deal with it right then. Instead, she forced herself to accept the fact that none of this was Ashe's fault. The guy hadn't broken any promises to her, because he hadn't made any. And she still needed his help with her family.

So she'd go back to the bar, and talk to him. The physical part of their relationship was going to have to end, but she'd find some other way to ensure his help. She didn't have any money, the Sabins' funds seized by the Council when they'd been banished, but there had to be something she could offer him. Who knew? Now that he'd gotten his fill of her, maybe he'd decide to keep helping her simply out of honor.

"Jules? Are you okay?"

"What?" She blinked, startled, and found herself standing in the middle of the path, staring up at Josh's worried face. God, she'd just been standing there, clutching his hand, so lost in her thoughts she'd probably looked catatonic. "I'm sorry. I, um, just have a lot on my mind. And I'm…hungry," she added, completely surprised by the husky words as they spilled from her lips. What on earth was she doing? She wasn't hungry. She'd had an entire bag of blood from the pack Gideon had left in their room before going down to dinner.

But she *was* jealous. And heartbroken.

Mistaking the pain on her face for hunger, Josh gave her an easy smile. His eyes burned a little brighter, the rise of desire in his warm scent impossible to miss.

"It's okay," he said, pulling her closer as he turned his face to the side, exposing the masculine line of his throat. "Take whatever you need."

He wasn't as tall as Ashe, but she still had to lift up on her tiptoes to reach him. Bracing her hands against his solid chest, she closed her eyes as she nuzzled his skin, her fangs pulsing as they lengthened. But as she drew in a deep breath, the warm scent filling her nose wasn't…the right one. He smelled good, but not…not like Ashe. He didn't smell like *hers*.

Like hers?

Ha! As if! A bitter sound erupted from her lips, that sharp burn of pain cutting deeper, and she reacted by sinking her fangs into Josh's strong throat, his blood hitting her tongue in a smooth spill of heat.

"No…stop!" a voice shouted in her mind. "This isn't right!"

"I'm sorry," she whispered, quickly sealing the small puncture wounds and pulling away. She was shaking so hard she could barely talk, but she slipped off his jacket and handed it back to him. "I'm sorry, Josh. Thank you…thank you for your offer. But I can't do this."

He lifted his hand, cupping her cheek as his pale gaze moved over her face, taking in each line of strain. "You look so sad, Jules. Is there anything I can do to help? Do you want to come and stay with my family?"

Tears burned at the backs of her eyes, roughening her voice. "Oh, Josh. That's so sweet of you. But I can't. It wouldn't be fair to—"

Her words broke off into a scream as a fist suddenly shot over her shoulder, connecting with Josh's face in a sickening crunch that knocked the vamp off his feet, sending him crashing back into one of the twinkling trees. With horrified eyes, she watched Ashe come around her side, stalking toward Josh's prone body.

"Ashe, stop!" she yelled, realizing he must have caught her scent outside the club and followed it to the park. Reaching out and grabbing on tight to his arm, she yanked with all her strength, struggling to keep him from throwing another punch. "His sister was my best friend! Don't hurt him!"

"I'm not gonna hurt him," he snarled, trying to shake her off. "I'm just gonna beat the shit out of him."

"No!" she shouted, shoving herself in front of him. "He didn't do anything wrong!"

"He had his bloody hands on you!" he growled, glaring down at her with a molten, glittering look of fury.

"Then beat up on me," she snapped, pushing against his chest. "But leave him out of it!"

"Beat up on…" Disgust washed over his angry expression. "I would never lay a finger on you, woman!"

"And you're not going to hit him, either," she said, fisting her hands in his sweater. She glanced over her shoulder at Josh, who had managed to pull himself up to his feet, the back of his wrist pressed to his bleeding nose. "Please, go," she said.

His brows were drawn together in a scowl. "You know this guy?"

She responded with a tight nod. "He's…with me. Helping me. Please, just go."

"You gonna be okay?" he asked, his gaze shooting over her head at Ashe with obvious concern.

"I'll be fine. Just go, Josh. And please, for your safety, don't tell anyone that you've seen me."

"I won't," he grunted, and she could see that he was afraid to leave her.

"I promise I'll be okay, Josh. But I'm sor—"

"Don't," he said, holding up his hands. "It wasn't your fault." The glare he cut toward Ashe made it clear whose fault he thought it was. A muscle pulsed in his jaw, his gray eyes burning with anger, but he agreed with a nod, then turned and headed back down the path, picking up the jacket he'd dropped on the ground as he walked past it. Juliana waited until he'd disappeared from sight, then turned her gaze up to Ashe, the air all but sizzling with the violent emotions arcing between them.

She still had her hands fisted in the front of his sweater, her breaths coming in a hard, angry rush that was identical to his. He started stalking forward, backing her into the same tree that Josh had crashed against after that powerful punch.

"Are you screwing him?" he demanded in an awful voice, slamming his fist into the tree's trunk just above her shoulder and splitting the skin across his knuckles. She blinked, staring at him in astonishment as the rich scent of his blood filled her head. His face was rigid, lips parted for the ragged breaths rushing from his chest. He wasn't just mad, he was furious. Burning with rage.

"What's wrong with you?" she whispered, releasing her hold on his sweater.

He started to say something, then looked from the deep imprint he'd made in the tree trunk, to his clenched, bloodied fist, and back to her face. His brows drew together in a deep line over his nose, his breaths coming faster as he asked, "Are you screwing him?"

Shock hit her so hard she didn't know whether to laugh or cry or tell him to go to hell. "Are you crazy? I've been in prison, Ashe."

His hands clenched at his sides as he clearly struggled to control his temper. With a low sound in his throat, he turned and paced away from her, then cut her a sharp look over his broad shoulder, his muscles straining the seams of his sweater. "Did you sleep with him before your banishment?"

Juliana crossed her arms. "Not that it's any of your business, but no."

His voice got lower. "Did you let him touch you tonight?"

Fury narrowed her eyes. "You, of all people, have no right to ask me that."

He turned toward her, his eyes burning like twin sparks of silver fire. "Either you answer the question, Juliana, or I go track his ass down and get it from him."

"He held my hand!" she exploded, so angry she could have slapped him. "But that's it!"

He stalked toward her again, his nostrils flaring as he pulled in a deep breath. "You're lying," he sneered. "I can smell him on you."

"I'm not lying, you bastard." She flung the words at him, each one biting and sharp. "It wasn't sexual! He gave me blood!"

"Blood?" He bared his fangs, looking ready to kill. "You took from his vein?"

"Yes!" she hissed, tears of anger and frustration in her eyes as she glared up at his rugged face. She wanted so badly to hate him for what he was, but even more for what he wasn't. Which was hers. "I thought you were getting a good meal from your little fuck buddy, so why shouldn't I get the same?"

"She isn't my fuck buddy," he snarled, shoving the words through his clenched teeth.

A bitter laugh tore from her chest. "Are you saying that you've never slept with her?"

He cursed, pacing away again. "Once." He cut her a sharp, dark look. "Once was enough. It was a few years ago. I never went back for seconds."

"Well, bully for you."

He pulled in another deep breath, and scrubbed his hands over his face a few times. A moment later, when he lowered them again and looked at her, Juliana was surprised to hear what sounded like a rough note of regret in his deep voice as he said, "All I did with Lacey tonight was talk."

"Right." Her snide tone made it clear she didn't believe him.

"Why would I lie, damn it?"

"You had to take her into the club's back room to *talk*? What's back there, anyway? Whips and chains?"

"It's just another bar," he muttered, starting up that restless pacing again, "with more tables and no dance floor." Rubbing at the back of his neck, he watched her from the corner of his eye. "And I went with her because I needed...I needed some space from you," he ground out, the thick words sounding torn from inside him. "It was too much. Everything we talked about."

Realization settled like a ghostly caress against her skin, and she trembled. "You mean you thought you'd use her to push me away," she stated, wrapping her arms around her middle, as if she could somehow hold herself together.

He stopped pacing, hands braced on his hips as he stared at the ground. He didn't deny what she'd said. Instead, he confirmed it. "I realized it was a dumbass idea before we even got into the back room," he admitted in a low voice. And then, very slowly, his head lifted, that bright gaze locking with hers. "And what about you?" he asked. "You had no right going to that guy for blood."

Juliana lifted her chin, refusing to feel guilty. "I can feed from whoever I damn well please."

His eyes narrowed to dark, piercing slits. "If I'm going to be the man fucking you, then I'll bloody well be the man feeding you."

"No," she argued, shaking her head. "That isn't our deal. In fact, considering everything that's happened, I think it's safe to say that our deal is off!"

His jaw tightened as he came toward her, muscles flexing beneath his sweater with raw, predatory power. When he spoke, his voice was little more than a threatening rasp. "Keep pushing me, Jules. I dare you."

She swallowed, torn between conflicting desires. On the one hand, she wanted to turn and run, unwilling to give him what he wanted. But on the other, she was dying to throw herself against him and claim every ounce of that hard, mouth-watering attitude for her own.

Before she could decide what to do, he got right in her face, looming over her, and said, "If you're not taking from me, then you'll continue to feed from the bagged blood Gideon brought us. Do you understand me?"

She was so angry she wouldn't have been surprised if steam started pouring from her ears. "So I have to keep drinking cold blood while you get it fresh?"

Something in his eyes flickered, frustration molding every word out of his mouth. "I've been drinking bagged blood for months now. It won't kill you."

Her jaw dropped, but then she quickly shook off the reaction. "It's a nice story," she muttered, turning her face to the side. "But I'd be an idiot to believe you."

"Damn it, look at me!" He took her chin between his forefinger and thumb, forcing her gaze back to his. "I didn't fuck her!" he growled. "I didn't even kiss her!"

"You just sucked on her neck, is that it?"

"No. I didn't." His breath shuddered past his lips, warm and sweet. "We talked, just like I said." His eyes narrowed again, and his voice dropped. "But even if I had, what would you be so pissed about? You've made it clear that I'm not allowed to suck on yours."

"And I'm glad I did!" she snapped, trying to sound tough. But her quivering chin ruined the effect.

Suddenly wrapping his hands around her upper arms, he pulled her against him as he lowered his head, his lips at her ear. "Damn it, I'm telling you the truth. I didn't do anything with the redhead. And do you wanna know why?" He took a deep breath, burying his face in her hair, and spoke in a ragged tone. "I didn't do anything because she wasn't the woman I wanted. She didn't smell right. She wouldn't have tasted right." He touched his tongue to the pulse hammering at the side of her throat. "What the hell have you done to me, Jules? I don't even know who I am anymore."

Something warm and soft started to burn in her chest. "You...you really didn't feed from her?"

He lifted his head, staring her right in the eye. "I didn't. But you fed from the boy. You owe me an apology, Juliana."

For a moment she thought about pointing out the fact that Josh wasn't a boy, then decided it would just be foolish to prod his temper. But she wasn't ready to accept his dictates. Not with the memory of him putting his arm around Lacey's waist and walking away with her still fresh in her mind. Just because he hadn't gone through with it this time didn't mean that he wouldn't the next. "I don't owe you an apology," she whispered, wetting her lips. "We've made no promises of fidelity to each other."

Her voice was soft, thick with pain, and Ashe hated himself for putting her through that. He'd known as soon as he'd gotten close to Lacey, pressing her up against a wall in the back room of the club, that he'd panicked and misread the signs. Juliana wasn't the mistake he'd needed to avoid—Lacey was. And now he had to find a way to make Juliana understand, to do some serious damage control, because he couldn't stomach the thought of her walking away from him.

Not just tonight. But ever.

"Do you know what's the first thing I'll want to do every time another man lays his hands on you?" he asked, digging his fingers into the soft mass of her hair and tilting her head back.

Her eyes narrowed to sharp, glittering points of light. "What?"

Very slowly, he said, "I'll want to kill him."

She blinked at the vehemence of his response. "You're joking, right?"

He rubbed his thumb over the smoothness of her cheek, thinking she was the most beautiful woman he'd ever known. "You don't think you're worth killing for?"

Her laugh was brittle. "Hardly."

For a moment, there was only the sound of their breathing and the wind gusting through the trees. And then he said, "I disagree."

She stared up at him, trembling, her eyes filled with the questions she couldn't put into words.

"I mean it," he rasped. "I would kill for you. Easily. Without remorse. Again and again."

"What are you saying?"

Recognizing the fact that he was standing at the edge of that cliff, ready to take that first life-changing step into the unknown, Ashe swallowed the lump of fear in his throat and gave her the words. "I'm saying that you're important to me, Jules. More important than any other woman I've ever known."

Tears filled her eyes, shimmering and bright. "You're…important to me, too. And I'm…sorry," she said with a hard swallow. "I was jealous. That was the only reason I fed from Josh."

"I don't ever want any other man's taste in your mouth. Only *mine,*" he groaned, his pulse roaring in his ears as he shoved the sleeve of his sweater over his forearm. Then he lifted his arm and pressed his skin against her mouth, her lips already parted for her panting breaths. He didn't wait for her to bite, shoving his skin against the sharp points of her fangs until they dug in with a tight pop. Her eyes went wide, then heavy, her feminine little hands suddenly clutching his arm, holding him to her mouth, her throat working as she swallowed. She took several deep, ravenous pulls, the drawing sensation reaching all the way down to his cock. He thickened, every lush pull making him harder, cranking his hunger up higher...and higher. He wanted the hot surge of his blood flowing through her body, washing away that other bastard's taste. Wanted to be in every part of her, filling her up.

"I need to be inside you, but I'm not fucking you against a tree," he scraped out in a thick voice, nipping the tendon at the side of her throat. "I need you in our room, Jules. Need you somewhere I can lay you down and spread you open, without worrying about some damn assassin shoving his claws in my back and trying to take you away from me."

Without waiting for her response, he tore his arm from her mouth and picked her up, carrying her against his chest. "Ashe, I can walk," she protested, hoping he didn't plan to carry her through the middle of the crowded nightclub. She brushed her fingers over her tingling lips, the mouthwatering taste of his blood still warm in her mouth, his unique, purely masculine flavor the most addictive thing she'd ever tasted.

"I know you can. But it'll take too damn long," he grumbled, his long legs eating up the ground. Within moments, they had crossed the road and he was setting her down outside the back door of the club, the look in his eyes warning her to move quickly.

"That desperate?" she teased, arching her brow at him.

"Woman, you have no idea," he grunted, ripping open the door and shoving her inside, his hand hot against her lower back. No more than a minute later, they'd maneuvered their way through the crowd, thankfully without running into either Josh or Lacey. Ashe used the key to unlock their door, his mouth already on hers as he pulled her against his chest and walked her into the room. He kicked the door shut with his foot, then reached back and flicked the lock.

They didn't even make it into the bedroom, his hands making short work of her sweater and bra as he herded her toward the small dining table wedged into the far corner of the room. Her jeans and panties had fallen only as far as her ankles, her knife still strapped to her calf and her boots still on, when he picked her up, kicked a leg of the table to knock it in front of the mirrored doors of a small coat closet, and laid her down on the chilly surface. Then he pushed between her legs, forcing them apart as he came down over her, his mouth moving over hers as he ate at her low moans, his tongue licking and swirling, driving her wild.

"Do you have any idea how worried I was when I couldn't find you?" he groaned, kissing his way down her throat, his tongue flicking against her rapid pulse before he worked his way to her breasts. The husky words shook with emotion, the heat of his mouth as he suckled on her nipple bringing a whimper of pleasure to her kiss-swollen lips. She dug her fingers into his silky hair, holding him to her. It was deliciously decadent, having his fully clothed body pressing against her bare skin, his hands stroking with rough urgency, as if he was desperate to touch her everywhere at once.

"Take my boots off," she panted, needing to wrap her legs around his hips. To feel him hard and thick against the place she needed him most. "Please, hurry!"

He drew his weight off her, but instead of doing as she'd begged, he flipped her over with ridiculous ease, putting her on her stomach. "Damn it, Ashe! What are you doing?"

"Shh," he rasped, gripping her hips. Before she even realized what was happening, her knees were on the table, her back arched, intimate bits on shocking display as he spread his hands over her bottom. Her breath caught as he slid his thumbs lower, through her swollen folds, and pulled her open. He made a thick, guttural sound in his throat that was sexy as hell.

"Always so candy-pink and juicy," he murmured, the rumbled words so soft she had a feeling he was talking to himself, lost in the view. She could feel the press of his gaze burning against her cleft, a strange feeling of vulnerability and power twining through her, making her want to fight just as badly as she ached to submit.

"Head up and eyes open, Jules."

At his rough command, she lifted her forehead from the table, her gaze locking with his in the mirror as she braced her upper body on her bent arms, the position pushing her hips up higher. She probably looked like some kind of commando porn actress, with the knife still strapped to her calf and her bottom in the air, her hair flowing around her flushed face in a wild tangle of waves, but it was obviously a look that worked for Ashe.

"That's it," he said with a growl. "Keep your eyes on my face. Just like that."

He ran his thumbs to the top of her sex, stroking over the tight bundle of nerves, and she sank her teeth into her lower lip, feeling as if he could see right inside her. Her lashes started to dip, until he snapped another husky command for her to keep her eyes open. Glaring, she said, "You love to give orders, don't you?"

His mouth curved with one of those sin-tipped smiles that always looked so good on him, his lips firm and sensual. "I just want you to see what you do to me."

"What *all* women do to you," she countered, suddenly compelled to make it clear this was nothing more than sex. Just because she believed he hadn't fooled around with Lacey earlier didn't mean he wouldn't run to another woman the next time things got too emotional between them. Like those two repelling magnets, they would keep veering apart, finding it impossible to be comfortable in anything more than a physical relationship.

"I don't want another woman," he argued, his eyes glittering like bright chips of lightning. "And sooner or later, you're going to believe that."

"Stop it. I don't want to fight with you, but lying is only going to piss me off again."

"Just think about it, Jules." She watched in the mirror as he lowered his gaze to her sex, the explicit position leaving nothing to the imagination. She could see the lust etched into the hard, masculine lines of his expression as he watched his thumbs stroking between her folds, her sex liquid and warm and pulsing. He rubbed the callused pad of one thumb over her tender opening, thrusting it into the slick heat, stirring her into a quivering froth of sensation. Then he pulled it out and wrapped both arms around her, yanking her upper body off the table and against his chest. "Why the hell would I touch another woman when I can have this?" he demanded, one big hand molding over her breast, the other burrowing between her spread legs.

She blinked at the erotic image they made in the mirror, and had to swallow as she tried to find her voice. "You can't...you can't have this forever," she heard herself say, unable to just give in.

His dark brows drew together in a fierce scowl. He hadn't liked her words, no matter how true they were. "I'll have it for as long as I want it."

"No, Ashe." The compulsion to defy him was impossible to resist. "That isn't how this works."

He held her tighter, as if she was already slipping away from him. "Damn it, why can't you just stop fighting me and let yourself go?"

"I...can't," she choked out, shaking her head, her long hair streaming over his chest. "Just because you're important to me doesn't mean I want you to have that kind of power over me. Over my emotions. It scares the hell out of me."

His nostrils flared. "And you don't think it scares me, too? I've been terrified ever since I spotted your little ass sitting on that damn patio in London!"

She wanted to scoff at that growled admission, but couldn't. Not when she could see the truth burning in his eyes. "This is so crazy. What's happening to us?"

"I don't know." His deep voice was tight, his expression etched with raw, devastating need. "But I can't stand you trying to push—"

The sudden shrill ring of his cell phone drowned out his words. "Ignore it," he muttered, burying his face in the curve of her shoulder, his mouth hot against her skin.

"Ashe," she moaned, trembling from the stroke of his thumb across her clit, her sheath pulsing around the fingers he'd buried inside her. But her conscience wouldn't let her choose pleasure over her family. "You have to answer it. What if it's Knox or someone with information?"

With a guttural snarl on his lips, Ashe stepped back and dug into his pocket for his phone. Punching the answer button, he put the phone to his ear and barked, "What?"

"Ashe, get the hell out of there!" Gideon yelled over the line. "Someone must have followed me to Nice. I just got a call warning me that a hit is coming for you and Jules at the club."

"Who was it?"

"Don't know, man. Didn't even recognize the voice. Just get the hell outta there!"

"Watch your back," he grunted, disconnecting

the call and shoving the phone back in his pocket. Looking at Juliana, who had already moved to her feet and was pulling up her jeans, he said, "Someone just called Gideon and told him that an attack is coming. We've got to go."

"Ohmygod! How did they find us?"

He started gathering their things together as he explained. "They must have had a surveillance team watching Gid in Marseilles, assuming I'd get in touch with him. Then they followed him here."

She was hooking her bra when a knock sounded on the door, her eyes going wide with fear, the warm color beneath her skin fading to white.

Ashe motioned for her to be quiet, then moved to the side of the door. Stretching his upper body across it, he took a quick look through the peephole, then muttered a sharp expletive. "It's your buddy," he grunted, cutting her a dark look. "Kid's got more balls than I'd have given him credit for."

"Josh? I have to talk to him," she said, yanking her sweater over her head.

"Not a fucking chance," he snarled, ripping the door open, prepared to order the punk to get lost. But before Ashe could mutter a single word, a bullet tore straight through the side of Josh's head.

CHAPTER ELEVEN

MOVING FASTER THAN SHE'D EVER seen him move before, Ashe pushed a screaming Juliana behind him as two vampires suddenly shoved their way into the room.

"I recognize your faces," Ashe growled, keeping his gaze on the men as he backed her against the far wall, putting the entire distance of the room between them and the two steely eyed males. "You're both in the Royal Guard at Court."

A deep shudder of revulsion tore through Juliana's dazed horror as those harsh words hit her ears. The last time she'd seen anyone from the Royal Guard had been the day the Court soldiers dragged her into the Wasteland, kicking and screaming.

"That's right," confirmed the sandy blond. He slipped his gun into the holster under his arm while the other guard dragged Josh's body into the room, and then shut the door. Blood poured from Josh's head in an ever-widening circle, but Juliana knew the wound wouldn't be fatal. Still, it infuriated her that these bastards had used Josh to get into the room.

"Since when do Royal Guards shoot innocent men?" Ashe's voice vibrated with fury. "For that matter, when do they accept assassination orders to kill innocent women?"

"We have no quarrel with you, Granger," the blond insisted, holding up his hands. He had a lanky build, unlike his partner, who was bald and stocky. "We just want to talk."

"Don't trust him," Juliana whispered, her intuition warning her that the blond guard wasn't what he seemed. There was something about him that reminded her of Raphe, but she couldn't say exactly what it was. He smelled like a Deschanel, and had the same pure gray eyes as she and Ashe did. But he didn't seem…right.

"Don't worry," Ashe muttered under his breath. "Considering the way he just put a bullet through your friend's temple, I've got a pretty good idea of why he's here."

"Sorry," she murmured, wishing Gideon's call had come in just a little sooner, so that they could have had time to get out of the room.

"We have no quarrel with you," the bald guard said to Ashe, repeating his partner's words. "We just want the girl."

"She's a pain in the ass," Ashe offered in a sarcastic drawl, releasing his talons, "but I'm afraid I can't just let you walk out of here with her."

A slow, bloodcurdling smile spread over the blond's mouth. "Is it going to be like that, then?" he asked, releasing his own talons. Juliana stared, trying to tell if they looked longer than they should, their width a little thicker.

Ashe's response was to take a step forward, his body seeming to expand before her eyes as he prepared for the fight.

She placed her hand on his back, and could feel the power thrumming through him, his muscles hard and at the ready. "Ashe, let me help you," she whispered, terrified that something was going to go horribly wrong. She knew he was an incredible soldier, but something about this whole setup felt…wrong.

"No!" he growled, keeping his eyes on the two guards who were still holding position on the other side of the small sitting room. "I can't fight and keep an eye on you, as well."

The bald vamp slid a look at his partner, and in the next second they charged, with Ashe meeting them in the middle of the room. The sound was horrific as punches and kicks connected, clothing and flesh ripping as deadly talons swung in powerful slashes. If the music playing in the club hadn't been so loud, she was sure the noise would have drawn the attention of the patrons downstairs. But as it was, they were on their own.

Keeping a careful eye on the vicious fight, Juliana reached down, pulling the leg of her jeans up and taking her knife from its sheath. She wasn't great with a blade, but she was thankful for the weapon, determined to help him if he needed it.

Clutching the lethal knife in her hand, she tried to edge her way around to the side of the room, thinking she could help by burying the blade in the bald guard's back, since he was closest to her. If she took him down, she knew Ashe could easily finish him off. But Ashe must have been watching her from the corner of his vision, because he immediately spotted her. "Goddamn it!" he roared. "I said to stay the hell back!"

She dropped back, just as he'd commanded, but she wasn't fast enough, the bald vamp twisting and lunging toward her. She flung herself toward the wall, but not in time to avoid the talons that slashed across her shoulder. Fire exploded across her skin, making her cry out, the stark sound swallowed by Ashe's bellowing roar. By the time she'd shoved her hair out of her eyes with her free hand, Ashe was gaining ground as he fought with an almost animalistic frenzy, driving the two guards into the corner. Blood flew, the scent of it ripe in the air, as the three men fought with savage skill. Ashe ducked to avoid a kick from the bald guard, then landed a blow that whipped the blond's head to the side. As his head turned toward Juliana, she saw the vampire's eyes flash crimson. And she knew.

Oh, God. She was right! The blond guard wasn't Deschanel. He was like Raphe, *exactly* like Raphe, which meant he could poison Ashe with those deadly talons he kept slashing toward his throat.

"Be careful!" she shouted, but she was already too late. Just as Ashe ripped his talons through the bald guard's throat, completely taking his head off, the blond threw himself at Ashe with such speed he was nothing more than a blur flying across the space that separated them. The impact of his body colliding into Ashe's cracked like thunder, both of them slamming into the far wall with so much force the plaster exploded around them, raining through the air in a hazy cloud of dust and fragments of drywall.

Coughing, Juliana waved her free hand in front of her face, struggling to see through the cloud of debris. She stumbled forward, knocking her shins into broken pieces of furniture, following the guttural sounds of the fight now taking place on the other side of the room.

Knowing she only had one shot at this, Juliana gripped the knife in her slick palm, blood pouring down from the wound in her shoulder, and edged closer as the air began to clear. The growls ripping from Ashe's throat were deep and feral, his strength as he battled his opponent truly breathtaking. But he didn't know what the assassin was, and now more than ever, she wanted to protect him from that truth. If the Delacourts had grown so powerful that Raphe's corruption had spread to the Royal Guards, they wouldn't hesitate to destroy Ashe and all that he held dear. Oh, she knew he would fight the bastards till the bitter end, but as long as there was still a chance she could save him from that nightmare, she would.

She didn't know if it was the right choice, or even a fair one. But it was the only one she could make based on her past. The only one her heart would allow her to make.

Taking a deep breath, Juliana focused her sights on the blond soldier, tightening her grip on the blade. He and Ashe were circling each other, their chests heaving, talons extended at their sides. Lifting her knife, she waited until the blond's back was to her, and then aimed for his throat. But he must have sensed the movement, because he spun at the last second, the back of his hand smacking her across her face. Ashe's furious shout rang through her head as she stumbled back, her blade only nicking the guard's arm.

No! I have to do this!

Juliana raised her arm again as the blond

lunged toward her, talons raised, ready to strike. But the blow never came. At the last second, Ashe threw himself at the guard, taking him to the ground. They grappled over the floor, punching and snarling, both of them covered in blood. Somehow, they ended up back on their feet, moving so fast it was difficult for Juliana to tell what has happening. She would have jumped into the fray, but was too afraid she'd stab Ashe by accident. She could hear herself screaming for him to watch out for the guard's talons, but then everything went strangely quiet as she watched Ashe suddenly stumble against the wall. He staggered and tried to brace himself, then slid to the floor, blood smearing on the wall behind him, as the blond turned, his eyes glowing bloodred in his face.

"You're going to be worth every penny, you meddling little bitch," he snarled, coming for her. Juliana held her ground until he was almost on her, then lifted the knife and plunged the blade into his throat, just beneath his jawbone. He staggered back, making god-awful noises as blood spurted from the wound, more blood gurgling in his throat as it came out his mouth and nose. Within seconds, he was dead.

Looking away from the gruesome sight, she rushed to Ashe and sank to her knees, tearing at his sweater so that she could check his injuries. Blood poured from the deep claw marks that were carved into his side. But the skin around the wound didn't appear to be poisoned. "Ashe, which guard made this cut?" she asked, wadding strips of his sweater together and pressing them against his shredded flesh.

"Bald one," he breathed out, and the sudden spike of relief made her dizzy. He was going to feel rough for a day or so while he healed, but he'd be okay, his body mending the injury with ease. But knowing how close it'd been made her sick with worry. She should have anticipated that Raphe would use every weapon in his arsenal to take her down, instead of relying solely on the Assassin's League.

"Are you okay?" he asked, his voice heartbreakingly weak.

"Don't worry about me," she muttered, applying more pressure to the wound in his side. "You're the one who's been torn open!"

A cocky smile twitched at the corner of his mouth. "Naw. It's just a flesh wound."

A burst of laughter escaped her tight throat, but it sounded more like a sob. "You idiot. I can't believe you're quoting Monty Python at a time like this."

"Jules, relax. I'm going to be fine. Just…help me get to my feet."

"Okay, but go easy," she told him, her voice rough with worry as she helped him to stand.

Searching for his cell phone in his pockets, she said, "I'm going to get you somewhere safe, so you can recover. Then I'm leaving."

"What?" he thundered, the bellowing sound immediately followed by a groan as he leaned more heavily against the wall. "The hell you are!" he growled, his pale face misted with sweat. "Damn it, I told you the truth. I didn't touch Lacey tonight!"

"It isn't that," she said, pausing her search for his phone long enough to meet his worried, pain-filled gaze. Her voice was thick with tears. "It's because I was…I was wrong to involve you in this. It's too dangerous. You need to get out now, while you still can."

"You think I'd run and leave you to deal with this shit on your own?" His lip curled, his dark eyes filled with rage. "What kind of man do you think I am?"

"I'm hoping you're a smart one," she said, reaching behind him to check his back pockets. "Trust me, you don't want to get involved with this mess. Your family has already been through so much, and this thing will come crashing down on their heads. You need to cut your losses now and let me deal with it."

Finding the cell phone, she yanked it from his

pocket and started to punch the button for his contacts, when he grasped her wrist. "What is it you're not telling me?" His dark eyes bored into hers, demanding the truth.

"What makes you think I'm keeping anything from you?"

"Because that's all you do is keep secrets. You don't know how to— Damn it," he cursed, sluggishly dropping to one knee.

"Oh, God," she cried, finally noticing the claw marks on the back of his right shoulder, the edges of the injury already turning black. "I thought you said that blond guard didn't cut you!"

"Didn't think he did," he muttered, the low words kind of slurred. "But my shoulder feels funny. What's hap—"

"You've been poisoned!" she choked out, helping him to the floor so that he was sitting with his back propped against the wall. With her heartbeat roaring in her ears, she searched frantically through his contacts until she found Gideon's number. Seconds later, the vampire answered, and she spoke in a tumbling rush. "It's Juliana. Your brother's been hurt. Do you know somewhere safe I can take him that's not too far from the club?"

"What happened?" Gideon demanded.

Pressing her free hand to Ashe's feverish brow, she said, "You were right. We were attacked again. Two Royal Guards this time. I don't know if they were working for the Assassin's League or for the Delacourts, but they were definitely trying to kill me."

Gideon said something loud and rough and foul, and she could hear people murmuring in the background, telling him he had to turn off his phone.

Knowing they were short on time, Juliana spoke quickly. "They're both dead, but I think one of the guards had dipped his talons in some kind of poison and Ashe has been infected. It's similar to something I saw in the Wasteland, and I have an idea of how to treat him. But he's probably going to be down for a few days."

"Okay, listen. You need to go to Essie's." He quickly rattled off an address in Nice, saying, "She's an old friend of my mother's. Essie's part witch and a healer, so she'll be able to get you anything you need."

"Do you trust her?"

"Essie loves Ashe like a son. I'm sure the only reason he didn't take you to meet her was because he didn't want to put her in danger."

And now it was going to happen, anyway, because she'd dragged Ashe into this. Regret coiled itself into a tight knot in her belly, but she forced it out of her mind, Ashe's safety the thing she needed to focus on now. "How long do you think it will take us to get there?"

"If you're walking, probably an hour." He exhaled a rough breath. "Damn it, I wish I could be there, but we're seconds from takeoff."

"Don't worry," she said, "I'll get him there, I promise. Just make sure they have fresh blood donors waiting. Women, men, it doesn't matter. He's going to need at least ten feedings."

"No!" Ashe groaned, suddenly snatching her wrist. His lashes fluttered, but he managed to open them enough to lock his dark gaze with hers. "No women," he rasped, his expression adamant. "Won't…drink them."

"Fine," she said thickly, taking Ashe's hand and giving it a comforting squeeze. "Make sure they're males. The stronger, the better."

"I'm on it."

"And Gideon."

"Yeah?"

Knowing they had to get moving, she looped Ashe's heavy arm around her shoulders, and said, "Tell them to hurry."

IT TOOK NEARLY AN HOUR, just as Gideon had predicted, for them to make it on foot to the address he'd given her, and it was the longest hour of Juliana's life. By the time they found the street the witch lived on, she and Ashe were both soaked in sweat and blood, their limbs trembling with exhaustion: his from the effects of the venom that had been introduced to his system, and hers from the strain of carrying their bags while supporting most of his weight as she'd all but dragged him down the dark, moonlit streets.

She hadn't been able to risk hailing a taxi. Not with all the blood soaking Ashe's clothing. She'd managed to get him dressed in a clean sweater and his jacket, but both were already drenched in fresh blood, as well as his jeans. Any taxi driver would undoubtedly report them to the police, and that was a complication they didn't need. More than once, Juliana wondered if she should have told Gideon to send a car, but was worried about getting into a vehicle with someone she didn't know. Her trust factor at the moment was down to zero, her paranoia rising. If it weren't imperative that Ashe have a place to recuperate, she wouldn't even be bringing him to this Essie person.

She'd hated leaving Josh like that back at the nightclub, unconscious and bleeding in their room, but knew he would heal in a few hours from the bullet wound that bastard had put in his head. On their way out, she'd told one of the staff that two assassins were dead and an innocent bystander had been injured in their room, so at least Josh wouldn't be left lying on the floor while he healed. Ashe, however, needed immediate attention, and she hoped that the woman Gideon was sending them to would be able to help.

When Juliana finally found the right house, Ashe barely managed to shuffle his feet along the walkway to the quaint two-story. They hadn't taken more than a few steps up the narrow walkway when the door burst open and a petite elderly woman came scurrying down the path in a pair of pink slippers, her gray hair pulled back in a heavy bun on the back of her head. She was wearing a pair of purple overalls on top of a tiger-printed shirt, the strange ensemble, combined with the hot pink slippers, looking somehow completely normal on her.

"My poor Ashe!" the woman cried, her scent a kind of soothing blend somewhere between witch and warm sugar cookies as she put her arm around his other side, helping Juliana support his weight. "Let me help you, honey."

"I'm Juliana," she said, her words tumbling over themselves as she tried to get them said. "He's lost a lot of blood and the poison is already spreading. He's getting weaker, and hasn't spoken for the last half hour."

"It's okay," Essie soothed, her tone soft but confident as they entered the cozy house. "Gideon said he was going to need blood. There are several vampires and shifters who I trust implicitly waiting upstairs to help."

"Thank God." Juliana would have gone ahead and given him her own vein, but knew from the research she'd done while in the Wasteland that too little blood could make the effects of the poison worse. In order for him to survive the first wave, Ashe needed to consume a massive quantity of blood, until the poison in his veins was diluted. Then, once that was done, it would simply be a matter of waiting out the second wave…and praying that he lived through it.

As they started toward the stairs, the witch's dark green gaze moved from Ashe's pale face, to Juliana's, and she smiled. "Strong ties bind the two of you together," she murmured, her tone warm with approval.

Juliana felt her eyes go wide, and rushed to correct her. "Oh, no. We're just…friends. We're not a, um…couple."

Essie's gaze seemed to glow with an eerie inner light. "Hmm. Maybe you are, child, but you just don't know it yet."

Before Juliana could launch another denial, Essie called out from the bottom of the stairs for someone named Jimmy. A moment later, a hulking brute of a shifter with a kind face made his way down the stairs. He took Ashe from them, handling his weight with ease as he carried him to the second floor, Essie and Juliana following behind. It took them only moments to get Ashe settled in one of Essie's guest rooms, while Jimmy hovered near the door, ready to be of service if they needed him. Stripping Ashe of his blood-soaked clothes, they cleaned and bound the wound in his side, as well as the infected one on his shoulder, using supplies from the first-aid kit Essie had laid out on one of the bedside tables. With that done, they quickly draped him in a sheet, and brought in the first male.

From the moment Jimmy had carried him up the stairs, Ashe seemed to have lost consciousness. It was as if he'd held on until the last possible second, knowing Juliana needed his help to get them to safety, but once there, he could do no more. He hadn't opened his eyes while she and Essie had worked on his wounds. Hadn't spoken a single word, his shallow breaths rattling in his lungs, while his color steadily faded until he was nearly as pale as the sheets, despite his raging fever. Juliana was terrified he wouldn't be able to feed, that they'd have to find some way to force the blood into his system, but as soon as the first vampire pressed his wrist to Ashe's mouth, he reacted with ravenous hunger, his fangs shooting out and piercing the male's flesh. He drank deeply, his hands holding the vampire's arm to his mouth, until Essie told him to stop, and then the next male came in. The process continued to repeat itself until Ashe's coloring slowly returned to normal, the wounds no longer bleeding as heavily as they had been, his body able to begin its healing process.

When he'd taken as much blood as the last male could offer, Essie said she'd give the two of them some time alone, and shooed everyone out of the room, closing the door behind her. Pulling up her sleeve, Juliana pressed her wrist against Ashe's bloodstained lips. "Now mine," she whispered, rubbing her skin against his lips, coaxing him to feed once more.

He pulled in a ragged breath, his eyes shooting open, the silver so bright it looked like liquid mercury shimmering around a single point of black. "Can't," he groaned, something like terror filling his breathtaking gaze as he stared up at her, his hands fisting at his sides.

"You have to," she told him, unable to understand why he refused. "I want you—"

Before she even finished the sentence, he caught her arm in his strong hands and drove his fangs deep into her flesh with a sharp pop. He rolled, almost turning over, her body pulled forward at an awkward angle as he held her wrist beneath his mouth, his fingers biting into her arm, holding her in place.

He drank deeply, making her light-headed, the strong pulls of his mouth and the way he gently worked his fangs in shallow thrusts, stroking in and out of the puncture wounds, reminding her of sex.

His hips rolled, legs shifting, dragging the

sheet down his body, and as he turned a little on his side, Juliana could see that he was getting aroused. Her own fangs burst into her mouth, heavy and aching, desperate for the feel of his skin and the taste of his blood. That short drink in the park hadn't been nearly enough, his flavor so warm and rich she could have easily become addicted.

The moment was incredibly erotic, steeped in breathtaking emotion and need, her pulse rushing thick and fast. But she knew this wasn't the time or place. Knew his suffering was only beginning. The realization filled her with rage, and Juliana silently cursed the ones responsible for this nightmare.

"Ashe, you have to stop."

He growled, obviously not liking the idea, but managed to wrench his fangs back, his tongue sliding over her skin to seal the wounds. His breathing was loud in the cool, quiet room as he released his hold on her arm and rolled into a sitting position. He was still a bit pale, but he looked better. She would have smiled, but she knew the worst was yet to come.

"Don't move," she told him, taking his hand in hers. "I've seen a poison similar to this used in the Wasteland," she lied. "That was only the first wave. The second is going to be much worse."

"I feel fine," he said, his intentions burning

in the silver glow of his heavy-lidded eyes as he swung his legs over the edge of the mattress, no doubt planning to pick up right where they'd left off, before Josh had knocked on their door. But the instant his feet hit the floor, the second wave slammed through him. His back arched under a powerful spasm that ripped through his body, his heavy frame crashing against the bed, every tendon and long line of sinew standing out in sharp relief beneath the sweat-slick surface of his skin.

And so the nightmare began.

Tears flowed down Juliana's face in an endless stream as the eviscerating pain tore through him in one tormenting wave after another. He thrashed on the sheets, his body raging with fever, while she and Essie tried to cool him down, stroking his limbs with cloths dipped in a bowl of ice water. Essie even tried dosing him with one of her special spells, but nothing they did seemed to work. Nothing lessened his mindless suffering. And as his raw, agonized shouts echoed throughout the long, harrowing hours of the night, Juliana's heart shattered into a million fractured pieces.

CHAPTER TWELVE

IN THE EARLY HOURS OF DAWN, Ashe finally drifted into a deep sleep. Juliana watched over him for several more hours, worried he might have a relapse. But when he continued to sleep peacefully, she made her way downstairs to grab a quick shower and feed on some of the bagged blood she'd tossed in her bag and brought with them. Since she knew Ashe's cell phone had a special chip that made it impossible to trace, she placed a quick call to the nightclub, relieved when the woman who answered the phone told her Josh had recovered and gone home with his friends. He'd probably never want to see her again, considering what had happened, but at least he was alive.

After that, she called Gideon to give him an update. Though he'd been on the phone with Essie several times during the night, Juliana felt she should call him, as well. Then she checked to make sure there weren't any messages from Knox, and headed back upstairs.

She wasn't gone for more than twenty minutes, and yet, when she returned to the room, she found Ashe swaying on his feet at the side of the bed. He'd managed to get his boxers on, but was trying, unsuccessfully, to pull on a clean pair of jeans he must have taken from his bag.

"What the hell are you doing?" she demanded, hurrying across the room toward him.

He lifted his flushed face and blinked several times, as if trying to bring her into focus. "Coming to find you," he said, the words a little slurred, as if he'd tied on one too many.

Catching a whiff of his breath, Juliana narrowed her eyes with suspicion. "Are you *drunk?*"

His eyes went wide. "Drunk? Nope," he said cheerfully, letting her help him back down on the bed. As she pulled off the one leg of his jeans he'd gotten to his knee, he went on. "I'm definitely not drunk, because I haven't had any beer. Or whiskey. Or scotch. Or rum. Or—"

"Okay, I get it," she murmured, snuffling a soft laugh under her breath. "You didn't drink anything."

"I didn't?" he asked her, kind of rolling and twisting his way over the bed, before stretching out on his back in the middle of the mattress, his arms flung wide. "That's weird. I thought I did."

Staring down at him from the side of the bed, Juliana arched a brow. "Okay, out with it. What did you drink?"

His grin was endearingly crooked as he turned his head toward her, the goofy expression making him look younger. Less strained. He even had a dimple! "Essie brought me something to drink a few minutes ago. Said it would help keep me asleep. But it wasn't liquor. Tasted foul, and now I'm…" He hiccuped, before saying, "Now I'm flying."

Juliana didn't know whether to laugh or groan. "You drank one of Essie's potions?"

"Uh-huh," he breathed out, his eyes already drifting closed.

"Poor Ashe," she murmured, sitting on the edge of the mattress and grabbing his hand. "You're probably going to have the mother of all hangovers later on. Didn't anyone ever teach you not to take candy from strangers?"

Both eyes popped back open. "It wasn't candy," he protested. "And she's not a stranger. She's an old family friend!"

She gave a kind of half snort, half laugh. "An old family friend, and a little cherubic-faced pusher."

He squinted, still trying to focus that hazy gaze. "Are you saying that sweet old lady doped me up?"

"What do you think?" she asked, lifting his hand to her mouth and pressing a soft kiss to his knuckles.

"I think she's brilliant," he said in a deep, drowsy rumble, watching her kiss his hand. "She told me she thinks you and I would be good together."

Lowering his hand to her lap, Juliana gave him a wry smile. "Which shows how little she knows, huh?"

He looked as if he was trying very hard to remember something. "I think she said you were afraid to let yourself feel anything for me."

"You think? You can't remember?" she asked, thinking he was absolutely adorable like this, even if the conversation was making her uncomfortable. Damn Essie for her meddling! A sweet little witch she might be, but she needed to learn how to keep her nose out of other people's business.

Ashe's dark brows scrunched with confusion. "Trying to remember everything she said, but my head's all…fuzzy."

Her voice was dry. "I'll bet it is."

Figuring he had only moments before he would be out for the count, she grabbed the sheet from the bottom of the bed, pulling it up to his trim waist, the white bandage on his side a stark reminder of what he'd been through. She asked him to lift his head, and leaned over, arranging the pillows for him. When she told him he could lower his head again, he did, his bright gaze focused on her face as he reached up and touched his fingertips to her cheek. Quietly, he said, "I just want to understand, Jules."

"Understand what?" she asked, her damp hair falling forward, the dark strands draping over his arm. It was odd, how after everything that they'd done together, the sight of her hair lying against his skin struck her as impossibly intimate.

He swallowed, and in an achingly soft voice, he asked, "Why would it be so bad?"

She knew he was asking about himself. About why she was afraid to start something with him. Something that was about more than sex. But there wasn't a simple answer. Her reasons were all tangled together, overlapping and bleeding into one another. Fear, regret, guilt. And a strong belief that it was better not to tempt herself with dreams she knew could never come true.

Before she could figure out how to put any of that into a response, his doped-up mind wandered onto a new train of thought. Pushing his hand into her hair, he trailed his fingers through the heavy waves, and said, "Christ. Why do you have to be so bloody beautiful?"

Her lips twitched with a smile. "I think you're just wearing beer goggles. Or whatever the equivalent would be for what Essie gave you."

He laughed under his breath, rubbing the ends of her hair between his thumb and finger. "I've heard of that. Wish it was true. But thought you were beautiful first time I ever saw you. Before I…" His voice trailed off, and he yawned.

"Before you what?" she pressed, stroking her fingers along the silky stubble darkening his jaw. It made him look dark and dangerous and deadly, which was fitting, since he was all of those things.

"Nothing." He reached up, grabbing her arms and pulling her down next to him, his body still remarkably strong even when he was flying high as a kite. Rolling onto his side, he nuzzled his face into her hair, his lips touching her ear as he asked, "Do you like how it feels when I'm inside you?"

Juliana hid her face against his throat. "That's not something we're going to talk about."

"We're not?" he asked, and she could have sworn he was smiling. "You're always so tough, Jules. I love that about you. 'Course, I love when you need me, too. Can't get enough of that."

"You need to sleep, Ashe."

"Okay," he said as he sighed, already sounding like he was drifting off, his arms cuddling her close. "But I'm gonna dream again. About getting my mouth on you."

"You've dreamed about that?"

"Mmm. And you're even better than I imagined. Hotter. Sweeter."

She wanted to ask him more, but felt guilty. His words were sounding more slurred, Essie's potion working deeper into his system. He probably wouldn't even remember a word of this conversation when the effects wore off.

Knowing it was the right thing to do, she tried to convince him to go to sleep again, but he wouldn't stop talking. "Do you think about me, Jules? I want you to. I want you to think about me…all the time."

She made a valiant effort to stay silent, but failed. "Do *you* think about *me?*"

He gave a husky laugh. "All the time. Want to make love to you. So bad. It's all I can think about."

"You want sex, not love," she pointed out. "And you're already having sex with me. Just like you've had sex with so many others."

"But you're different." She could feel his frustration as his muscles went hard; could hear it in the grittiness of his voice. "Those other women never meant anything to me. But you…I want you to be *mine* when I'm fucking you. Want it…to be different. I want you to *belong* to me. Want to be able to do anything I want to you."

"You do a lot as it is," she said with a smile, his words reaching into her chest and taking hold of her heart.

"Want more, though. Want to own every inch

of you." He paused…his chest lifting with a deep, shuddering breath. And then he said, "I *do* own every inch of you. I just haven't claimed them yet."

Her breath caught. "What do you mean?" she demanded, trying to draw back so that she could see his face. But he kept her pressed against his chest, one hand buried in the back of her hair, the other on her lower back.

"You're mine," he rasped. "By right."

"No," she argued, her jaw quivering. "By right, I'll belong to the man who I make Burn."

He pressed his lips to the top of her head, his deep voice drowsy with satisfaction. "Hmm…and that would be me."

Ohmygod…this can't be happening.

Her breath not only caught, it seized in her lungs. "Ashe?"

"Shh. You don't know, so don't let me tell you, 'kay?"

She would have laughed at the absurdity of that statement if her heart weren't trying to pound its way through her chest, her pulse rushing so fast she felt light-headed. "Ashe, what are you saying?"

He exhaled in an audible rush. "Been Burning for you for months now, Juliana. Even been taking something to make it hurt less—but it isn't helping. Tried a lot of women, too, but that didn't help, either. All I could think about was you. Drove me crazy."

She trembled, unable to believe what he was saying. And yet, she knew it was true. She could *feel it* deep inside, down in her blood and her bones and her soul. "I don't...I don't know what to say," she breathed out, her voice thick with the desire that was suddenly pouring through her veins. "How...long?"

"Months...and months...and months. And you're probably gonna be mad if I tell you this other thing, so don't remember. 'Kay?"

"Tell me what other thing?"

"I didn't sleep with anyone at your compound."

Juliana stiffened against him, her voice sharp with disbelief. "Ashe...I saw you."

"You saw what I *wanted* you to see," he drawled. "Did a lot of kissing, but that was all. And since female vamps don't provide as much heat as other species, I had to make you think I was sleeping with a lot of them, since I was running so hot. But the truth is that I couldn't get hard for another woman when you were so close." His chest shook with another quiet laugh. "All those women you live with probably think there's something *really* wrong with me. But since they didn't know for sure, they didn't want to admit to anyone else that I hadn't nailed them. Whole situation would have been funny as hell, if I hadn't been in so much pain."

She pressed her forehead against his chest, her shoulders shaking with laughter even as her eyes burned with tears. "God, Ashe. I don't know what to say."

"S'okay." His arms pulled her a little closer, his hands molding her against the front of his body, the feel of his rigid erection making it clear she wasn't the only one aroused by the conversation. "Now that we're sleeping together, it's so good it's all I can do not to shove my fangs into you, hard and thick and deep, and make you mine. Can't get enough of the way you feel under me. So small and tight. So...*perfect*..." His voice trailed off, and she drew her head back, checking to see if he'd finally fallen asleep. Which he had.

In fact, he'd fallen asleep with a smile on his face.

Nuzzling against his chest, Juliana pressed her ear to his heavy heartbeat, his stunning confessions buzzing through her mind in a continual loop. She didn't know if he would remember any of what he'd told her when he woke up, but she knew that she'd never forget it. Not for as long as she lived, whether that was a matter of days...or decades.

She was tired and wired at the same time. Too shocked to sleep, but too exhausted not to.

And terrified that the last of her defenses had just been utterly destroyed.

IN THE EARLY AFTERNOON, Ashe came back into the bedroom with a towel wrapped around his waist, careful not to make any sound and wake Juliana. She was still snuggled in the bed, her dark hair mussed from sleep, cheeks pink from the heat blasting out of a nearby radiator.

He should have been aching from the top of his head to the soles of his feet after suffering through the effects of that bloody poison, but he wasn't. He'd removed his bandages before he'd showered, and his wounds were almost completely healed thanks to Juliana's quick thinking.

He also should have had the hangover from hell. God only knew what Essie had given him to knock him out. But, in fact, he felt oddly lucid now that he'd showered and shaved, as if seeing clearly for the first time.

And what he saw was a young, hardheaded woman who drove him out of his mind with frustration and lust, anger and tenderness, twisting his emotions into so many knots he didn't know up from down most of the time anymore.

She might not trust him with her secrets yet, but she wasn't Gretchen. Unlike that bitch from his past, Juliana was worth fighting for. And as he thought of the way she'd cared for him during his illness, of the way she'd held him and whispered in his ear, telling him how much she needed him to pull through for her, he knew without any doubt that letting her push him away would be the biggest mistake of his life. She cared. She just didn't know how to deal with the fear of being hurt, same as him. But he didn't have any choice except to figure out how to deal with that fear. He didn't know where this thing between them was going exactly, but damn it, he needed the time to figure it out.

Yeah, it hurt to be so close to her with the Burning scalding his veins, but it was better than the alternative, because he had a feeling that losing her would quite likely break him.

That realization would have had the old Ashe running as hard and as fast as he could, determined to protect his heart. But the new Ashe—the man who'd woken up that afternoon with his hand clasping hers, his head filled with hazy memories of the way she'd held him and comforted him— that man was ready to find his balls and stick with this thing, determined to see where it might lead.

The thought made him smile.

After this third attack on her life, he was worried and frightened and so hungry for her he could barely see straight—but for the first time in what felt like a long, hollow forever, Ashe thought he just might be happy.

And he needed to hold her so badly he was shaking with it.

As the early-afternoon sunlight slipped around the edges of the blinds on the room's lone window, he carefully stripped the sweat-soaked sheets off the bed without waking her, moving her body from one side to the other. Next, he covered the mattress with one of the soft crocheted blankets he found in the simple wooden chest at the foot of the bed. Then he tossed his towel on the floor, stretched out on the bed and gathered Juliana's slight body into his arms, both of them lying on their sides, face-to-face.

Ashe didn't know how long he simply lay there holding her, watching her sleep, while listening to the sounds of a quiet rain beginning to fall. He thought of how incredible it'd been when she'd given him her blood the night before, and how hard he'd had to fight not to inject the serum into her vein. He honestly didn't know how he'd found the strength to resist, the fear that she might hate him for it afterward the only thing that had stopped him.

When she finally began to stir, he stroked the delicate length of her spine with slow, gentle touches, waiting for the moment when she would open her eyes and look at him. He wanted to see what her gaze would tell him in those first, unguarded seconds, when she found herself lying in his arms. She made a small, sleepy sound that made him smile again, her nose scrunching as she shivered, stretched…and finally lifted those thick, curling lashes.

She looked right at him…and he groaned, undone by what he saw shimmering in those luminous depths.

Cursing a hot, husky string of swearwords under his breath, Ashe ripped off her shirt and bra, then covered her mouth with his, unable to wait. He needed her taste, damn it. Her breath. Needed to drown himself in her. But she gasped, breaking her mouth from the kiss as she pushed him to his back. He started to protest, when she lowered her head, pressing those soft, velvety lips against the hammering pulse at the base of his throat. Every muscle in his body went hard with anticipation, his mind dazed as he wondered if she was going to…

Oh, shit, he thought, as she trailed her mouth lower, pressing sweet, teasing kisses to his chest, across a nipple, then lower, to his ribs. A dizzying surge of blood rushed to his cock, the swollen shaft pulsing and tight and heavy, and he knew there was no way in hell he was going to be able to hold this.

"I need to be inside you," he growled, his voice more guttural than he'd ever heard it. "Get those damn jeans off. I can't wait."

"You have to," she whispered, kissing her way down lower, over his abdomen, her tongue flicking over his navel, and another surge of blood rushed to his cock, making him even harder, thicker, his skin stretched hot and tight around the rigid shaft. He shuddered, covering his eyes with the heels of his hands, his face going hot, as if he was some green-eared teenager anticipating his first blow job.

Would she like his taste? Like the way he felt in her mouth?

A harsh laugh jerked from his throat. He couldn't ever remember worrying about things like that in the past, simply taking his pleasure as if it was his due. But this was Juliana, and damn it, that made it different. He wanted her to feel the same urgent, wrenching need that he did. Wanted her to be consumed by the same primitive, demanding hunger.

And if the sexy little moan she gave as she wrapped her hands around him and ran her soft tongue over the ripe tip meant anything, then she did.

"Tell me what you like," she whispered, running her lips down one side, her tongue flicking against the sensitive veins that wrapped the dark, ruddy shaft.

Ashe opened his eyes and lifted his head, desperate to see it…to watch her lips and tongue touching that most primal part of him. He might have been able to wrap an air of civilization around him for the most part, but there was nothing civilized about his cock. It was long and thick, the size too much for a lot of women, but Juliana didn't seem put off or worried, her hot little mouth closing over the swollen head so eagerly, it nearly stopped his heart.

Struggling for his voice, he rasped, "I love all of it. Everything. It's so good you're killing me."

"You're going to have to be more specific than that," she said with a smile.

"Seriously." His voice got deeper. "Just…do whatever you usually do."

"That won't work," she said, this time with a muffled laugh.

"Why?" he grated, barely able to think straight. He couldn't remember his own damn name, much less give her instructions on something this important. He was dying here!

"I can't do what I usually do," she told him, rubbing her cheek against him, "because I've never done this specific act before. So, um, it'd probably be a good idea if you don't set your expectations too high."

Ashe shook his head, thinking he mustn't have heard her right. "What?"

She lifted shining eyes to his face, her smile turning wry. "I said I've never done this before."

"You can't be ser…" His voice trailed off as he took a long look at her blushing cheeks, an adorable blend of embarrassment and excitement burning in her silver eyes. If any other woman had told him such an outrageous claim, he would have called her a liar. But staring at Juliana's pink face, he knew, instinctively, that she was telling him the truth. At least about this.

A jolt of lust shot through him, so violent and strong he nearly came then and there, his cock pulsing hard in her grip.

She gave a soft laugh. "I think you like that. Don't you?"

He tried to say yes, but his throat was too tight, his ears roaring. Bracing himself on an elbow, Ashe reached down and put his hand on the back of her head, watching with rapt awe as she let him bring her face closer to the full, glistening head. "Lick it," he said, the guttural command scraping his throat.

She flicked her tongue over the tip again, taking the drops of moisture there into her mouth, and he had to grit his teeth. Then she opened her lips over the straining crown, her tongue licking and rubbing, as she breathed through her nose and started taking him in. He made a low sound deep in his throat, pleasure shooting up his spine as his hips surged, pushing him a little deeper. She almost panicked, her hand tightening on the base of his shaft. But then she swallowed…and took some more, the feeling of being in her hot little mouth so good it nearly killed him.

"Get your hair out of the way," he told her, his voice raw. "I need to see it. Need to see you sucking me."

She used her free hand to pull her hair over her shoulder, her mouth still working him over with that lush, wet suction, her cheeks hollowing as she did a fluttering pull on her way up that made him groan. He ran his finger along the edge of her mouth, her lips stretched wide to accommodate his width, her shimmering eyes staring back at him through her lashes. It was the sexiest damn thing he'd ever seen, pushing him even closer to the edge. "Get up here," he growled, needing to make sure she was ready for him before he lost it.

She drew her head back, trailing those soft lips down the side of his shaft. "What?" she whispered, her voice thick with pleasure.

"I want you up here," he ground out.

"Stop distracting me." She shot him a quick smile before she trailed her lips down the other side.

Ashe pulled in a deep breath, then slowly let it out. But it didn't help. "I'm not joking, Juliana."

She gave another soft laugh. "I'm sure you aren't."

He was losing it, damn it, and the little witch

was enjoying herself. "If you don't get your ass up here in the next five seconds," he said, pushing the words through his gritted teeth, "I won't be responsible for what happens."

Her response was to cover him with her mouth again, taking him even deeper than she had before, and a harsh roar tore its way out of his chest, echoing through the room. In the next instant, he jackknifed and pulled her off him, her high-pitched squeal joining his savage growl as he turned, tossing her onto the bed. He came up on his knees beside her, ripping her jeans and panties off, then knelt between her slender thighs, spreading them wider.

"So wet," he groaned, pushing two thick fingers inside her, loving the way she held him. Going down on him had obviously gotten her off, because she was soaked, her back arching as he worked his fingers in deeper. "And so damn tight," he growled, leaning over and taking one of those strawberry-pink nipples into his mouth. He sucked on the tender peak while he worked his fingers in and out, hoping to God she was ready for him, because he was done waiting.

With a gritty curse on his lips, Ashe replaced his fingers with his cock and shoved inside her, the feeling so incredible he had to lock his jaw to keep from shouting. Heat crawled its way up his chest, adding to the fire in his veins as he worked himself in deeper, and deeper, until she'd taken every inch of him. Then he started to move, riding her with hard, hammering thrusts as he braced himself on rigid arms, his gaze locked tight on the erotic sight of his body driving into hers. It was hard and fast and furious, and he'd have been terrified it was too much for her, if she weren't clutching his hips, pumping up against him, her tight little sex already pulsing around him. She climaxed screaming, the sweet convulsions rippling along his shaft, squeezing him tight, and he pounded into her even harder. The bed creaked and groaned, slamming against the wall as his release thundered down on him. He raised his gaze, needing to see her face, to stare into her pleasure-bright eyes as it ripped through him with explosive, mind-shattering force, his body all but turning itself inside out as he pumped into her, giving her everything that he had.

When he finally collapsed onto his side, dragging her with him, he was still shuddering, his muscles twitching with residual pulses. He tried to drag air into his aching lungs, and couldn't. But hell, who needed air anyway? He could just keep floating on this surreal wave of satisfaction and die happy, without a care in the world.

Except that he needed to protect the fiery little female lying in his arms. That was definitely worth living for.

"So what's the plan?" she asked, the touch of her lips making him smile as she pressed a kiss to his chest.

It took him a moment, but Ashe finally got his sluggish brain to work. "We're going to drag our asses out of this bed, grab some food, and hop a train over to Toulouse."

"What's in Toulouse?"

Wishing he could stay inside her all day, but knowing they needed to get going, he carefully pulled himself out. "Another old family friend," he said, answering her question. "Her name is Mo and her son Alex is a computer whiz. I called her when we were at Knox's and asked if she could get him to try and hack into the Council's private financial records. Specifically Lenora Delacourt's."

Juliana braced herself on an elbow, her gaze wide with surprise. "You really think she might have paid for the assassination orders with one of her personal accounts?"

He shrugged as he rolled to his back. "If she's arrogant enough, there's a good chance. And I know Raphe is too arrogant by half. It would be just like him to use his mother to set the transaction up, allowing him to hide behind her status." He reached up and tucked her hair behind her ear, rubbing his thumb against her temple as he said, "Mo sent a text through on my phone this afternoon. That's what woke me up. She said she's got something to show us."

"Do you trust Mo?"

He answered without hesitation. "With my life."

Her lips curved with a soft smile. "Then let's go see what her son has been able to find."

Juliana started to climb off the bed, intending to get ready, when he grabbed her arm, holding her in place. "What is it?" she asked, looking back and seeing the seriousness of his expression.

His gray eyes glittered with emotion. "If I asked you to stay with Mo's family while I get to the bottom of this, would you?"

"No," she answered, shaking her head. "I couldn't do that. It wouldn't be right."

"I talked to Gideon while you were sleeping. We both think that whoever called him last night with that warning is probably the same person who helped you escape the Wasteland. For them to know that attack was coming, it's got to be someone close to the Delacourts, and I have a bad feeling about it." He sat up, a scowl settling between his dark brows. "This entire situation is unacceptable. I don't want anything to happen to you."

"It won't." She pried his fingers off her arm and carried them to her lips, kissing his battered knuckles. "You're the one I'm worried about. I hate that I dragged you into this. I feel so guilty."

"Don't," he said in a low voice. "You didn't do anything that wouldn't have happened anyway."

She cocked her head to the side. "What do you mean?"

He kept his gaze locked tight with hers. "I mean I would have learned about your escape eventually, and once I did, nothing in heaven or hell would have been able to keep me from coming after you and making sure you were safe."

In that moment, she wanted so badly to ask him about the Burning, but knew he didn't remember any of their shocking conversation from that morning. If he did, he would have already said something. So she settled for simply saying, "Would you have really come after me?"

"Oh, yeah." The truth of those husky words smoldered in his eyes, and Juliana felt something warm and wonderful unfurl inside her, glowing like a burst of light in the center of her chest.

"By the way," he murmured, the look in his eyes turning dark and sensual, "did I remember to thank you for saving my life?"

"No, but I'll think of a special way you can thank me later," she teased, laughing when he made a playful grab for her as she scrambled off the bed, a blissed-out smile on her face that felt strangely comfortable, as if it belonged there.

And as she rushed to get ready, that smile never once left her lips.

CHAPTER THIRTEEN

IF ASHE HAD EVER felt this good before, he couldn't recall the occasion. The Burning was still simmering through his veins, but for the moment, the need seemed to have been tempered by the feel of Juliana's slender hand gripped in his. It was almost as if his body sensed his capitulation in the near future, and knew it wouldn't be long before it got everything it wanted.

The idea should have scared the ever-loving hell out of him, but after the way she'd cared for him and stayed by his side, he only found his smile getting wider, his chest so light he felt ready to float off the friggin' ground. Something was happening to him, changing him and reshaping him, like shaking off his old skin and stretching to life inside a new one. Everything looked brighter, scents sharper…richer, the world exploding around him in a burst of color and light and beauty.

He was waxing poetic like a damn idiot, but he was too ramped up to worry about it. He just wanted to enjoy the afternoon as they headed to Mo's, the smiles Juliana kept sliding him making him restless with excitement. He just wanted to keep wallowing in this feeling, soaking it in.... And he wanted this shit with the Council and the Delacourts behind them so he could focus all his time and energy on the woman walking at his side. He was determined to strip all the secrets down between them, getting it all out in the open, so that they could both see just what they were dealing with.

Then, together, they could figure out what they were going to do with it. With each other.

Ashe knew that meant he'd have to tell her about the Burning, and though it made his damn knees shake to think about it, he would man up and do it. If he was going to demand she open up to him, then he could bloody well do the same for her, no matter how fucking vulnerable it made him feel. She'd either be happy about it...or run screaming.

And if she ran, he'd just go after her stubborn little ass and drag her right back. Then he'd put his mind to work and figure out a way to make her fall in love with him. He didn't think it would be easy, but then, he'd been alive long enough to know that nothing worth fighting for ever was.

Feeling her shiver as a cold breeze tugged at their jackets, Ashe wrapped his arm around her shoulders and pulled her against his side. They'd traveled to Toulouse by train, and were walking the mile from the station to Mo's house. "We don't have much farther to go," he said. "Mo's is just around the next corner."

"And to think that I complained about the Wasteland being cold," she drawled, snuggling closer to his side. "But at least the sun is shining here. You can't imagine how much I've missed the sunshine."

Ashe watched as she tipped her face up to the sky, a pang in his chest as he pictured her spending so many years in that hellhole of a prison, where the sun was seldom brighter than a faint glow. Feeling as if he had his heart stuck in his throat, he said, "Whatever I have to do, Jules, I'll make sure that you never have to go back there."

Her brow creased with concern as she shifted her gaze to his. "I just hope that you don't end up there with me."

"What do you mean?"

He could feel the tension moving through her shoulders. "I've been thinking about what happened last night. If word gets out that you killed one of those Royal Guards in Nice, the Council is going to send the Förmyndares after you."

"It depends on what kind of headway Gideon

is able to make at Court," he murmured, "but it's always a possibility."

She shot him an incredulous look. "How can you be so calm about it?"

He shrugged. "Because I'll deal with whatever they throw at us. I'm not going to feel bad that those bastards are rotting in hell. And if the Förmyndares end up coming after us because the guards are dead, then I'm willing to accept that."

Her voice was strained. "But did you think about that at the time? That by choosing to fight them, instead of handing me over, you were probably destroying not only your career, but your life? Because if we fail to find the evidence we need, that's exactly what's going to happen!"

Hating to hear her so upset, he stopped and pulled her against his chest. "First of all," he told her, staring down into her shimmering eyes, "there's no way in hell I ever would have let those bastards take you. And secondly, you let me worry about my life and career. I know what I'm doing, and I'm… I feel good about my choices, Jules. I feel…right."

She sniffed, saying, "I just don't want anything to happen to you."

"It won't." Lowering his head, he pressed a soft, tender kiss to her lips, then gave her a smile. "Now stop worrying. I swear I know what I'm doing."

Moments later, they were walking into Mo's, the familiar scent of tea and cookies filling his nose, reminding Ashe of the times he'd visited there as a child. He kissed Mo on the cheek, then made the introductions, and could tell his old friend was as charmed by Juliana as he was.

Knowing how secretive Mo's son Alex was when it came to his work, Ashe left Juliana sipping tea in the conservatory while he went down to the basement, where Alex had his computers set up. Despite being a self-proclaimed computer geek, Alex looked more like a surfer, with pale blond dreads reaching his shoulders, his lanky body eternally dressed in shorts, T-shirt and flip-flops, no matter how cold it was outside. The two vampires gripped hands as they greeted each other, and then Alex told Ashe to take a seat in the extra chair he'd pulled up to his workstation, so that he could bring him up to speed on what he'd been doing.

"After you called my mom," Alex said, tucking a dread behind his ear, "I started digging into the Council's financial records, pulling up as much account information as I could find." He swiveled his high-tech monitor around so that Ashe could see the numerous lines of numerical data filling the screen. "I've already gone through the private accounts assigned to the individual Council members, and they were all clean. Even Lenora's."

Ashe blew out a rough breath, and said, "Shit."

"No, it's okay. Keep listening," Alex told him. "In addition to the personal accounts, there are always hundreds of secret miscellaneous accounts tied in with the Council's system, and that's where they hide things they don't want going on public record. A certain number are for mistresses, others for money laundering. You name the vice, and they've probably used one of those accounts to pay for it."

Ashe could only imagine what kind of look was on his face. "Are you telling me that you have actual proof that the Council is laundering money?" he asked, his voice gritty.

Alex leaned back in his chair, put his hands behind his head and waggled his brows. "I have proof of lots of things. Trust me, man. If you knew what I know, your brain would have melted by now."

"Christ," he muttered, pulling his hand down his face. The implications of what Alex was saying were huge, especially if the money they were laundering belonged to Raphe Delacourt.

"So, anyway, as I was saying—" Alex's fingers moved with lightning speed over his keyboard "—there are a shitload of these secret accounts just waiting to be explored by geniuses like me." He nodded at the monitor, where a new list of data was filling the screen. "These are most of them. I started going through them yesterday, one by one, which was way beyond tedious." He shot Ashe a cocky smile. "But it paid off."

"How?" Adrenaline punched his system, sending him to the edge of his chair. "What'd you find?"

Alex tapped away at the keyboard again, and the lines of account numbers disappeared until only one remained on the screen. Narrowing his eyes, Ashe studied the data. There was only one transaction listed under the account, being paid to a Carlos Chacal in the amount of ten million pounds.

Holy hell...

He swung his gaze to Alex, who was still smiling. "Is that what I think it is?"

"Oh, yeah," Alex drawled, clearly enjoying himself. "Carlos Chacal is a name that the League sometimes uses, referencing Carlos the Jackal. Guess even assassins can have a warped sense of humor, eh?" He pointed a finger toward the screen. "I'd be willing to bet my favorite body part that this is the payment on your lady friend's life."

"So who used this account?"

"That's what I have to figure out," Alex said, leaning back in his chair again. "They funneled the money in through a bunch of different offshore accounts, trying to cover their tracks. But I'll crack it."

"How long do you think it'll take?" he asked.

Alex scratched the blond stubble on his chin, and said, "For anyone else, I'd say at least a week, if not longer. But since it's you, I'll keep working on it till I've got an answer."

They both moved to their feet, and Ashe slapped him on the shoulder. "I owe you, man. Big-time."

Alex gave him a sly grin. "You can thank me by letting me borrow that Ferrari you were driving the last time I saw you."

Ashe laughed. "You trace that transaction," he said in a low rumble, "and you can forget borrowing it. I'll *give* you the damn thing."

Leaving an inspired Alex hunched over his keyboard, fingers moving with supernatural speed, Ashe walked back upstairs, where Mo was waiting for him. They talked for a few minutes, and then he made his way back to Juliana.

She was still in the conservatory, but instead of sipping tea at the table, she was now sitting in the middle of the floor with three of Mo's grandchildren. The four of them were coloring with crayons, telling funny stories and jokes, the little ones rolling with laughter, clearly delighted with her.

Shaking his head, Ashe lifted his hand to his chest, rubbing at the funny feeling that was tingling there as he watched this different side of her. It made him think of the family he had never wanted. But he could see a dream of it in his mind. A beach with lapping waves and warm sunshine. Laughter filling the air as his wife built sandcastles with their daughter and son. A little dark-haired girl with rosy cheeks and a grinning boy who had a bit of the devil in his eyes.

Looking up, Juliana saw him standing in the doorway, a radiant smile spreading over her beautiful face. "Did Alex find what we need?"

He had to swallow twice before he could say, "He's close. As soon as he's got something concrete, he's going to let us know."

"Where's Mo?"

Pushing his hands in his pockets, Ashe rested his shoulder against the door frame. "She's looking something up for me."

"Oh?" she asked, as the children's nanny came in and took them off for dinner. But not before each one had given her a hug and a kiss on the cheek.

When they were alone, he said, "Her husband Henry collects all kinds of clan medical journals, and even writes some of his own. He's out of town right now, but she's going through the journals up in his study, trying to identify the poison that was used on me last night."

"What?" she gasped, the blood suddenly drain-

ing from her face as she dropped the crayons box in her hand and lurched to her feet.

Before he could say anything more, Mo moved past him in the doorway, a large, open leather volume in her wrinkled hands as she sat at the table. "Here it is," she murmured, running her finger down the page. "I found something, Ashe, but it's so odd. According to Henry's journal, the only poisoning he's ever heard of with the same type of symptoms you had came from the poison that's carried in a Medeiros vampire's claws and fangs."

"That is odd," he murmured. "It must be three hundred years since the Medeiros were marked for elimination." Ashe knew, because he'd been taught about the fallen Medeiros line during his studies at the Förmyndare academy. Originally, there had been two clans that were classified as vampires: the Deschanel and the Medeiros. The two species shared certain characteristics, but unlike the Deschanel, the Medeiros were more violent in their hungers, often draining their victims to the point of death. They were considered colder, harder and far more unpredictable than the Deschanel. A dangerous distinction, especially in light of the fact that unlike their Deschanel cousins, the Medeiros could turn humans with their bites, their darker characteristics magnified in the changelings, who were often so violent and vicious they killed anyone they came into contact with.

For centuries, the Deschanel did their best to control the Medeiros, monitoring their behavior. But as time passed, the line became more dangerous, until the decision was made to exterminate the Medeiros in order to protect the secrecy of the clans. It was considered a dark spot on the legacy of the vampire clans, and one that Deschanel scholars still debated today.

Mo continued reading from the page. "It says here that the poison collects in pits which are located beneath the skin on the vampire's wrists and in their throats, just under their jawline. If you stab them in one of the venom pockets, it kills the vampire almost instantly."

"Son of a bitch," he cursed, cutting his gaze toward Juliana, who was standing in the center of the room with her hand over her mouth, her eyes wide with panic. His memories of the battle against that blond guard were dim at best, but one thing he could clearly recall was sliding down that bloody wall, his gut twisting with fear for Juliana as he watched her thrust the knife into the guard's throat. Just under the bastard's jawline.

"How the hell did you know to do that?" he growled, fisting his hands at his sides to keep himself from crossing the room and doing something he would later regret.

Juliana lowered her hand, licking her lips as she cast a nervous look toward Mo, who had gotten up from the table and was quickly leaving the room, the door closing softly behind her. Returning her gaze to Ashe, she swallowed, and said, "I…I didn't. I just got lucky."

His expression darkened with rage. "Don't lie to me. Not anymore! You didn't stab him there by accident. That much I remember. You aimed right for that specific spot!"

"Okay, fine. I knew!" she shouted, her insides twisting with agony from the way he was looking at her. "I knew what he was!"

With a guttural groan, he lowered his head into his hands, shoving his fingers back through his hair, his body rigid with tension. "How?" he demanded, forcing the words through his gritted teeth. His head shot up, his dark eyes burning with raw, savage fury. "How the hell did you know? And why didn't you tell me?"

She spoke in a breathless rush. "I'll tell you everything. I promise. But we can't talk about this here," she whispered, pain lacerating her heart as she realized she was on the verge of losing him. "Not unless you want to put Mo and her family in danger."

He didn't say anything more; he just turned and left through the door that Mo had used. A minute later, he came back into the room with their bags over his shoulder. "Move it. Now."

Juliana slipped into her jacket and made her way to the front door, following him outside. The wind had picked up since their arrival, dark storm clouds rolling in hard and fast. The sidewalks were empty as they headed down the street, back toward the station, the blustery weather keeping everyone indoors. She had to practically run to keep up with Ashe's long, angry strides, the waves of rage pulsing off him so intense she could have sworn she felt them blasting against her.

Nearly ten minutes of strain-filled silence had passed before he finally said, "I want an explanation, Juliana. And I want it now."

She fought to smooth out her choppy breaths, her thoughts so scattered it was difficult to find the right words. "The D-Delacourts," she stammered, her jaw shaking. "Raphe…and his m-mother. They're Medeiros."

He ran a shaky hand down his face, muttering something foul under his breath as he kept walking.

"They hide it somehow," she continued. "But I…I don't know how."

Grabbing her arm in a brutally hard grip, Ashe suddenly yanked her off the sidewalk, pulling her along behind him as he headed into a small, wooded park that was thankfully empty.

The pain in his chest was so damn raw he was sucking wind, his lungs working like a bellows. Christ, he felt like such a fool! All this time, he'd been trying to work out what kind of evidence her parents had against the Delacourts, and she'd known all along. They'd obviously discovered the truth about the Delacourts' bloodline, threatening to expose them. That would certainly explain Lenora's willingness to risk censure from the Council for their unauthorized deaths. As well as her determination to see the Sabin family destroyed before his investigation into their sentencing stirred up questions she didn't want anyone asking...or finding the answers to.

He couldn't believe Juliana had kept something this important from him. He felt as if she'd taken a sledgehammer to his breastbone, the blow even sharper for the way it'd come on the heels of watching her play with Mo's grandchildren, his head filled with fantasies about their future. A future that would never happen now, because he couldn't stomach the thought of tying his life to a devious little liar.

Staring down into her tear-filled eyes, he swallowed the lump of rage in his throat and said, "I want the full story, Juliana."

She huddled within her jacket and lowered her gaze to his chin, as if she was afraid to look him in the eye. Then she took a deep, shuddering breath, and said, "I met Raphe Delacourt on my nineteenth birthday." Her voice was soft, and eerily hollow. "He was very charming, and despite the whispers I'd heard about him, I was...I was infatuated. I didn't believe he was a criminal, even though I'd heard people gossip about how he made his money. But I didn't want to listen to vicious rumors. Instead, I made sure to visit certain places where I knew he'd be, and it...it wasn't long before he started...pursuing me."

Disbelief roughened his voice. "And your father allowed it?"

Her eyes slid closed and she gave a dry, brittle laugh. "Hardly. He was furious. He forbade me to so much as talk to Raphe. But, of course, I was young enough to think he was wrong...that I knew what I was doing. So I...I started meeting with him in private."

Ashe's fangs burned for release, while some kind of dark, primitive sound tore from his throat.

Deep down inside, he'd secretly feared that it would be something like this. Maybe that was why he hadn't pushed her harder, all those times they'd talked about her past. Maybe on some instinctual level, he'd sensed that the truth wasn't something he'd want to know, the idea of Jules in bed with his worst enemy making him ill.

Choking on the bitter taste in his mouth, he

forced himself to say, "So you started screwing him."

She opened her eyes, locking her tormented gaze with his. "Not…exactly. We started dating. But we…we weren't sleeping together."

Oh, hell. Just how stupid did she think he was? "You really expect me to buy that bullshit? Raphe Delacourt has a reputation worse than mine. There's no way he would have dated you without getting in your pants."

"Whether you believe it or not, it's the truth. We dated for months without anything happening." She turned her face to the side, staring into the trees. "I'd already had a few serious boyfriends, so I couldn't understand what his issue was. He seemed to think I was this fragile little creature he needed to protect, and it drove me crazy. But I put up with it because I thought he loved me."

Ashe's head started to pound, a cold ache twisting through his gut as he listened to her story.

"I even had this crazy idea that he wanted to… marry me." A bitter smile touched her lips. "But then I was out with some friends, and I saw him on a date with another woman. That was when I realized that the entire time we'd been together, he'd been getting sex elsewhere. I was young and stupid and hurt enough to convince myself that the mature thing to do was to show him that I was woman enough for him. So I…I went to his house that night to prove that he didn't need those other women." Her jaw shook, her face getting paler as she said, "I got what I wanted, and we ended up in bed together. But then…things went wrong. Raphe…changed, taking his Medeiros form."

Ashe choked back a sharp curse, his mind supplying enough gruesome detail for him to imagine how terrifying it must have been for her. He'd read back at the academy that when a Medeiros male shed his control, he became something that was more monster than man.

After a moment, Juliana went on. "Obviously, I realized something wasn't…right. That Raphe wasn't a Deschanel vampire, as I'd believed. So I got the hell out of there and did what all frightened young girls do. I ran home and told my daddy what had happened." She shifted her tear-filled gaze back to his, huddling deeper into her jacket. "If I'd been thinking straight, I'd have realized how furious my father would be. But I was too…upset. I told him everything, and he was the one who figured out Raphe's true species, based on my descriptions. Believing my life was in danger, he convinced my mother that they had to go before the Council immediately and launch a formal accusation against Raphe. But on their way to the Court, Lenora's guards intercepted them and they were killed." She drew in another shuddering breath, then slowly let it out. "I should have known that Raphe's mother would do whatever it took to protect him. If I hadn't run… If I'd just stayed and let Raphe kill me, then no one would have suffered."

"*You* would have suffered," Ashe stated in a low voice, wanting so badly to believe her. But he…couldn't quite do it, the ability slipping through his fingers like wisps of smoke. All he could think about as he looked down at her was that a beautiful little liar had played him all over again. Her excuses didn't matter. Why should he believe them, when he couldn't believe anything else she said?

Responding to his comment, she wiped the tears from her cheeks with her sleeve, saying, "I've been suffering ever since I told my parents what happened that night. And the guilt has been eating me alive ever since."

He cocked his head to the side, studying her through his lashes. "Yeah, that guilt of yours is one of the first things I ever noticed about you. Which makes me wonder if what you've just told me is really the way it happened."

She blinked, looking as if he'd slapped her. "What do you mean?"

He wouldn't have thought Juliana would whore herself out for Raphe Delacourt's wealth, but hell, what did he really know about her, anyway? Who knew if she'd just been playing him from the moment he found her sitting out on that patio in London? Who knew what was real, and what was simply the talent of a cunning actress?

"I mean, are you sure you didn't plan to get your share of Raphe's dirty money, no matter how it was earned? Maybe even join up with him, like a modern-day Bonnie and Clyde? Until, of course, you found out he was more than just a playboy criminal who liked to fuck younger women." His voice got harder. "Are you sure you just didn't get in over your head? Though I guess you should get some credit for not going through with it, once you found out his dirty little secret. Screwing a criminal for his money is bad enough, Jules. But spreading your legs for a monster, just so you can grab a few bucks? That's as low as it gets."

Tears poured down her cheeks as she took a step back from him, her expression stricken. "I thought he l-loved me," she said, her voice cracking. "I didn't want his money, and I didn't believe he was a criminal. But even if he was, I'd thought I would be able to help him change."

His low laugh was mean and ugly. "First rule of relationships, Jules. Never try to change your lover. Accept them for exactly what they are—criminal, murderer, liar—no matter how sick it makes you."

Very quietly, she said, "I know you think I'm a

scheming liar, Ashe, but I'm not. I'm not like that woman who hurt you." She brushed her tears away with trembling fingertips, and went on. "Every single person who knows the truth about the Delacourts has suffered. My parents...my family. It's even the cause of Micah's suffering. The woman who poisoned him—he was with her because he was trying to get information about Lenora. That's the only reason I didn't tell you. I didn't want you to know because it's like a curse! I was only trying to protect you!"

"Bullshit. You just didn't trust me with the truth! This whole investigation has been nothing but a fucking waste of time!"

"That's not true," she argued. "I still need proof of the assassination orders to take them to the Council. That hasn't changed. If I try to go before them and make the same claims about Lenora's bloodline that I did before, they'll laugh in my face." She took a step forward, lifting her chin. "And *you* of all people have no right lecturing me about trust and the truth!"

He clenched his jaw. "Just what the hell is that supposed to mean?"

"It means I know about the Burning!" she shouted.

Ashe staggered back, feeling like he'd been kicked in the gut. "How the hell did you—?"

Her eyes glittered. "You told me yourself.

When you were under the influence of the potion Essie gave you."

He swallowed, shaking, desperate to think of something to say...of a way to make this right. But in the end, only one hoarse, guttural word fell from his lips. *"Fuck."*

CHAPTER FOURTEEN

THEY DIDN'T SAY MORE THAN a handful of words to each other as they traveled by train back to the coast, staying in one of the little seaside towns not far from Marseilles. In fact, Ashe hadn't talked to her much at all since she'd admitted that she knew about the Burning. Juliana had sat beside him on the train, so close, and yet never had the distance between them seemed so vast. She told herself the rift shouldn't have come as a surprise. After all, she'd known just how ugly his reaction would be if he ever learned the truth about the Medeiros and her relationship with Raphe.

But that didn't mean that it hurt any less.

As they made their way inside the slightly up-scale bar where Knox had arranged for them to stay, she breathed a quiet sigh of relief. The tense walk from the train station had only gotten worse when Ashe thought he saw one of his Förmyndare buddies tailing them as they'd made their way through the busy town center. He'd automatically yanked her inside a crowded nightclub, pulling her through the writhing crowd of half-dressed dancers. When they'd made it to the back of the club, he'd trapped her against the wall between two other couples and taken her mouth. The hard, anger-flavored kiss had been purely for cover, but Juliana had still responded, trying to tell him with her body what she couldn't convince him of with her words. But he wasn't listening. When he was satisfied that no one had followed them inside, they made their way through the club's back exit and continued on, pretending the kiss had never happened.

But now she was done pretending...and she was done with the silence.

She held her tongue as they climbed the stairs up to their room on the second floor, but the moment Ashe had closed and locked the door behind him, Juliana slipped off her jacket and said, "Are you ready to talk yet?"

He shot her a dark look before tossing his own jacket onto the foot of the bed and walking to stand before the room's large bay window, essentially turning his back on her. "Be careful," he said in a low voice, the breadth of his shoulders accentuated by the way he stood with his hands pushed in his back pockets, staring out into the inky darkness. "Because I really don't think you're going to want to hear anything I have to say."

"Ashe, please. Just listen to me," she pleaded. "I'm sorry that I wasn't honest with you before, but I swear that everything I've told you today is the truth. I never meant to hurt you. I just wanted to protect you, for as long as I could."

He turned to face her, the look in his eyes so angry it made her flinch. "Are you sure it wasn't Raphe Delacourt you wanted to protect?"

"I understand that you're determined to think the worst of me right now, but I swear to you I'm not trying to help Raphe." She lifted her hands in confusion. "I'm not even sure how that would be possible."

So much fury was carved into the rugged, masculine angles of his face, it made something clench into a painful knot in her chest. The urge to shrink back from his anger was strong, but she forced herself to hold his hostile gaze as he said, "That worthless piece of shit needs to be taken down, and now I know how to do it." He took a step toward her, his regard deep and measuring as he studied her expression. "What's the real story, Juliana? Are you sure you didn't want me to know about the Medeiros so that you could protect him? You still carrying some kind of torch for that twisted son of a bitch?"

Oh, God.

She pressed a fist to her chest, but she couldn't stop the devastating well of emotion that suddenly poured up from inside her, nearly a decade's worth of anguish and grief twisting her features. "Just stop!" she screamed, her throat clogged with tears. "You don't know what you're talking about. If you had any idea what that monster put me through, what he did to my life, you wouldn't do this to me. I hate him!"

He didn't say anything, but his jaw hardened as he took in the sight of her tears.

"Ashe, please believe me," she cried. "I swear I'm not lying to you. I just…I wanted to keep anything bad from happening to you. Every person who has learned the truth about the Delacourts has suffered. I knew that if you learned what they really are, you wouldn't stop until you'd found some way to destroy them. Even if it killed you. I just wanted you to be safe!"

He made a hard, thick sound of frustration. "Goddamn it, Jules. Did it never occur to you that I could take care of myself? I didn't need your protection. I needed your honesty!"

"I know. And I'm sorry. But I wouldn't change what I did, even if I could. I wasn't trying to hurt you. I'm not like Gretchen, and I'll do whatever it takes to make you believe that. I only lied to protect you, not use you. And you've lied to me, too."

"We're not going there," he growled, turning

his face to the side. His profile looked as if it'd been carved out of stone, his chest rising and falling with his ragged breaths.

Wetting her lips, Juliana accepted that the only way she might reach him was by tearing open her soul and baring the last of her secrets. It might backfire and blow up in her face, but she was willing to take the risk if it meant having a chance with him. "You can trust me, Ashe. I swear that you can. And I'll…I'll tell you the truth about everything to prove it to you."

He turned his head, his heavy-lidded gaze sliding slowly back to hers. "You mean there's more?" he drawled, his husky tone sending nervous chills down her spine. "What now, Jules? You have proof of Big Foot? The Loch Ness Monster?" He lifted his hand and snapped his fingers. "No, wait. I know. Alien abductions, right? Are we going to share secrets about little green men?"

Juliana could feel the color leach from her face as she wrapped her arms around herself. "You can be an ass if you want—it isn't going to make me run. I just…I want you to understand why I was so protective. I want you to know what they're capable of." She swallowed, forcing the words from her tight throat. "You see…the banishment to the Wasteland wasn't—"

"It's too late," he growled, cutting her off. "I don't want to hear any more."

Standing near the foot of the bed, she said, "Ashe, please."

"I'm serious," he ground out, shoving his hands in his front pockets. He started to pace before the dark window, his powerful muscles coiling and flexing beneath the soft cashmere of his sweater. "Let's just leave it and try to get some rest."

"Are we at least going to talk about the Burning?" she asked, wiping her damp cheek with her sleeve.

He cut her a sharp, warning look from the corner of his eye. "No, we're not."

"Just tell me one thing," she whispered, her heart pounding to a deep, painful beat. "Is the Burning the only reason you made that deal with me? Was it only because you needed to…ease yourself?"

He rubbed his hand over his mouth, then exhaled a rough breath. "This isn't a conversation we need to be having right now."

She licked her lips again, and could taste the salt of her tears on them. "It was quite a risk you took, sleeping with me when you had no intention of claiming me."

His breaths were coming a little faster, a muscle pulsing in the hard line of his jaw. "I wanted you and I took you," he scraped out. "Nothing could have stopped it from happening."

Even though Juliana knew she should stop talking, she couldn't hold the husky words inside. "I've heard the need for a Burning male to release the serum in his fangs is excruciating. Your control is impressive, Ashe." A bitter smile touched her lips. "But then, it probably helped that you don't even like me."

He slanted her another narrow look. "Don't do this."

Her own temper started to fray. "This isn't fair," she snapped, irritated that the blasted tears wouldn't stop even when she was angry. "I'm opening myself up to you completely, and you're still blocking me out. Still blaming me, as if my reasons mean nothing to you." Her voice was getting louder. "Do you always bury things you aren't willing to deal with behind a wall of rage? Do you always have to control every bloody situation?"

He was on her before the last word had even left her mouth, taking her down to the bed and crushing her beneath his body. "You never know when to stop pushing, do you?" he growled, pinning her wrists over her head and taking her mouth in a kiss that was hard and hungry and raw, before tearing his mouth away. "Do you see any control now, Jules? Do you?"

She stared up into the glittering depths of his eyes, his gorgeous face right over hers. "The Burning—"

"Fuck the Burning. I wanted you before it even

started. From the first goddamn moment I ever saw you!" Pulling in a deep breath, Ashe tried to claw onto his control, but it was shattered, violent hunger and an eviscerating tangle of emotions ripping through him, breaking him down. "The heat in my veins came later," he choked out, trying to make her understand. "It might have made things more painful for me, but it didn't make me want you more. I already wanted you so much I bloody ached with it!"

"Then why didn't you tell me?"

"Because I didn't trust you! I still don't!" he shouted, his fangs dropping from his gums with a searing burst of heat. He tried to fight it, but couldn't. Before he even knew what he was doing, he'd lowered his head and was running his lips up the tender side of her throat. The scent of her skin made him crazed, the beat of her pulse roaring inside his head as if it was his own. "After what you've done, I doubt I could ever trust you," he added. "But strangely enough, none of that seems to matter worth a damn, because I still want to mark you as mine so badly I can taste it."

She turned her head to the side, moaning his name as her body shivered with need, and Ashe knew that she was his for the taking. That she wouldn't fight him. He could drive his fangs into that pale, fragile skin and release the serum right into her vein, while her hot blood poured like liquid pleasure over his tongue, sweet and warm and rich. He was so damn tempted to do just that, if only he could find a way to get past his anger. But he…couldn't. It'd braided itself into his friggin' system, seeping into his blood and bones and cells. He was angry with her for not trusting him and for thinking he couldn't handle an arrogant prick like Delacourt. For having ever let that miserable bastard put his hands on her in the first place.

But more than anything, he was furious that she'd made him start thinking this thing between them might actually have a chance. For making him believe in her, when she'd been lying to him all along.

The only answer was to do something to make her push him away, because he didn't have the strength to do it himself.

And it had to be done now, because he was only seconds away from losing it.

Forcing himself to release her wrists, Ashe pulled away from her body and moved to his feet at the foot of the bed. Scrubbing one hand over his jaw, he said, "Tell me something, Jules. Were you as easy for Raphe as you are for me?"

She blinked up at him, looking confused. "What did you say?"

He raked his gaze over her body, then locked it with hers. "I asked if you were as easy for Raphe as you are for me? Is that why you wanted him so badly? Because he could flip your switch without even touching you?"

"You son of a bitch," she whispered, her expression stricken as she quickly scrambled off the side of the bed.

"Just answer the damn question."

Folding her arms around her body, she shook her head and stared back at him with glistening eyes, looking as if he'd just stabbed a knife between her ribs. "No," she said in a low, whispery voice. "I wasn't…easy for him, Ashe. But if you want all the gritty details of our night together, then I'll tell you."

"Can't wait," he said, though he was starting to feel a little sick inside.

She lifted her quivering chin, and said, "Raphe was already losing control by the time he pushed inside me." Her trembling was getting worse. "And by the time he was done, I was almost dead. He'd clawed me, ripping my flesh all the way down to the bone in some places. And when he reached his release, he nearly tore my throat out."

Ashe could feel his blood draining out of his face, while a cold drop of sweat slipped down his spine.

"I was barely conscious when I ran from his house," she said, her gaze shifting to some distant point on the far wall as she continued her story. "That's why I wasn't with my parents when they died. Instead of traveling to Court with them, I was at home, recovering from my injuries. And after my parents were killed, Lenora went before the Council and told them that..." Her voice cracked, and she took a deep breath, hugging herself tighter as she started to rock on her feet, completely lost in the memory. "Lenora told her fellow Council members that I had used my body to seduce her son in the hopes of gaining a child from him. A child she said I would use to black-mail Raphe and demand the Delacourts' support in my family's supposed scheme to take over the Council. Then she...she argued that I should be kept from ever committing such a crime again. So they carried out the necessary procedure before we were sent to the Wasteland. And all so Raphe and his mother and however many other Medeiros are working with them could keep their little secret."

A blinding, gut-wrenching rage unlike any-thing Ashe had ever known tore through his body, nearly bringing him to his knees. "Are you...are you telling me that those bastards used a sacrifi-cial knife on you? That they cut out your womb with one?" A Deschanel couldn't heal from an injury inflicted by one of the Council's sacrifi-cial knives, which was why they were often used during punishments.

"Of course they did." She brought her shimmering gaze back to his. "What choice did they have? By the time I had to stand before them, I was healed from my injuries. It was just my word against Lenora's." A bitter smile twisted her lips. "And I was just a scheming little liar, right?"

"Don't," he groaned, a piercing sliver of cold stabbing him through the heart. He felt like the biggest bastard alive for every ugly, hurtful word that had come out of his mouth that night.

Her smile fell, and it suddenly felt like she was staring right through him, her voice barely audible as she said, "I knew it was crazy…thinking this thing could work between us. How could it, when I'm already dead inside?" She pressed one hand low on her belly, the look on her face a million miles away. She was closing down on him, right before his eyes, and it scared the living hell out of him.

"Damn it, Juliana. I'm sorry." He started to make his way toward her, but she quickly held up her hands, the silent gesture asking him to stay back. He wanted to ignore it and grab her anyway, keeping her locked in his arms, but she looked like she might crack if he touched her.

"I'd like to take a shower now," she said in that same eerie monotone, making her way around him.

"Jules, please," he whispered, his chest aching as he watched her walk away. "I don't know why I acted like—"

"It doesn't matter," she said, walking into the bathroom and closing the door behind her.

Feeling like he'd had a hammer taken to his skull, Ashe just stood there and stared, until he heard the lock click. Then he dropped down on the foot of the bed and buried his head in his hands, wondering what was wrong with him. Revulsion for the things that he'd said to her coiled through his insides, making him ill.

Damn it, he should have just listened to her when she'd been trying to explain her reasons! But he'd let pride and jealousy control his mouth, spouting words that he could never take back. And all because he'd allowed his past to color his perception of Juliana from the start, when she'd only been trying to protect him.

An anguished groan ripped its way from Ashe's chest as he compressed his head between his hands, wishing he could kick his own ass. He deserved that and more for judging her so unfairly and for making her cry. For pushing her to relive such traumatizing memories.

Another tormented groan worked past his lips, his muscles tremoring with rage. There were no words for the fury that poured through him when he thought of what they'd taken from her.

He wanted blood for what they'd done to her… for what they had made her suffer. When he was done with the Delacourts, he was going to take on the Council next. No way in hell was he going to let those spineless old men get away with what they'd done. Lenora might have been the one who demanded Juliana's punishment, but those fucking inept bastards had given her the authority to carry it out. Whatever her hold over them, it must be a strong one. The Council's power was standing on a rickety house of cards, and after what he'd learned tonight, Ashe intended to bring the whole thing crashing down.

Knowing there was work to be done, he exhaled a ragged breath and finally lifted his head, his gaze sliding toward the closed bathroom door. He hardened his jaw as he stared. It was going to take time to heal the hurt he'd caused Juliana, but he'd find a way to do it. And in the meantime, he'd find a way to put an end to this nightmare once and for all.

Needing to talk to Gideon, he pulled his cell phone from his pocket and saw that he had several missed calls, but no voice mail messages. Though a few of the calls were from a blocked number, there was also one from his brother. There were no bars showing on the phone's screen, which meant that he'd missed the calls because he didn't have reception in the room.

Damn it!

Moving to his feet, Ashe pushed his phone back into his pocket and scrubbed his hands down his face. Then he grabbed his jacket from where it'd been knocked on the floor, and walked over to the bathroom door. "Gideon tried to call my phone but I don't have any reception in here," he said, raising his voice so that she could hear him over the running water. "I'm going to run downstairs to see if I can get reception outside, but I'll come right back. Okay?"

He listened for her response, but wasn't surprised when she didn't give him one. He was going to have a long, uphill battle to win her back, but he'd do whatever the hell it took. Crawl after her on his knees and beg her forgiveness for days on end. Destroy the Delacourts until they were nothing more than a stain on the ground. Whatever it took, he'd do it, because she was that important to him.

Juliana had marked him in a way that was deeper than the lust, deeper even than the Burning, as if she'd laid claim to the innermost parts of his soul. To everything that he was, and all the things he would ever be. Hell, she was the most vital, important thing in his world, and losing her would destroy him, because he…

Oh, Jesus. The truth exploded into his brain like a bloody rocket. He *loved* her. Had fallen

madly, head over heels, out of his freaking skull in
love with her. Pressing a shaky hand to his stomach, Ashe took a deep breath as the stunning realization swept through him in a hot, shivering
rush. He had to reach out and brace a hand against
the wall until his head stopped spinning, his lips
twitching with what would have been a smile if
he weren't feeling like such a bastard for how he'd
acted.

Still trembling from the mind-blowing knowledge that he'd lost his heart to the beautiful little
vampire, he grabbed the key on his way out of
the room. After locking the door behind him, he
walked down the stairs and headed toward the
front entrance. A woman near the door gasped
when she caught sight of him, and a grim smile
lifted a corner of his mouth. He probably looked
like he'd been kicked in the face, his self-loathing
over how he'd treated Juliana blasting out like a
neon sign for the entire world to see. The only
thing that could make it worse would be dealing with Gideon's smart-ass attitude, but he didn't
have a choice. He needed to find out what his
brother had to say, and then tell him what he'd
learned from Alex and Juliana, in case something
happened to him and he didn't make it.

Making his way outside, Ashe stood at the
side of the building and took out his cell phone,
relieved to see that he had reception again. He

punched Gideon's name on his contacts list and waited for his brother to answer, keeping a careful eye on his surroundings. He'd talked to Knox earlier, and the shifter had warned him that he'd heard the payment on the assassination orders against the Sabins had just been raised to twenty million. For that kind of money, they were going to have every two-bit criminal on the continent gunning for them, eager to get their hands on the prize.

Gideon's phone rang seven times before his brother finally answered.

"Ashe?" Gideon asked, sounding a little breathless.

His eyes narrowed with suspicion. "Where are you? Are you alone?"

"Hold on a sec." There was some soft murmuring, the sound of creaking floorboards as a door closed, and then Gideon said, "Okay, it's just me. What's up? You and Jules okay?"

Understanding his brother had just left some woman's bed, he said, "It's good to know you're working hard at Court to help me out, Gid." His tone was dry. "I really appreciate it."

"Hey, you have no idea how hard I've been working," Gideon shot back, sounding insulted. "I'll have you know that a woman's bedroom is one of the best places to get information!"

With a sharp sigh, he said, "Christ, whatever.

Just make sure you can't be overheard, because I have something important to tell you. But first, what were you calling me about? I have a missed call from you on my phone but you didn't leave a message."

"For some reason your voice mail wasn't picking up. But it was nothing big. I just wanted to hear how it went at Mo's," his brother explained, "since you suck at staying in touch."

"Sorry," he grunted, pulling a hand down his face. "But things got...shit, it's a long story."

"Yeah?" Gideon sounded concerned. "You didn't run into more assassins, did you?"

"No. But I've learned something you're going to find hard to believe." He explained about the Medeiros poison and the Delacourts' bloodline as quickly as he could, pausing only when Gideon would mutter a foul string of curses in response to something Ashe had said. "That's why they're so desperate to destroy Juliana and her family," he concluded, his rough tone betraying his fury. "If Raphe's getting ready to use his mother to make a power play, the last thing he needs is the truth about the Medeiros coming out. He needs to be positioned first, and then God only knows what he plans to do. With the full authority of the Council in his hands, he'll control a contingent of Royal Guards that's large enough to wage war on any species of his choosing."

"You really think it will come to that?" Gideon growled.

"I think he's power hungry enough to lose sight of what's sane," Ashe replied. "God only knows what his endgame is, but it won't be pretty."

"I hate not being there to back you up," Gideon said in a hard voice. "You sure you don't want me to come back?"

"No. Now it's more important than ever that we have things in place. I don't want the Sabins stuck in that hellhole the rest of their lives for something they didn't do."

Gideon's tone was gruff. "Just promise you won't let anything happen to you. I know I give you hell, but it'd fucking break me if I lost you, man."

Coughing to clear the lump of emotion in his throat, he said, "Same here. But if something happens and you don't hear from me, make sure you contact Alex. I'll be counting on you to get that evidence before the Council."

"Nothing's going to happen to you," Gideon muttered. "Because if it does, I'll have to kick your ass."

"You'll have to get in line," Ashe responded with a low laugh, and then he disconnected the call.

Since he couldn't access the blocked number that had called him, Ashe slipped his phone back in his pocket just as a group of scantily dressed women strolled by, sliding flirtatious smiles in his direction. He gave them a bland smile in return, completely uninterested, another thought working its way through his brain as he headed back inside. In addition to earning her forgiveness, he would have to find a way to put an end to Juliana's doubts about his ability to be faithful. Because his devotion to her was a given.

Knowing that the best thing he could do was open up and tell her how he felt right now, before she had the time to rebuild her defenses against him, he hurried up the stairs, his hands shaking with nerves as he unlocked the door and entered the room. Then his heart nearly shot its way through his chest, because he knew, in an instant, that something was wrong. The room was too silent, the bathroom door hanging open. He ran over, thinking that maybe she'd fallen on the slippery floor and hit her head, but the bathroom was empty. Spinning around, Ashe scanned the rest of the room and noticed that Juliana's bag was gone.

With bile rising in the back of his throat, he tore out of the room, trying to convince himself that maybe she'd just gone down to the bar for a drink. But by the time Ashe had searched the entire building and made his way back to their room, without finding any sign of her, the truth was sharply, painfully clear. Juliana had either run from him…or she'd been taken.

He prayed to God it was the first, terrified it was the second…and knew damn well that either way, she was gone because of him. He'd screwed up and let her slip right out from under his nose—but he wasn't going to stop searching until he'd found her.

With the pounding rhythm of his heart roaring in his ears, Ashe grabbed his bag and raced downstairs, shoving his way through the crowd as he hurried from the bar, out into the quiet darkness of the night, determined to do whatever it took to get her back.

CHAPTER FIFTEEN

THINK, DAMN IT. STOP panicking and start using your damn head!

Right. He knew that was what he needed to do, but as he prowled around the side of the bar, Ashe could feel his control slipping. Struggling to stay focused, he pulled in deep breaths through his nose, searching for any trace of Juliana's scent. But there was nothing. Just the faint stench of spilled alcohol and the briny scent of the nearby Mediterranean.

Desperation started pumping through his veins.

"Please let her have run away," he prayed under his breath. "Please don't let her have been taken."

But as badly as he wanted to believe she might have given in to her anger and run from him, it didn't fit. Juliana was too smart to risk her safety that way. Which meant that someone had gone into that bloody bar and taken her. But who? If it'd been another group of assassins, wouldn't they have left her body in the room? The Förmyndares, then? Was that who had her? Had they finally caught up with them?

Taking his cell phone from his pocket, he made a quick call to Gideon and told him to check in with the Förmyndare headquarters to see if any captures had been reported. Disconnecting the call, he returned the phone to his pocket and edged around the back corner of the building, into the darkened alley that ran between the bar and a row of warehouses that looked as though they'd been converted into apartments. Scanning his surroundings, Ashe ran down the middle of the alley in one direction, then turned and went in the other direction, still frantically searching for her scent.

"Goddamn it," he snarled, ready to head back out to the main road and keep searching there, when the wind surged and he thought he detected the scent of another vampire. Scanning the alley, he caught sight of a man stepping out of the thick shadows at the far end of the bar, Ashe's night vision picking out features that seemed vaguely familiar.

He narrowed his eyes. "Who the hell are you?" he growled, crossing the space between them in a long, aggressive stride.

Instead of backing away, the man stepped forward, hands raised in front of him, and Ashe got a clear view of his face. Cleft chin, straight nose, and shaggy, reddish-brown hair. The build was right, too. Tall and muscular, his body moving with the same predatory strength of all male vampires, lean muscles coiling beneath a white shirt and black jeans. So like a Deschanel…but with a monster's heart.

Son of a bitch.

A deep, snarling roar ripped up from the depths of Ashe's chest as he dropped his bag on the ground and charged toward Raphe Delacourt. Though he had seen Delacourt from a distance on several occasions, and had viewed numerous photographs of the infamous criminal, this was the first time he'd ever been face-to-face with the bastard.

"Where is she?" he growled, tackling Raphe to the ground and throwing a hammering right hook at the vampire's jaw. "What have you done with her?"

"If you ever want to see her alive again, you stupid fuck, then stop fighting me and listen! I'm not the bad guy here. It's my mother! She's insane. She's the real power behind my whole goddamn operation, just using me as a cover. She's the one who took Juliana. Not me!"

"You lying piece of shit," Ashe bellowed, smashing another punch across Delacourt's face.

"I'm not lying," Raphe snarled, blocking Ashe's

next punch. "I know where she is, but we have to hurry!"

"The only thing I have to do is beat the living shit out of you!"

Ashe landed another bone-crunching punch, and Raphe suddenly twisted in some kind of Brazilian jujitsu move that threw him off. They both hurried back to their feet with their arms raised, but while Ashe's hands were fisted, Raphe was holding one with his palm out, the other wiping blood off his chin. "Just wait!" the guy shouted, turning and spitting a mouthful of blood from his split lip onto the concrete. "Damn it, I'm here to help you. I swear it on my honor!"

"You don't have any honor!" he ground out, landing another punch against the bastard's face. With a foul curse, Raphe blocked his next punch, but Ashe came in hard and fast with a punishing sequence of blows, pinning the asshole against the rear wall of the bar. Trapping him there, Ashe braced his forearm against Raphe's throat, cutting off his air. It wasn't a move that could kill a vampire, but it was still painful as hell. And he was pissed enough to make it hurt, rage flowing through his veins like a liquid flame. It was poisoning his mind, everything colored with a red, orange-tinted haze, flavored with fury.

"Listen to me—" Raphe wheezed, clawing at his arm.

"I said enough!" he barked, pressing his arm down tighter against Raphe's throat as his talons slowly slipped from the tips of his fingers.

He could have easily ended it then, digging his talons into the skin under the bastard's jawline and ripping open his venom sac, releasing the Medeiros poison into his system. The only thing that held him back was Delacourt's eyes. They were a dark, muddy gray, proof that Raphe hadn't fed before coming to confront him. In their world, that was a sign that he'd come in peace, and not aggression. That he'd purposefully constrained his strength as a show of good faith—one that Ashe couldn't ignore, no matter how badly he wanted to.

Only an idiot would confront a Förmyndare without first loading up on a blood high.

An idiot...or a man who was telling the truth.

But he couldn't forget what Juliana had suffered because of this asshole.

"Do you know what those bastards did to her after you'd torn her apart?" he snarled, shifting his hold on the vampire so that the tip of his thumb talon was pressed against the kill point on Raphe's throat. "They cut her open because of you!"

For an instant, Raphe's eyes flashed crimson, then returned to that same cloudy gray. "What are you talking about? Her punishment was banishment!"

"Yeah," Ashe sneered, getting right in Delacourt's face. "But not until after your mother had them cut her fucking womb out! And you stood by and did nothing, just so you could save your own ass."

"I did everything I could," Raphe argued. "Who do you think sent the damn guards to work at the Sabin compound? I've been arranging for her protection for years!"

"Bullshit. You've been living the high life for the past decade, while she suffered in that miserable shit hole." He lifted his knee, jamming it against Raphe's groin. "I should just smash these in," he sneered, applying more pressure, "because you aren't a man. You're a fucking little mama's boy, too dickless to stand up and do the right thing."

Delacourt's face was going red, a thin circle of crimson beginning to glow around his pupils. "You think I want the life I've had? Like hell. I've been pushed around by that woman since the day I was born."

"You could have fought back," Ashe argued, keeping his talon jammed under his jaw.

Violent emotion twisted Delacourt's features. "You don't know what you're talking about!"

Ashe's nostrils flared. "So now you've finally found the balls to make a stand? Is that what I'm supposed to believe?"

"It's…complicated." Raphe shoved the words through his gritted teeth. "I'm screwing up my life with this stunt, but I don't want to see Juliana die any more than you do. I can't just stand by and let my mother kill her!"

Ashe broke away with a vicious snarl, his body rippling with fury. "Talk," he growled. "And make it quick."

"Several of my mother's guards kidnapped Juliana tonight," Delacourt scraped out, rubbing his sore throat. "My mother's been researching your family ever since you started asking questions about the Sabins. Her spies have been watching the houses of everyone you know. When you visited that place in Toulouse today, her spies followed you back here. Just like they followed your brother to Nice."

Retracting his talons, Ashe paced from side to side with restless aggression, keeping his gaze locked on Delacourt's face. "Why should I believe you?"

"Because I'm the one who's been helping you, you jackass. I got Juliana out of the Wasteland, and I warned your brother about those guards that attacked you. You have to believe me, you arrogant son of a bitch, because I'm your only hope!"

"Where did they take her?" he demanded, almost wishing this bastard was lying, the idea of Jules being at the mercy of Lenora's crazy henchmen making him want to rip something apart with his bare hands. And he'd be happy to start with the asshole standing in front of him.

"She's at one of my mother's homes on the out-skirts of Marseilles. It's not far from here, but we have to hurry. My mother's on her way back from Rome as we speak."

Ashe made a hard, thick sound in his throat, his eyes narrowed to sharp, piercing slits. "If you're so intent on saving Juliana, why didn't you stop them?"

Raphe's jaw tightened with frustration. "I must have done something to tip my mother off, be-cause she tried to divert my attention tonight. By the time I figured out what was happening, I tried to get here in time to stop them, but I was too late. Hell, I even tried calling your cell phone, but it wasn't working." He pulled his car keys from his pocket. "The only good news is that they'll have to wait for my mother to arrive before they get to work on her."

The idea of them "getting to work" on Juliana made Ashe want to retch, his fear like an actual physical thing in his body. "What's the address?"

Raphe told him, and Ashe grabbed his bag. "If you're lying," he said, slanting a deadly look toward the vampire, "I'll track you down and feed you your own entrails."

He started to head back out to the main road,

intending to borrow the first car he came across, hotwiring the engine, but Raphe grabbed his arm. "Wait! I have to go with you."

"Not gonna happen," he snarled, yanking his arm out of Delacourt's hold.

Frustration roughened the guy's words. "Don't be an ass. You *need* me. I'm the only way you'll get inside that place without her guards ripping you to shreds."

Curling his lip, he sneered, "You're actually willing to go in there and fight for her? Why the hell should I believe that, when you've never been willing to fight for her before? Why the fuck should I trust you?"

"Because I could have gone ahead and killed you both several times now," he shot back. "Thanks to my mother's watchdogs, I've known where to find you all week. But I didn't because I want her alive, damn it! Just as badly as you do!"

Ashe could see the truth of those words in Delacourt's furious gaze, jealousy coiling like a sinuous snake through his system. He choked it down, shoving it to the back, knowing it would just screw with his head when he needed to stay sharp for Juliana. Exhaling with a soft, serrated curse, he scraped out seven words that he'd never thought he would be saying to Raphe Delacourt. "Then I guess we're doing this together."

THEY MADE THE TRIP in record time, Delacourt's low-slung Lamborghini Gallardo handling the winding French roads with sharp precision. With his elbow braced on the passenger's-side door, Ashe rubbed his hand over his mouth, struggling to put his chaotic thoughts in order. To make sense of this surreal madness.

"If you're the one who's been helping Juliana," he asked, sliding his gaze toward Delacourt, "then why couldn't you just give her the damn evidence that she needed?" They were clipped, hard-edged words. "And why didn't you just tell her it was you? That you were the one helping her?"

The vampire's chest rumbled with a bitter laugh. "First of all, telling her I was the one trying to help her would have sent her screaming in the other direction." He slid Ashe a wry look. "Why the hell do you think I'm bringing you along with me now? She'd never believe I was trying to help if I went in there on my own."

"And here I thought you were bringing me because if the shit hits the fan, you won't be able to handle your mama's guards all on your own."

His response was dry. "Well, there is that."

"And the reason you couldn't just give Juliana the information she needed to prove there were assassination orders out on her family?"

Shifting the car into a higher gear, Raphe said, "I couldn't give you more because I didn't have anything more. I had no idea which account my mother placed the payment from. I only knew she was the one who did it."

"Why now?" he asked. "Why her sudden determination to see them destroyed after all this time?"

"Because she hates the Sabins with a passion. As she sees it, Juliana almost took me away from her. She's been plotting that woman's downfall for nearly a decade." He steered the Gallardo around a hairpin curve, then went on. "But she never made a move until now, because she didn't want to push her luck with the Council. But that situation is changing. She's been digging up dirt on her fellow Council members for years, and now she's got those old bastards by the balls. Except for Selingham, which is why she got rid of him." He cut Ashe a harsh glare. "Still, she probably wouldn't have risked her power play by messing with the Sabins, until you started digging into things."

Ashe brushed off that irritating remark, saying, "So you bust Juliana out of the Wasteland and then just leave her at the mercy of the Assassin's League?"

"I didn't just leave her," Raphe argued, his knuckles turning white as he gripped the wheel. "I've intercepted two assassination attacks that you don't even know about. And stopped another one that was headed for her family. But it hasn't been easy with my mother watching every damn move I make!" He slanted Ashe another blistering scowl. "And I told Juliana to find you. I didn't plan on her fighting this thing on her own."

"About that," he rasped, grasping for the door handle when Raphe took the next turn at full speed. "Why *me?*"

Raphe gave a rusty laugh, wiping the back of his wrist over his busted lip. "Because I knew you were interested. That's why."

Ashe's dark look demanded an explanation.

"You're not exactly subtle, Granger. You've been hounding the Court for information about the Sabin family for a year now. I knew you'd help her. And you helped keep the pressure off me for a while, since my mother assumed you were the one who'd helped Juliana escape from the Wasteland."

Irritation roughened his voice. "Why not just tell Jules where to find me in London? Why the whole setup at that restaurant?"

Delacourt gave a stiff roll of his shoulder. "I needed to be able to see—"

"You were watching us?"

"Damn right I was," he snapped. "I wanted to make sure you didn't turn your back on her."

"Bullshit," he growled. "You just wanted to watch the drama. And if you were watching, you could have offered some help with those bloody Lycans."

"I would have stepped in with the Lycans," Raphe said, "but you had it well in hand."

Ashe cursed something rude under his breath that made the other man laugh, and then with a sobering cough, Delacourt said, "By the way, I wanted to let you know that I'm sorry for what happened to your cousin. It wasn't my choice to have Sanders killed. It was my mother's."

He wondered how the hell he and Gideon had failed to realize it was Lenora Delacourt who was controlling her son, and not the other way around. With a sharp sigh, he asked, "Just what the hell is your mother after anyway?"

"Believe it or not," Raphe murmured, "she wants to see the Medeiros back in power."

"She's fucking insane!"

A wry smile twitched at the corner of Raphe's mouth. "I didn't say she was well-balanced. Just ruthless."

Hoping they didn't have much farther to go, desperate to reach Juliana, Ashe asked, "Just how many of there are you, anyway?"

"Thanks to my mother, there are hundreds of Medeiros now hiding among the Deschanel. It's why she's never mated. She sees herself as a breeder. Not only has she had countless offspring with different males, but she controls who the other Medeiros breed with, as well. She's claimed authority over the line, using her position on the Council to cover for her 'children' whenever one of them has a lapse."

"You mean whenever one of them kills," he bit out.

Delacourt nodded, his profile grim.

"And what about you?" he rasped. "She cover up your kills, as well?"

Raphe pulled back his shoulders, his voice tight. "Believe it or not, I have better control than that."

"You didn't with Juliana," he accused in a low, furious slide of words.

"That was a…special circumstance," Raphe muttered, his expression bleak. He slowed the car and steered into a small turnoff that was barely wide enough for the Gallardo. "We're not far from the estate," he said, changing the subject as he parked in the shadow of a towering oak tree. "We should go the rest of the way on foot."

They climbed out of the car, and Ashe followed Delacourt through the wooded grounds. Considering the harrowing circumstances, the weather should have been raging with the foul, destructive force of a storm. But instead, the sky was exceptionally clear and bright, the glitter of the stars like watchful eyes staring down on them from above.

They discussed the best way into the house, deciding to take a side entrance that Delacourt believed would be the least guarded. Working together, they took down the two guards standing watch at the wide double doors and quickly made their way up to the second floor of the historic château.

"I know which room they're keeping her in," Raphe said in a low voice, leading the way down a long, ornate hallway with a mirrored ceiling and silk-covered walls. When they reached the eighth door on the right, Raphe pulled his key ring from his pocket, found the right key and inserted it into the lock.

Then he stepped aside, motioning for Ashe to enter first.

With his heart pounding, Ashe pushed open the door and stepped inside, frantically scanning the room for Juliana. He spotted her slender form pacing in front of a dark window, and relief punched his chest with such a powerful blow he nearly staggered backward into Raphe.

"Ashe?" she cried, already running toward him. "Oh, God, you found me!"

They came together in a hard, clutching embrace in the middle of the room, their hands stroking and searching, as if trying to make sure the other was unharmed. "How did you…?" She shook her head as she stared up at him, her big eyes bright with shock. "I don't understand!" she whispered, her sweet voice quivering with emotion. "How did you know where to find me?"

"I had a little help," he muttered, crushing her against his chest as he buried his face in her hair. "Christ, woman. You frightened the ever-loving hell out of me. I was so damn scared that I'd lost you."

She was hugging him back, but he could feel her tension as she sniffed, no doubt detecting the scent of another male. "Ashe, who's with you?"

Exhaling a rough breath, he kept her in his arms as he turned to the side, the change in position giving her a clear view of Raphe standing in the open doorway, the male's expression a primitive mix of jealousy, frustration and soul-deep yearning.

A hard shudder racked her trembling frame, and she sucked in a wheezing breath. "What's… Why is… What the hell is he doing here?" she gasped.

With a soothing touch against her spine, Ashe said, "I need you to take a deep breath and calm down, angel. It's okay. I won't let him hurt you. I know it sounds crazy, but he's the one who helped me find you."

"What?"

"It's a long story. But Delacourt's the one who brought me here."

"That doesn't make any sense! Why would he do that?" she demanded, shaking like someone with a high fever, her teeth chattering. She was going into shock, and Ashe cut a warning glare toward Delacourt.

"Give her an explanation. Now!"

Raphe stepped into the room and shut the door behind him, his tall form rigid with tension as he turned to face them. "I brought Granger here because I care about what happens to you, Juliana." His throat worked as he gave a hard swallow and wet his lips. "I know...I know you probably find that hard to believe, but it's true."

Juliana gaped. "Is this some kind of sick joke?"

The vampire shook his head. "No joke. I... Christ, I don't know how to do this," he rasped, shoving his hand back through his hair, "so I'm just going to say it. Despite what happened between us, I want you to know that I loved you."

"YOU *LOVED* ME?" Juliana swayed, unable to believe what she'd just heard. "What the hell do you mean you *loved* me? You tried to kill me!"

He couldn't seem to find the right words to explain. "I wasn't...I know that's how it seemed, but I—"

"How it *seemed?*" she choked, cutting him off. "You tore me to shreds, you bastard!"

She tightened her hold on Ashe's strong arms

as Raphe took another step toward her. He still looked so much like the man she'd known, except that his playboy's smile had been replaced by an expression of raw anguish. "Juliana, listen to me!" he pleaded. "If my intention had been to kill you, I'd have released my venom. But I didn't. What I did was lose control, because you're...because you..." He broke off with a frustrated curse and slanted a shuttered look toward Ashe, before locking his gaze back on hers. "Juliana, there's... there's a reason the Medeiros only mate with our own kind."

She blinked, unable to believe he would try such a ridiculous lie. "I know your past. You had affairs with dozens of human and Deschanel women, if not more!"

"That was fucking," he growled, his hands curling into hard fists at his sides. "I didn't feel anything for them. You were different."

"You're lying!"

"Damn it, I loved you!" he roared, the guttural words echoing through the room.

With a snarl, Ashe released his hold on her to take an aggressive step forward, but Juliana stilled him with her hand on his arm. "It's okay," she said in a soft voice. Then she looked at Raphe and said, "You had a hell of a way of showing your love." Tears clogged her throat. "Do you have any idea what they did to me?"

His face went pale. "I didn't. Not until tonight, when Granger told me." He came a little closer. "Juliana, I can never tell you how sorry I am. I never meant…I never meant for you to suffer. I knew I shouldn't touch you. I *knew* it. Knew that my feelings for you would test my control. I tried to fight it, but when you came to me that night, I couldn't resist."

"You should have tried harder," Ashe growled.

Raphe's tormented gaze cut to Ashe, his lip curled in a sneer. "So says the man who can't keep his hands off her."

"That's different," he said quietly, his eyes burning with a fierce, possessive fire. "She's *mine*."

Raphe flinched, looking as if he'd just been punched. "You mean…?"

Ashe gave an affirmative jerk of his chin, and something like pain washed through Raphe's eyes. "I'm…glad," he said haltingly. "It means…that you'll be cared for, Juliana."

"I can take care of myself," she said, lifting her chin. She refused to look weak in front of this man.

A sad smile twisted the corner of his mouth. "I know you can. I'm the one who was weak, and that weakness cost you." He shook his head again, his deep voice thick with emotion. "I just…I want you to know that I'd give anything to go back and change that night."

"Why didn't you just do something, Raphe? If you really cared about me, you could have gone before the Council and told them your mother was lying about me."

"Because he was saving his own ass," Ashe muttered.

"Not mine," he said. "My sister's."

Juliana blinked. "What did one of your sisters have to do with it?" she asked, aware that he had numerous half brothers and sisters on his mother's side.

"Her name is Jessica and she's my father's daughter," he explained. "The girl is only thirteen, the product of an affair my father had with a human female. The woman died during the birth, shortly before my mother had my father killed. Suspecting that my mother was plotting against him, he had begged me to take care of the little girl if anything ever happened to him, but my mother got to her first. She's been holding Jessica prisoner ever since, hiding her away from me, threatening violence against her if I don't do as she says."

"Oh, God," she whispered with horror.

"Juliana," he said, his gaze imploring her to understand, "I want you to know that I *did* try to help you after that night. When I learned that my mother was planning to execute your entire family before their case could even be tried before the Court, I leaked the information to the Council. That's why the Council took your family into custody before the sentencing." His breath shuddered past his lips as he added, "When my mother realized what I'd done, she said that Jessica would have to pay the price for my betrayal, and she cut off one of the child's fingers."

Before Juliana could say anything, they each caught the sound of footsteps coming from the hallway.

"That's enough time spent on explanations," Ashe said quietly, taking Juliana's hand as he looked at Raphe. "We need to get her out of here. Now."

Raphe handled the guard they'd heard in the hallway, and together the three of them hurried down the main staircase, ready to make a run for one of the exits at the side of the house. But just as they reached the bottom of the stairs, the massive front doors swung open and Lenora Delacourt stepped over the threshold, flanked by eight of her private guards. Ashe knew at a glance that the guards were Medeiros vampires, their eyes already burning with a crimson glow, their talons the same thick consistency of the Royal Guard he'd fought at the nightclub.

As the eight guards began shifting into their

Medeiros forms, gaining another foot in height and nearly forty pounds in muscle, their skin darkening to a deep, gleaming shade of red, Lenora moved forward.

It was strange, looking at her angelic appearance, and knowing she was such a maniacal bitch. She was dressed in a stylish white pantsuit and black heels, her dark hair falling in long, glossy waves over her shoulders. She was petite, probably reaching only five feet without the heels, her pale skin smooth and flawless, despite the fact she had to be over three hundred years old. As he and Raphe had made their way through the woods, the vampire had told him that Lenora was a child at the time of the mass Medeiros executions.

"You protect Juliana," Raphe said at his side, while keeping a careful eye on his mother. "I'll handle the guards. Just…promise that if something happens to me, you'll find a way to protect Jessica."

"You'll handle *all* of them?" Ashe made a rude sound deep in his throat. "You might be tough, Delacourt, but you're not *that* tough. Unless, of course, you're not really planning on fighting them." His tone was thick with suspicion.

"I've gone this far," Raphe snapped. "I'm not about to back out now."

"Of course he's not," Lenora drawled, her unsettling crimson gaze locking with Ashe's. "My son allowed you to kill two of my favorite Royal Guards in Nice. And he's been helping the little whore hiding behind your back. He knows I won't forgive him for this." She looked at Raphe and lifted her brows. "Isn't that right, darling?"

"I'm not your fucking darling."

Her smile looked brittle enough to crack. "Not anymore. It's a shame Jessica will have to pay for your disobedience. If I weren't so determined to see you bleed out on this floor tonight, I would have made you witness her torture."

"You are one twisted head case," Ashe muttered.

"And you, Förmyndare, are a troublemaker," she drawled, sliding that crimson gaze back to Ashe. "But you won't win with this little crusade of yours. Soon, the Medeiros will be in power, and your kind will suffer for their crimes."

Ashe narrowed his eyes. "The Medeiros were destroyed for a reason."

"We were slaughtered!" she burst out, her calm facade shattering beneath a violent wave of rage. "I was just a child when my family was executed. I escaped with a few others, and we hid, living like animals. But we planned, and began to search for others of our kind. And now there are more of us than you'll ever know!"

As she finished her impassioned speech, her guards stepped forward, ready to do battle as

Lenora turned her mad gaze on her son. "You've ruined everything, Raphe. I only kept that little Deschanel bitch alive tonight because I planned on teaching you a lesson. I was going to make you watch me carve her into pieces, feeding them to my boys here."

"You sick bitch," Ashe snarled, and together he and Raphe charged forward, meeting the Medeiros guards in the center of the great, high-ceilinged room. He roared for Juliana to stay back as they slashed and tore their way through the guards. From the corner of his eye, he watched as Raphe took his Medeiros form and neatly sliced one guard's head from his shoulders, then had to turn and block a powerful blow aimed for his throat. Blood arced across the gleaming hardwood floor as Ashe drove his talons beneath another guard's jaw, ripping open the bastard's venom sac. Lenora held back during the gruesome battle, allowing her guards to do the fighting. They were some of the strongest opponents Ashe had ever gone up against, but no way in hell was he going to let them win. He hadn't survived a bloody war with his friends in the Specs team only to stand back and allow this psycho bitch to start another one.

And he sure as hell wasn't going to let her lay a finger on his woman.

Fighting back to back, he and Raphe made

short work of the remaining guards, and as the last one fell to the floor in a bloody heap, Raphe turned toward his mother. "It's over," he rasped, his chest heaving from the ragged force of his breaths. "Surrender, and I'll let you live."

"Like hell," Ashe growled, a scowl wedging between his brows as he noticed Juliana edging her way around the side of the room. The wild look in her eyes worried him, since she had her bright gaze focused on Lenora.

"It's the only way," Raphe argued, failing to notice Juliana. "I'm not saying she doesn't need to be punished for her crimes. But as long as she knows where the other Medeiros are hiding, she needs to be kept alive."

Lenora seethed with rage. "You would do this?" she snarled at Raphe. "You would turn your back on all your kind? And for what?" she screeched, pointing at Juliana. "For that troublesome little whore?"

"Watch your fucking mouth," Ashe warned in a low, deadly tone. But Lenora wasn't listening.

Wishing she could reach one of the heavy swords that hung high on the room's pale walls, Juliana continued to edge her way toward Lenora. If Ashe gave in to Raphe's demand and allowed the woman to live, she knew it would be up to her to take the bitch down. It would be too dangerous to put her in the custody of the Council, who were obviously as corrupt as they were spineless.

"You're not worthy of the Medeiros blood that runs through your veins!" Lenora screamed at Raphe, releasing her talons. "You never have been."

Raphe shuddered with fury. "No," he forced out through his gritted teeth. "What I haven't been worthy of is my *father's* blood that flows through me. You're just a poison that's destroyed everything in this world I ever cared for!"

"Then I might as well finish the job," Lenora hissed, turning her hate-filled gaze on Juliana.

As Lenora ran toward her, Juliana could hear Ashe shouting for her to get back, his long legs racing across the floor in his desperation to reach her. But Raphe had been closer to the place where she stood, and it was his body that leaped in front of her just as Lenora struck. Juliana let out a high-pitched scream, everything seeming to happen in slow motion as she watched Lenora's claws rip across Raphe's throat, nearly taking his head. Blood spurted in a thick spray, pouring over her as his body crashed into hers, taking her to the ground. Her hoarse cries echoed through her head, so loud they drowned out all the other sounds around her. But she could see Lenora, a maniacal smile on the deranged woman's face as she quickly turned to face off against Ashe. Terrified for Ashe's safety, Juliana was trying to push Raphe's lifeless body to the side, when she saw one of the heavy battle swords swing through the air. It struck the side of Lenora's neck, taking her head from her shoulders in the blink of an eye. Her lifeless body slumped to the floor, blood spilling over her pristine white suit in a thick, sluggish pour.

And then Ashe was tossing the sword aside as he crouched down on his knees beside Juliana, his face tight with concern. He lifted Raphe's body away from her, and pulled Juliana into his arms. Holding her tightly, he carried her to the far side of the room, away from the bloody carnage, before setting her back on her feet.

"Is it over?" she asked, staring up at him in confusion, her mind overwhelmed by all that had happened.

He nodded, looking as if he very much wanted to pull her back into his arms, but was…unsure it was where she wanted to be.

"Thank God," Juliana whispered, covering her face with her hands as the enormity of what they'd been through crashed over her. She took a hitching breath, trying to hold it together, but couldn't. Giving in to the burning need inside her, she threw herself against Ashe's chest…holding on to him as tight as she could.

And that was when the tears started to fall.

CHAPTER SIXTEEN

TWENTY-FOUR HOURS LATER, Juliana and Ashe still hadn't slept.

After the battle at Lenora's château, they raced to Rome. With the evidence that Alex had dug up in their hands, the Granger brothers confronted the Council and gave the leaders absolute hell. They demanded all the high-ranking officials within the Deschanel Court be present, and before the end of the meeting, all charges had been dropped against Juliana's family. In addition, the Sabins' lands and wealth were restored, with interest. Thanks to Ashe's friends, word of this wonderful news was already on its way to the Wasteland, and a private Court escort would arrive within days to transport her family back to their nesting grounds.

Though Ashe had wanted nothing less than the Council's blood, Juliana and Gideon convinced him to take the official route and file charges against the corrupt leaders. An investigation was currently under way to determine how the charges should be handled. Before it was over, Juliana had a feeling the Council would have undergone many changes, but it was about time. There needed to be fail-safes in the Deschanel system of government to keep what had happened to her family from happening again—as well as to ensure that maniacs like Lenora Delacourt never again attained positions of power.

In addition, an official search was being conducted for the remaining Medeiros. Once the vampires were tracked down, they would be given a choice: live under clan law within the Deschanel Court, where they could be monitored...or imprisonment. The investigative team would start by searching Lenora's château near Marseilles for any documents or information regarding the Medeiros, and Juliana asked Gideon to make sure that Raphe's body was given a proper burial.

Ashe also assigned a group of Förmyndares to search for Raphe's sister, Jessica, and she prayed that they found the girl soon. The soldiers were checking all of Lenora's properties first, and hopefully it wouldn't be long before Jessica was rescued and returned to her mother's family, who had been thrilled when Ashe contacted them with the news that a search had begun. They'd feared Jessica had been killed when she'd been kidnapped, and were praying for her safe return.

When the last of the arrangements were finally in place, they shared a quick meal with Gideon, who was relieved to have his brother back in one piece, before heading off to find a hotel. Though Ashe wanted to take her to the apartment he kept in Naples, neither of them was in any condition to make the journey, as exhausted as they were. Instead, Ashe told their taxi driver to take them to the Hotel de Russie, where he booked them a suite for the night. They showered separately in the suite's two luxurious bathrooms, and while Ashe was taking a call from one of his friends on his Specs team, Juliana slipped into a T-shirt and panties and pulled back the covers on the bed in the smaller of the suite's two bedrooms. She was closing the curtains on the windows, when she heard him say, "Is the fact that you're in here meant to be some kind of message?"

God, she thought, closing her eyes as she savored the husky timbre of his voice, thinking it was the sexiest thing she'd ever heard. Then again, everything about Ashe Granger was sexy-as-sin… and twice as wicked.

Turning around, Juliana opened her eyes and found Ashe standing in the doorway with one shoulder propped against the door frame, his tall, mouthwatering body covered in nothing but a tight black pair of boxers. He had a few scrapes from the battle with Lenora's guards, and more bruises than she could count, but they only accentuated his dark, dangerous beauty.

Coughing to clear the knot of lust from her throat, she managed to find enough of her voice to say, "I thought it might be a good idea if I gave you some space and slept on my own tonight."

He crossed his arms over his broad chest, studying her with a deep, measuring gaze. Quietly, he asked, "Why's that, exactly?"

She licked her lips, wishing she'd kept one of the hotel's bathrobes on. "Well, things are different now."

His eyes narrowed. "Like hell they are."

"Ashe, please," she whispered, not even sure of exactly what she was asking him for. "I wasn't trying to upset you."

As if sensing how unsettled she was, he softened his expression. "You're a free woman now," he murmured, smoothly changing the subject. "Have you thought about what you want to do?"

Baffled, she said, "I don't have a clue."

"If you hadn't been banished, what would you have done with your life?" he asked.

"I…I don't know," she answered, the question making her feel ridiculously anxious. "I was such a different person back then. Just a naive girl with foolish dreams."

His smile was gently encouraging. "Dreams are never foolish, sweetheart."

She touched her fingers to her throat. "It was so long ago, I hardly remember. I…I guess I would have wanted to keep painting. I loved art." Fear slipped down her spine, all those lost years spinning out before her. "But I couldn't now. I mean, it's been years since I've even tried to draw anything."

Sensing her panic, he came to stand in front of her, his warm scent dazzling her senses. "There's no rush," he told her, the tender look in his eyes making her breath catch. "I just…I want you to tell me whatever it is you need to be happy. If you'll tell me, I swear I'll move heaven and earth to make it happen."

Juliana pulled her lower lip through her teeth, just like she always did when she was troubled. Though her heart was dangerously opposed to the idea, she knew she had to be strong and do the right thing. "Ashe, I…I appreciate what you've done for me and my family. So much more than I can ever possibly make you understand. But we both know that this…*thing* between us was only temporary."

"No, we *don't* know that." He caught her hand and pulled it to his mouth, his breath curling hotly inside her palm as he pressed a tender kiss to her skin. "I'm so sorry, sweetheart. For everything that you've been through, and for all the awful things I said to you last night. I know I was an ass, and you can spend the rest of our lives making me do penance. But I'm not going to let you just push me away. I *can't*."

She opened her mouth, trying to think of what she could say to convince him he was just feeling guilty, and that he didn't really want to be with her, when he rubbed his thumb over her knuckles and asked, "Do you still care about him? Is that it?"

"What?"

"Raphe. Do you still care about him?" he rasped. "That was a pretty intense confession he made last night. I just wondered if it'd…if you…"

She struggled for a moment, trying to figure out how to explain the way she felt. "No," she whispered. "I…I guess I feel sorry for the life he had, and I'm sorry for the terrible way that he died. But I…I don't have those kinds of feelings for him."

His eyes went dark with emotion. "I'm glad. I mean, yeah, it'd make me jealous as hell, but it's more than that. I wouldn't…" He paused, exhaling a shaky breath as he gently squeezed her fingers. "I wouldn't want you to suffer because he was gone."

"It's okay." She lifted her hand, cupping the side of his face, loving the silky heat of his skin.

"Thank you for coming for me last night, Ashe. The day was so crazy, I don't remember if I told you that. But...thank you."

"Nothing could have kept me away," he said in a low, velvety rumble. "Just like there's nothing in heaven or hell that could keep me away from you now."

"Nothing," she whispered, "except for a cold, hard reality."

His eyes took on a molten gleam as he stared down at her. "Reality is you and me," he told her. "Together. Forever. So you had better start getting used to it."

"What about trust?" she asked, closing her eyes as she sniffed back tears. "How can you want me if you don't trust me, Ashe?"

"Jules, look at me." He waited until she lifted her lashes, his voice a hard scrape of sound as he said, "I was an idiot. I'll shout it to the rooftops if I have to, but I know that won't be enough. But look at it this way," he offered with one of those deliciously crooked smiles. "You can make me pay for it for the rest of our lives." The smile slipped away, and his voice got rougher. "And I give you my word, on my soul, that I will never let you down again."

"This is crazy," she said unsteadily, completely undone by what he'd said, as well as the mesmerizing way he was looking at her. "We...we have to be sensible, because we both know that you wouldn't want me if it weren't for the Burning."

With a quiet snort, he pressed her palm against the heavy beat of his heart. "You don't know anything, sweetheart."

Her response was soft. "I know *you,* Ashe."

He took a deep breath. "No. You know the man I've *been.* But you don't know the man I could be, damn it. The one *you* make me."

She spoke in a frightened, breathless rush. "But you'll…you'll eventually find a way to have the Burning undone."

A slow smile tucked its way into the corner of his mouth as he shook his head. "That will never happen, Jules, because I'm not interested in having it undone. I even stopped taking the 'inhibitor' I'd been given."

She blinked with confusion and shock. "When? Why?"

"I threw it out when we were at Essie's. And why do you think?" he asked, shrugging his massive shoulders. "I love you."

She stared, stunned. "But you…you like your variety."

Insult tightened his expression. "Let me get this straight. You think I'm going to fall in love with one woman and waste my time screwing around with another one? Jesus, Jules. What kind of jackass idiot do you think I am?"

"I don't think you're an idiot or a jackass. I just thought…"

He snorted again. "That's your problem, sweetheart. You're always thinking everything to death. For once, just turn your brain off long enough to listen to the rest."

"I can't," she breathed out. Her eyes burned with tears. "Bad things happen when I do that."

He took her face in his hands. "Wrong. A bad thing happened, and it wasn't your fault. And now something good has happened, and you've got to learn how to accept it."

The first tears spilled down her cheeks. "Oh, God, Ashe. I don't know if I can."

Watching the movement of his thumb as he brushed her tears away, he said, "When Gid and I were little, we asked my grandfather to explain the Burning to us. He told us that the magic happens for a reason, but that fate isn't something that's always kind. That sometimes men end up in situations that are more hell than heaven."

"What are you saying?" she asked, her voice little more than a croak.

He brought his gaze back to hers. "When this started, I thought I was being punished."

"And now?"

His lips curled, eyes crinkling with a breath-taking look that was both tender and suggestive. "Now I know I must have already paid for my sins, because Burning for you is the most amazing thing that could have ever happened to me. I know I don't deserve you now, Jules. But I'll do whatever it takes to become a man who *does*."

With a hard swallow, she said, "You really want me?"

His eyes were bright. "I want you. More than… Christ, I want you so badly, I can't even put it into words."

"Oh, God." She wrapped her fingers around his strong wrists, completely destroyed, her heart melting into some kind of warm, glowing flame in her chest. She shivered and trembled, lips tingling, eyes hot from the sting of tears. How the hell did he do this to her?

Lowering his head, he rested his forehead against hers as he said, "I know you're scared. And probably still mad at me. But I won't give up on you, Jules. Ever. I'll do whatever it takes to make you love me. I'll—"

"Ashe—"

He raised his head, his hands warm against the sides of her face as he stared deep into her eyes. "Damn it, let me finish. I'll—"

"I already do."

"Do what?"

Her smile was wobbly. "Love you."

He blinked. "You love me?"

"Yes!" She gave a watery laugh. "That's what I'm trying to tell you."

His mouth tilted at a rakish angle. "Then tell me again. I'm listening now."

Knowing this was the most incredible moment of her life, Juliana wet her lips, and said, "I love you, Ashe Granger. So much that it hurts."

And with those simple words, she let loose a storm of hunger, his mouth ravaging hers with wild, devastating skill, her thoughts scattering like the windblown seeds of a dandelion. But she somehow managed to focus on the words she knew she had to say. "Wait!" she gasped, turning her face away as she tried to catch her breath. "We haven't talked about children."

Panting, he asked, "What about them?"

Juliana forced herself to meet his gaze. "Ashe, you know I can't have any. I...I won't be able to give you sons and daughters. I won't—"

"Jules, stop." He wrapped his arms around her, crushing her against his chest. "I hate, *hate,* what those bastards did to you, but don't think for a second that changes the way I feel about you. If you decide you don't want a family, I'll accept that and I'll understand. But if you decide that you do, then, honey, there are millions of children in the world who need parents who will love and cherish them."

She stared back at him, trying to put her intense, incredible feelings into words. But it was impossible. So she simply grabbed him instead, pulling his head down to hers and kissing him with all the love and fiery passion he'd ignited inside her. He growled, rubbing his hands over her hips and pulling her closer, while she clutched his broad, muscular shoulders, squeezing the tough muscles.

Lifting her into his arms, his voice was breathless as he said, "I want to be with you, Jules. Today. Tomorrow. Every month and year and decade that goes by. I want every morning and every night. I want it all. I don't ever want to be apart from you." He kissed her lips as he laid her down on the bed, his tongue slipping inside her eager mouth, slow and deep and tender. Then he came down over her, and tenderness bled into raw, heart-pounding hunger, their hands desperate for the touch of bare skin as they ripped at the thin layers of cotton separating them.

When they finally broke apart for air, Juliana watched his dark head lower over her chest, her breaths coming faster, sharper, as she felt the touch of his tongue against a swollen nipple, then lower, nuzzling hungrily against her cleft. He tasted her with deep, ravenous licks, his low growls of satisfaction vibrating against her, adding to the hot, shimmering glow of bliss pouring through her veins.

"God, you're incredible," he groaned, his lips moving against her clit as he spoke. Then he gave a tender nip with his teeth, followed by a provocative swirling suction that nearly brought her off the bed. "I'm addicted to the way you taste. Can never get enough of it," he told her, his deep voice thick with lust…and *love*. She could feel it in the way he touched her. In the mouthwatering warmth of his scent. The ragged tones of his voice. He thrust that wickedly clever tongue inside her, penetrating her with slow, savoring strokes until she was begging and moaning. Her nails dug into the hard, thick muscles in his shoulders as she pleaded for him to fill her…to come inside her, until he pulled away with a harsh, animal sound rumbling deep in his chest, his expression as he came down over her carved with breathtaking need.

His magnificent body trembled, the muscles in his strong arms bunching hard and tight beneath his dark skin as be braced himself over her, staring down at her through eyes of fire. She'd never seen so much hunger. So much raw, visceral need.

"You're *mine*," he growled, pressing the heavy tip of his cock against the slick, tender place where she needed him most. And then, with his jaw clenched tight, he drove into her, burying every fever-hot inch of his massive shaft hard and deep.

"I love you," she whispered, the husky words

causing him to stiffen and pulse inside her. He lowered his head into the crook of her shoulder, the provocative scrape of his fangs against her vulnerable throat making her arch beneath him. He pulled back his hips, shoving back into her with a thick, hammering thrust as his fangs suddenly pierced her flesh. Liquid fire raced through her veins as he pulled against her throat, drinking her in, and then he tore his mouth away with a breathless gasp.

"This is why I've been drinking nothing but bagged blood for so long. No one tastes right but you. So hot and sweet." He sank his fangs in again, forcing deeper, hotter, more voluptuous waves of ecstasy through her body with his desperate feeding as her own fangs burst into her mouth, heavy and aching. Then he pulled back his hips and fangs once more, making her whimper.

"I'm giving you the serum with my next bite, but I want you to bite me at the same time," he said roughly, rubbing his lips against her throat. "You ready, Jules?"

"God, yes," she cried, so excited she thought her heart might burst. Then she could have sworn that it did as he sank his fangs in at the exact moment he drove savagely inside her body. She screamed from the pleasure, from the scorching burn of heat as the serum rushed through her veins, her craving for him impossible to ignore as she turned her head and buried her fangs in his strong, corded throat. As his blood hit her tongue, exploding over her senses, Juliana started to come, the orgasm slamming into her with such ferocity she felt stunned. It was as if the molten heat in his veins was pouring into hers, his body shuddering as he followed her over into that blinding, shattering madness. She could feel him in every part of her. In her mind. In her body. Her thoughts and her moans. He filled her completely, crushing out the loneliness and shadows with his sharp, burning heat, incandescent waves of pleasure blasting through her, giving her new life…new dreams. A shining, vibrant hope for the future.

As the fabric of their souls was bound together, she could feel her life being intertwined with his, uniting them in a connection that could never be undone. Nothing in her life had ever felt more right…or as perfect, and in that moment, Juliana suddenly realized that the magnets had been flipped. Instead of pushing apart, they were now drawn together. Body, heart and soul.

They both pulled their fangs free at the same time, their ragged breaths filling the quiet room as he nuzzled the side of her throat, his heart pounding heavily against hers in a deep, drugging rhythm. "I love the way you hug me," he groaned, still moving inside her with slow, pleasure-thick lunges, as if he couldn't bring himself to stop. "It's like…like I've finally found my home."

Emotion washed over her at his gruff words, blissful and surreal, like a dream that would carry her away. But his arms were solid and strong, wrapping her in a tight, possessive hold. She felt so safe, so loved, that tears burned in her eyes.

"Oh, angel. Don't cry," he whispered, pressing his lips to her cheek, his tongue taking her tears into his mouth. It was so sweetly intimate that she started coming again, pulsing warmly around his shaft, and he growled, thrusting against her, giving her more of his seed, his body shuddering as he wrapped her in his arms and crushed her against him.

"Christ," he groaned in a raw voice, when the rhythmic spasms of pleasure had finally eased. "I think you're trying to kill me."

Juliana laughed, the sound freer than any she'd ever made. Somehow they'd come through the storm…and survived. Stronger, happier. She knew old fears would creep in on her from time to time, but she didn't doubt that Ashe would sense the moment they did, easing her with his touch and his smile.

Minutes later, when he'd finally found the energy to draw his head back, he stared down at her with eyes that were like bright chips of lightning, more beautiful than anything she'd ever seen. "I'm going to make you so incredibly happy," he told her, the solemn words like a vow.

"I'll make you happy, too. I promise I will."

A slow, sin-tipped smile curved his lips, and she felt his body already hardening inside her. "Sweetheart," he rasped, his hips beginning to move in that slow, devastating rhythm, "you already do."

EPILOGUE

WITH A SMILE OF SWEET anticipation curving her lips, Juliana moved from her dresser to the suit-cases that were laid out across the sprawling king-size bed she shared with her husband. Tomorrow was their first wedding anniversary and Ashe had surprised her the week before with plane tickets to the private island where they'd been married. It would be a second honeymoon for them, their days spent making love on a blanket in the sand, while the crashing sound of the waves filled their heads and the sun beat down on their glistening skin. They were leaving in the morning and she couldn't wait.

Though they'd bonded that incredible night at the Hotel de Russie in Rome, Ashe had waited until they'd traveled to his apartment in Naples the next day before he proposed to her, using his grandmother's ring. It was a square-cut emerald surrounded by diamonds and she loved it. But then, she would have loved the plainest of bands, simply because he'd given it to her.

Their wedding had been held in the spring, on a private Caribbean beach, with soft white sand beneath their feet and the warmth of the sun bathing them in a golden glow. All their family and friends, with the exception of Micah, had come to share the momentous occasion with them, the guys in his Specs team and their wives staying for an entire week to help them celebrate. Even Knox and Essie, along with Mo and her family, had made it to the wedding, a grinning Alex still exuberant over the Ferrari Ashe had given him.

For herself, Ashe had promised to give her sunshine and happiness after the cold years she'd spent in the Wasteland, and he'd more than succeeded. Juliana smiled so often these days, and so easily, every moment with Ashe a treasure that she held dear to her heart. It still amazed her, the fact that he was hers and hers alone. But she had no doubts about his devotion. Every day, her husband showed her how much she meant to him, from the simplest romantic gestures to the darkly provocative ones that brought a flush to her skin just from thinking about them.

The only part of her past that pained her still was her inability to give Ashe a child. She was painting again, much to her husband's delight, and had made strong friendships with his friends and their wives. They'd even made their home in a beautiful house that Ashe had bought for her not far from the Specs team's headquarters in the Lake District, and Gideon stayed with them whenever he was in town. Even Micah was doing better, undergoing treatment at a nearby facility, and she and Ashe visited him often. Gideon had also managed to find Raphe's little sister, and the girl was flourishing under the love and care of her family. But despite how blessed she felt, Juliana couldn't help but feel that there was something *more* meant for her and Ashe. That they were meant to have a family to cherish and protect and shower with love.

The door to the bedroom opened behind her, and she added a bathing suit to her luggage before turning to greet her husband. He'd been out all morning, taking care of some mysterious errand, and now that he was back his eyes were glittering with excitement as he crossed the room to her and pulled her into his arms. "Do you love me?" he asked huskily, his deep-grooved grin unbearably beautiful as he stared down at her upturned face.

"You know I do," she told him, wondering what on earth he was up to.

He touched his lips to hers, smiling. "You're about to love me even more."

"Not possible," Juliana protested, giving a playful nip to his lower lip.

"We'll see," he teased, telling her to close her eyes.

Her pulse was starting to quicken. "Ashe, what's going on?"

Stepping away from her, he said, "Just trust me and close your eyes, sweetheart. I promise you won't regret it."

"Fine," she murmured, feeling ridiculously nervous as she lowered her lashes.

"Now, before I give you your surprise—"

"I thought our trip back to the Caribbean was my surprise," she said, cutting him off.

She could hear the smile in his voice as he said, "I'm afraid the trip's going to have to be postponed for a bit."

They were postponing their trip? Her mind raced as she tried to understand what was happening.

"Who is that?" she asked, aware of someone coming into the room, and then leaving, pulling the door shut behind them. But though they were alone again, she could detect a new scent in the room with them. It was something sweet and lovely and warm, and she started to tremble.

Ashe's deep voice was achingly tender as he said, "Everything's wonderful, Jules. There's nothing for you to worry about. Just hold out your arms for me, okay?"

She was still worrying her lower lip with her teeth when she felt a soft weight being laid in her arms. "Careful, now," he murmured. "She's only three weeks old."

With a soft gasp, Juliana opened her eyes and found herself staring down into the precious face of a beautiful little baby girl. Big gray eyes blinked up at her with childish wonder, one tiny hand grasping on to a long strand of her hair.

"Ohmygod," she said unsteadily, unable to take her eyes off the lovely newborn.

With his hands caressing her trembling shoulders, Ashe lowered his head and pressed a gentle kiss to her tear-covered cheek. "Are you happy, sweetheart?"

It took three tries before she was able to find her voice. "We have a…daughter? She's ours? Forever?"

"Yes." Ashe lovingly placed his big hand on the little girl's fuzzy head of hair. "Her parents, who were Deschanel, were killed by some human vampire-hunters a few days ago and there was no other family to take her in. So if you want her, she's ours."

"Want her?" she cried, cradling the little girl's soft weight against her heart. "Oh, God. She's so perfect and beautiful and I love her already."

"I thought you might," he whispered, his own voice thick with emotion.

Juliana lifted her tear-filled eyes to his handsome face. "I hope you know how much I love you. How important and precious you are to me."

"You're my life," he groaned, his breath hitching as he took her face in his shaking hands, his silver eyes glistening with more love and devotion than she could have ever imagined. "You're my heart and my soul, Jules. From now until forever. All I want is to make you happy, to spend my life with you, and to raise a family with you. I know it won't always be easy, but I swear that I will *never* let you down, and I will *always* be true to you, in every way. You're the only woman I'll ever want, that I'll ever need. You're the last thought in my head when I fall asleep at night, and my first thought when I awaken. You're my sun and my moon and my stars, and I will *always* work hard to be the kind of husband and father that you and our children deserve. And I give you my word that our daughter is going to have more love than any child's ever known."

As the tears of joy poured down Juliana's cheeks, her husband curved one strong hand around the back of her neck, pressed his forehead to hers and, in a husky, love-roughened voice, he continued to describe a bright, dazzling vision of their future, painting the images in her mind with his breathtaking words....

And it was the most beautiful thing in the world.

* * * * *

A sneaky peek at next month...

NOCTURNE™

BEYOND DARKNESS...BEYOND DESIRE

My wish list for next month's titles...

In stores from 17th August 2012:

☐ A Wolf's Heart – Vivi Anna

☐ The Enemy's Kiss – Zandria Munson

In stores from 7th September 2012:

☐ Bride of the Night – Heather Graham

Available at WHSmith, Tesco, Asda, Eason, Amazon and Apple

Just can't wait?

MILLS & BOON®
Book Club

Free Book!

Get your free book now at
www.millsandboon.co.uk/freebookoffer

Or fill in the form below and post it back to us

THE MILLS & BOON® BOOK CLUB™—HERE'S HOW IT WORKS: Accepting your free book places you under no obligation to buy anything. You may keep the book and return the despatch note marked 'Cancel'. If we do not hear from you, about a month later we'll send you 3 brand-new stories from the Nocturne™ series, two priced at £4.99 and a third, larger, version priced at £6.99 each. There is no extra charge for post and packaging. You may cancel at any time, otherwise we will send you 3 stories a month which you may purchase or return to us—the choice is yours. *Terms and prices subject to change without notice. Offer valid in UK only. Applicants must be 18 or over. Offer expires 31st January 2013. **For full terms and conditions, please go to www.millsandboon.co.uk/freebookoffer**

Mrs/Miss/Ms/Mr (please circle)

First Name

Surname

Address

_____ Postcode

E-mail

Send this completed page to: Mills & Boon Book Club, Free Book Offer, FREEPOST NAT 10298, Richmond, Surrey, TW9 1BR

Find out more at
www.millsandboon.co.uk/freebookoffer

Visit us Online

0712/T2YEA